The Fate of a Crush

MARIE MCGRATH

Also by Marie McGrath

Novels

The Many Faces of Charlotte Barnes (My Book)

Honey Cove Series (My Book)

The Fall Changes – Book 1

The Winter Heals – Book 2

The Spring Renews – Book 3

The Summer Unites – Book 4

Anthologies

Christmas Magic (My Book)

Phantoms (My Book)

Happily Ever Never (My Book)

For the latest news and updates, please check out Marie McGrath's newsletter. Signups can be found on her website.

Twitter: @Marie_McGrath_

TikTok: marie_mcgrath_author

Instagram: marie_mcgrath_

Website:

https://mariemcgrathauthor.wixsite.com/books

ISBN: paperback 978-1-956183-85-6
Library of Congress Control Number: 2022943526
Any references to historical events, real people or real places are used
fictitiously. Names, characters, and places are products of the author's
imagination.
Cover Design by Alt 19
First Printing Edition 2022
Published by Creative James Media
Pasadena, MD 21122

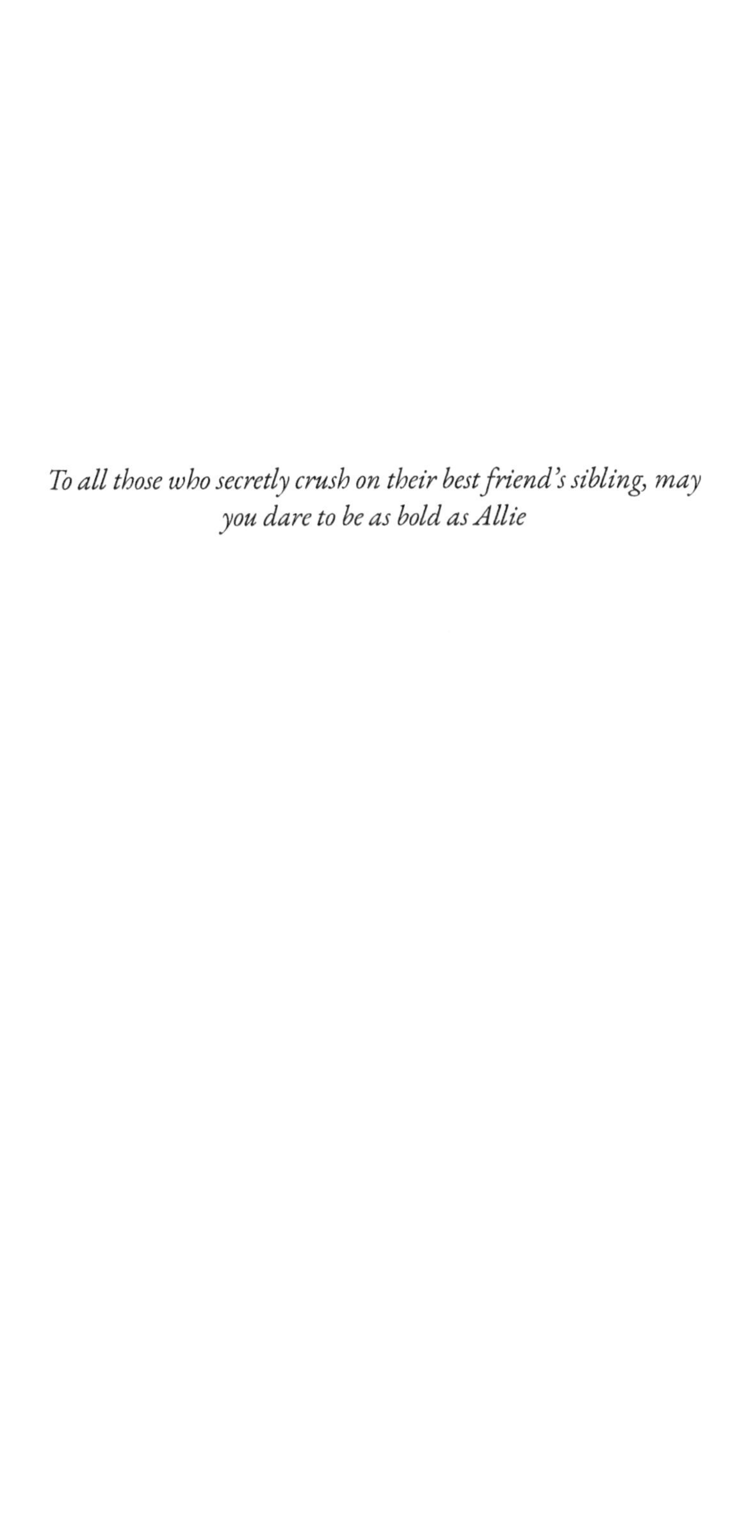

To all those who secretly crush on their best friend's sibling, may you dare to be as bold as Allie

Chapter One

I knew falling in love with my best friend's brother was a bad idea, but I just couldn't help it.

Hunter Baylor was dreamy, wonderful, and amazing. The only problem? He was absolutely off limits because he was Mia's brother. And well, Mia was my best friend since ... well, forever.

"Allie, are you even listening to me?" Mia asked.

"Hmm? Yeah of course."

Mia crossed her arms. "Oh really? So, you agree?"

Whoops. "Yeah, absolutely."

Mia threw the pastel-green pillow at my head. "You weren't paying attention! There's no way you'd agree with them if you heard what I said."

"I'm sorry, Mia. Start over."

"I said that my parents are letting Hunter bring a friend to our summer vacation. I don't want one of his meathead friends ruining our fun, yanno?"

I giggled. "I mean I've been coming with you guys for years. I can't imagine how they could argue against him having someone too."

Mia snorted. "Please, you're family. God, I hope he doesn't invite Richard; he's the worst."

"There's like what ... two weeks left until the trip? Why don't you just ask?"

"Definitely not. I'd rather die. If he thinks I don't like his answer, he will purposely bring Richard. No. I'll just wait to see."

"If you say so."

Mia was right. Richard was nothing like Hunter, but I supposed it could be worse. Besides, who cared who he brought if Hunter was there?

Mia's bedroom door flew open and banged against the wall.

I nearly jumped off the chair.

Mia's brows furrowed. "Hunter! What are you doing?"

Hunter chuckled from the other side of the doorframe. "Jumpy much?"

"No, more like I wish you would respect my privacy. The door is shut for a reason."

"Relax. Mom told me to tell you two dinner is ready. Blame her for the broken privacy."

I stared at Hunter as he left Mia's room and headed for the stairs. His tank hugged his body. Goosebumps erupted over my arm. I quickly rubbed them away before Mia saw. The first rule of liking your best friend's brother was that she could never know. The second? I could never do anything about my feelings. But man did I want to.

Mia stood and walked to the door. "You ready to eat?"

I nodded and followed her downstairs.

Mia's house was like my second home. I knew every room, every corner. We would all eat dinner together in their dining room. No meals in the Baylor house were held in front of the TV, unless for some reason her parents weren't home.

The dining room was connected to their kitchen, but still

had a wall that divided it from the rest of the family room. Their house was cozy, and personally, I loved the style Mia's mom used to decorate the house.

The walls to the dining room were a slate blue with a long and fabulous wooden table. The legs of the table were white, and the wood was a dark stain. The chairs were white and upholstered with gray cushions. It was simple and elegant. Or at least that was what she used to describe it to Mia's dad after she redid it. Mia thought the whole renovation was ridiculous, but I rather liked the updates. The only other decorations in the room were large plants in the corner and a chandelier above.

It reminded me that the purpose of the room was to connect, nothing more.

Mrs. Baylor set the final platter onto the table. There was a large bowl of spaghetti, a pan of garlic bread, and freshly grated cheeses.

I inhaled the delicious scent as I sat in my usual seat next to Mia and across from Hunter. Their parents sat on the ends.

"This smells amazing, Mrs. Baylor."

"Oh, Allie, thank you, honey. You flatter me too much."

"Never. Compared to my meals at home, you know these are like four course meals."

Mrs. Baylor waved me off as the blush on her cheeks rose. She would never admit it, but I knew that she loved my praise about her food.

Mia leaned closer to me. "You brown noser. Stop making me look bad with my mom. She's going to send me home to your house and keep you if you keep going at that rate."

I took a sip of my water. "Maybe ... maybe not."

Mia gasped. "That's what you want isn't it?"

I giggled. "No. But when can it hurt to have your mom in a good mood."

Mia tilted her head. "Good point."

Hunter plopped into the chair across from me, as Mr. Baylor sat to my left.

My eyes darted back to my empty plate. If I stared at him too long, those gorgeous almost-emerald eyes would suck me in. They were magical, even if Mia had almost an identical copy. Hunter's eyes were different. The green drew me in like a current and I couldn't get caught. Not now, not ever.

"Let's eat," Mrs. Baylor said.

Another Baylor family tradition was that each plate or bowl of food was passed around the table, starting with Mr. Baylor. He lifted the large bowl of spaghetti, scooped out what he wanted and passed it to Hunter.

He effortlessly lifted his spaghetti onto his plate, his arm muscles rippled as he handed the bowl to his mom. Once she safely held the bowl in her hand, his eyes looked ahead, meeting mine.

My stomach flipped.

Out of habit, I turned to look at anything else to focus my attention. Thankfully, Mia was oblivious to any kind of awkwardness. Not only was she entranced in her phone, but I had crafted my shield delicately over time.

I hadn't always liked Hunter Baylor, but as he became older and left middle school, it was undeniable his boyish features became manly. His baby weight turned into muscle. Eventually, his body only chiseled more and more.

In eighth grade, Mia had invited another girl to a sleepover to join us for her fourteenth birthday. At the time, Hunter had turned sixteen several months before. Maureen was only a school acquaintance—someone Mia had a few classes with.

During the sleepover, Maureen had disappeared, and Mia began to search the house for her. We found Maureen sitting on Hunter's bed, batting her eyelashes at his charm.

Mia's eyes bored a hole into Maureen, and she has never showed up at any event again.

I realized then that if I wanted to maintain my friendship with Mia, I could never switch to Hunter's side. So, I shoved the flutters, the goosebumps, and the jelly legs as far down as I could and that's where I locked them away.

I twirled the noodles around my fork and waited until they were perfectly set to take a bite. Spaghetti was one of the worst things to eat in front of people, especially someone you had feelings for.

"Are we all excited to go to the beach in a couple weeks?" Mrs. Baylor asked.

I nodded and smiled.

"Good! This year will be fun. It's the biggest house we've rented yet on the beach."

I poked Mia, who only shrugged.

Mr. Baylor wiped his mouth with a napkin. "Have you settled on who to bring, Hunter?"

Hunter who had been devouring his spaghetti, looked up. "Yeah, sure," he said as he choked down his mouthful.

Mrs. Baylor leaned closer. "And?"

Mia squeezed my knee as we all waited.

"Richard."

Oh man.

"Such a nice young man," Mrs. Baylor responded.

Mia stifled a snort.

I knew what she was thinking. I could practically hear the curses shouting from her mind. This was not good. Not good at all.

* * *

I leapt from the table when dinner was over with an excuse about getting home. I was sure that Mia had planned to complain about Richard, but honestly, I didn't want to listen to it right then.

The Baylor's house wasn't a long walk from my own. We lived in Rosewood Estates—a neighborhood close to school in Chesapeake Hills, Maryland. The neighborhood had mostly well to do homes, except at the entrance, which was where my house was located. My parents weren't poor, but they certainly weren't as well off as the Baylors. Mr. Baylor was a mechanical engineer, while Mrs. Baylor was an interior designer.

Our moms had met at an HOA meeting and then again a few short months later at a birthing class. When they realized that their children would be the same age they stuck together —making our two families inextricably linked.

My walk felt like forever as I trudged the short distance. The humidity of a July afternoon was at its worst and I was practically soaked by the time my house loomed in front of me. My hair splattered against my face from the humidity.

Finally, I reached my yard—our red front door beckoning me inside where it was cool and dark. I pushed open the door and listened for my parents. They were both Biology professors at the local college, Rosewood, and should have been home by now.

"Mom? Dad?" I shouted.

"In the office, Allie!" Mom said.

I dropped my bag on the dark laminate floors and moseyed through the hallway until I reached the last door on the left. Mom and Dad both shared an office, which had originally been a spare bedroom.

Mom leaned over her desk poring over a book splayed out in front of her. She glanced up at the sound of my footsteps. "Hey, Allie. How was Mia's?"

I flopped down on the pale-green chaise lounge in the center of the room. "Good. We discussed the trip in a couple weeks and practiced for volleyball tryouts."

"That's great honey. Are you hungry? I have more work to do to prepare for tomorrow's classes, but I could order us something. Your father won't be home for another hour or so."

"I'm fine. I ate at Mia's house. Mrs. Baylor cooked spaghetti."

"Okay, well if you change your mind let me know," she said without glancing up.

I stood and leaned toward her, kissing her head gently. "Thanks, Mom. I'll be in my room."

She patted my hand and kept her steady gaze trained on the book.

How Mom and Mrs. Baylor ever managed to have anything in common enough for Mia and me to be friends was beyond me. Mom was a studious, geeky type of a person. I knew she hated the word geek, but to be honest, nothing else suited her. She could stare at a microscope slide for *hours* and not move an inch. If that plus her incessant need to learn everything she could didn't make her a geek, then I didn't know what else would make someone qualify.

Gently, I closed the door and headed toward my bedroom —the only room upstairs. Our house was a ranch style home, with most bedrooms on the first floor, but the builder had wanted to add a loft to this design. As I got older, my parents decked it out to be my room and I loved it.

The stairs creaked as I ascended, then I opened my white door. My room was still in a disarray from two nights ago. Mia had raided my closet, deciding on outfits I should bring to the beach. She was convinced that this year was our year for catching the eyes of boys vacationing. I couldn't tell her that I didn't care about random strangers, but if the outfits worked for them, maybe they would work for Hunter.

Piece by piece, I piled the clothes onto my bed and grabbed the hangers left in the closet. As I straightened it out, images of Hunter danced around my mind.

Some may think I was obsessed, but they just didn't

understand how amazing he was. Sure, he could be a typical brother to Mia, and I guess if I had a brother, I wouldn't want my best friend to take his side, but it wasn't my fault he was gifted with desirable qualities. If anyone should be to blame, it's his parents and maybe even Mia for being my best friend and causing me to spend so much time with him.

How could I be held responsible for an inevitable consequence of our friendship?

I slapped my hands together in satisfaction. Now with a clean floor, I could relax. I was never one for a mess, even as a child. If I made a mess, I cleaned it up. It was who I was. Mia on the other hand couldn't be more different. Her room consistently had an inch high layer of clothes. I had no idea how she knew what was clean or dirty, but it suited her, so I never fixed it.

The evening summer light streamed through my window as I sat on my bed and opened my laptop. My tabs from the last time I was home were opened. One caught my eye.

It was Richard's social media page. Why would this page be up? I hadn't used my laptop before we left, which made even less sense that Mia would have been looking at this. Something about the whole situation didn't add up but getting it out of Mia would be near impossible. If there was one thing that had never changed about Mia as we got older, it was how stubborn she was. If she decided something, there was no changing her mind. If I had any hope of figuring it out, I'd have to lead her to the idea.

I shook my head and closed the laptop. Maybe things would be more enlightening on our vacation.

Chapter Two

Green blobs blurred past the window as I snuggled closer in my blanket. We officially were on hour four of our trip to the beach and I was over the car ride already. It was possible that part of my mood was due to Hunter driving his own car to the beach and missing the mandatory six hours of close confinement with us.

Mia sat with her earbuds in, jamming out to some playlist she made right before we left. I could have asked her to share, and she would have, but the disappointment of not being around Hunter was more than I could fake now.

So instead, I continued to watch the scenery outside the SUV window blur past me. We would stop when we got to North Carolina, but either way, the drive was boring when I couldn't be close to Hunter without it seeming like I had ulterior motives. It may have been weird, but when I couldn't outwardly show how I felt about him, I had to take what I could get.

Last year, Mia and I had sat in the back row, while Hunter took over the middle row of seats. He had played card games with us and told silly jokes. He even talked to us a little about high school since it was to be our freshman year, but his absence on this ride was worse somehow.

Mr. Baylor met my gaze in the rearview mirror. "Hanging in there, Allie? Need to stop or anything?"

I shook my head. "I'm good. Just can't wait to be there."

Mrs. Baylor laughed. "You and me both, Allie. This trip gets longer and longer every year."

"Absolutely."

She turned and smiled, then refocused out the front window.

Mia still sat on her side of the SUV absorbed in her playlist and phone. At this point, all I could do was read my book and wait for the remaining time to pass before we stopped for gas and some basic necessities before heading to the rental house.

A cool hand pushed my arm. "Allie. Allie, wake up! We're here!" Mia screamed.

I blinked a few times trying to get my eyes to adjust before climbing out of the SUV. Mia had already run around to my side before I managed to open the door. I replaced my bookmark in my book, after having fallen asleep while reading, placed it on my seat and exited.

The humidity and afternoon sun beamed down onto my air-conditioned face. The warmth felt good after being in a deep freeze. Mia's parents always kept the air conditioner on high during the trip. I didn't mind though, it was an inexplicable feeling being that cold and stepping into the sunlight, at least until I thawed out and started to sweat.

Hunter beeped the horn on his green convertible as Richard leaned from the window. "Outer Banks baby!" Richard shouted.

Mia glared at Richard and rolled her eyes. "God, he is so

ridiculous. I hope our rooms are so far apart this year. I can't stand him."

"Have you seen the house yet?" I asked.

"Nope. Mom and Dad are keeping it all hush hush this year. I have no idea how many rooms it is or if it's close to the water this time or not."

Mia's family always rented a house for the trip. A few times we had been remarkably close to beach, while others we had to drive to the beach from the house. No matter what though, the house was always spectacular.

"I guess we'll find out soon enough."

Hunter parked the convertible in a spot a few rows up from the gas pumps.

Mr. Baylor pumped gas into the SUV, while Mrs. Baylor disappeared inside.

Mia watched Hunter and Richard with a look of disdain etched across her face.

I had never seen her react so aggressively toward one of Hunter's friends. With everything I knew about the profile being on my laptop and how she acted, something was up, but I couldn't put my finger on it quite yet.

I shut my eyes and stood with my arms outstretched soaking in the sun. Before I knew it, the week would be up, and I wanted to bask in all its glory before I had to go back to Chesapeake Hills and school.

School wasn't the worst thing in the world. At least I would have volleyball tryouts but still, I didn't want to say goodbye to summer just yet, even though this trip's purpose was to do just that.

An elbow lodged its way into my rib cage. "Ow!" I peered at whoever had done the damage, surprised to see Hunter barely a few inches away from my face.

"Did you break on the car ride down?" he asked.

I squinted into his beautifully tanned face. "What? No."

He cocked his head to the side. "Could have fooled me. You're standing out here by yourself with your arms out and your eyes closed. You look like you're trying to catch snowflakes. All that's missing is your tongue out."

"I'm trying to warm up and it feels nice. Mia was just here, and you're here, so I'm not alone."

He chuckled. "Sure, Duncan. If you say so." He strolled back to his convertible twisting his lanyard around his fingers as it swung in the air. His muscles flexed with each movement in a hypnotic fashion.

I shook my head and forced my gaze down. What was I thinking? I couldn't openly ogle at Hunter when Mia could see me. If she saw my face and traced my gaze to her brother's butt, she would kill me.

Mia skipped from the gas station door with a handful of packages. She tossed me a small sugary snack. "They didn't have much, but I know you can't resist the powdered donuts."

"Thanks. This is perfect, but did you happen to—"

Mia interrupted me by tossing a Coke in my direction.

"You are seriously the best."

Mia grinned. "I know."

We hopped back in the SUV as Mr. Baylor put the cap back on the gas tank and grabbed his receipt.

Mia chomped down on her Takis. How she tolerated them was beyond me. I wasn't a spicy person, but she could eat a whole bag and barely break a sweat.

"Are we close?" I asked.

Mia stopped midbite. "I think so. Mom didn't really tell me much, but I swear I can almost smell the beach. So that's something."

"You swore you could smell the beach when we were in Virginia."

"And your point? Virginia has beaches!"

"I know, silly, but not the right ones."

Mr. and Mrs. Baylor hopped in the SUV and turned the key.

"Ready ladies?" Mr. Baylor asked.

Mia hooted and I followed suit.

He chuckled. "I'll take that as a yes."

I giggled sending white powder from my lips. Soon we would be at the house and then the vacation could really start.

* * *

The house was bigger than any of the others I could remember. It was called Destiny. Every house was named, for what, I had no idea, but alas this was the name of ours. The siding was navy blue with white trim. A large staircase led to the second floor of the house, while the driveway had a small overhang to pull the cars under and walk in on the ground floor.

In all, the beach house had three stories with balconies on both sides and off the bedrooms. It was more than I could have hoped for.

Mia sighed. "This house is legendary. Let's sneak in and steal the better room before the boys do."

I followed her around to the side while her parents sorted things in the back of the SUV. The boys hadn't pulled up yet.

A short hallway led into a large game room filled with a pool table and foosball. A small bedroom led off the main room.

Mia peeked inside and then shook her head. "Definitely not, we'd never get any sleep being right here."

I agreed, but she missed my nod. She found the steps and ran up to the second floor. Off the stairs was a sitting room overlooking the pool. From this sitting room there was a bedroom with bunk beds on both sides. Both rooms looked identical with furniture and a bathroom off each room. One room was decked out in dark blues and greens, while the other was more reds and oranges like the sunset.

"What do you think?" I asked.

"Let's do the blue and green. This orange is a bit much."

I giggled and followed Mia back to the left side of the second floor and set my backpack on the one bottom bunk, while Mia placed her hat on the other bottom bunk.

Mia flopped on the bed and spread out. "This is the life."

I smacked her leg. "Let's go to the top floor, I wanna see the view."

We went up one more flight of stairs and had a panorama view as the kitchen was off to the right and the master bedroom was on the left. As far and as wide as we could see was sand and blue sky through the many floor to ceiling windows.

I took a deep breath. "Wow."

Mia's eyes were wide, and her jaw slackened as she stared. "Yeah. Best house ever."

"Mia! Allie! Come help with all the bags. You can explore later!" Mrs. Baylor shouted.

Mia sighed and trudged down the stairs. I stared for a few more seconds until I followed her too. The sun only had a few more hours of daylight and I knew the Baylors wouldn't be pleased to unload in the dark.

Hunter's green convertible pulled up next to the SUV just as we stepped down the final stair.

I wondered what they would think of the house. Not that I could find out or pay attention to it, Mia huffed at the sight of Richard and practically stomped away. This would be a long week if she stayed prickly.

The backseat was full of my pillow and blanket. I grabbed my suitcase from the back of the SUV and loaded my pillow and blanket on top and wheeled it up the stairs. It took four trips up and down the stairs to unpack the back of the SUV and the trailer. The next day we would go to the grocery store to stock up the house, but tonight it would be a dinner of grilled hot dogs and mac n' cheese. The classic meal for the first night at the beach house.

"I'm starving. Mom packed way more than normal this year."

"More people, more stuff?"

Mia harrumphed. "Yeah probably. Too bad the people aren't better. Whatever. If they think they're dominating the four wheelers or the game room they've got another thing coming."

"Really, Mia? Since when do you play pool? And besides, we aren't sixteen yet. We can't really drive the four wheelers."

Mia cocked her eyebrow. "When has that ever stopped us? I'll ride them if I want to ride them."

I raised my hands, palms out. "Whatever you say."

The door to the bedroom burst open, Hunter and Richard overwhelmed the space in the doorway.

We sat up on the bunks. Mia glared at them, while Hunter's eyes danced with orneriness.

"This is a nice room. Who says you two get it?" Hunter asked.

Mia crossed her arms. "Finders keepers."

Hunter's eyebrows shot up. "Is that so? You really want to play it that way?"

"It's a room, Hunter. The on the other side of the house is the exact same. We already claimed this one."

"Just because you both laid on the bed, doesn't mean you claimed it."

"Our stuff is already in here, just get out and go put your stuff in the other room."

Richard gave Hunter a wink. "We could easily move *their* stuff to the other room."

Oh crap. Richard shut up, just stay silent.

Mia's gaze sharpened. "Excuse me? Or you could get out of our room."

Hunter chuckled and patted Richard's shoulder. "Nah, let them keep the room. I have other ideas."

They backed out of the doorway and shut the door.

Mia growled once the door was fully shut. "What is it with him? He thinks he can do and say whatever he wants. He's on vacation with *my* family. He needs to figure out where his place is."

Mia continued ranting, but I stayed silent. There was absolutely nothing I could say that would calm that fire or not make myself the target. It was better if it stayed focused on Richard. I didn't need to be a casualty too.

Chapter Three

"Dinner's ready," Mrs. Baylor shouted.

My stomach grumbled. After putting away all my clothes in the drawers and setting my bed up the way I wanted, I was ravenous. I headed for the stairs, even though Mia was still in the bathroom.

Hunter came around at the same time.

We almost collided.

He outstretched his hand. "You first."

"Thanks." My cheeks flushed, heat crawling up my neck. Why did I blush so much around him? It didn't mean anything that he let me go ahead. He was being a gentleman.

Mrs. Baylor passed us plates, then let us scoop out our portions of mac n' cheese and grab hot dogs as we pleased.

Mr. Baylor already sat at the table, scarfing down what was probably his second hot dog from the grill.

There was something about a grilled hot dog that just tasted so much better than any other kind.

Mia came to my side and bumped me as she grabbed her plate. "Didn't wait for me I see."

"Everyone for themselves when it comes to dinner."

She laughed. "Fine, but I'll remember that next time."

I sneered at her playfully, then took my plate to the table.

Mr. Baylor smiled. "All unpacked?"

"Yep," I said then took a bite.

"Good. Any plans for tonight?"

Hunter sat across from me.

Yikes. Why did his proximity have to kick start my heart rate?

"Probably finishing a book," he said, then smirked.

"No," I said.

Mr. Baylor chuckled. "Nothing wrong with reading."

"Of course not," Hunter said.

"For your information, I don't *read* all the time."

Mia plopped into the chair next to me. "Yes, you do. But I still love you anyway."

I harrumphed. Did everyone have to make me out as a nerd too?

Mrs. Baylor took her seat at the opposite end of the table, leaving a chair open next to Hunter. "Where's Richard? The food will get cold."

"He'll be up in a few minutes. Was on the phone."

I caught Mia's eyebrow raise, before she covered her expression.

I sunk my fork into the mac n' cheese, then took the bite. The cheesy goodness made my heart sing. No matter how old I got, I would never shy away from mac n' cheese and its comfort.

Not to mention, the more I focused on my plate, the less I had to stare into Hunter's gaze. Why did he have to sit across the table from me?

"Well, your father and I will be going to bed early tonight after that drive. Plus, we are leaving early to get food from the grocery store. So, you kids behave tonight. Don't get into too much trouble."

Hunter saluted, while Mia rolled her eyes.

"Of course, Mrs. Baylor."

She smiled. "I know I can count on you, Allie." She pointed her fork to her children. "Not sure about those two."

I giggled.

"Me?" Mia asked. "Allie's the one who's the bad influence."

Hunter snorted. "Yeah right, Duncan doesn't have a bad bone in her body."

Heat crawled up my cheeks. Thankfully, Richard had finally come up the stairs, cutting off Mia's comment. I didn't want to hear it anyway. I didn't want the attention. It always made it harder to protect my feelings.

Richard sat across from Mia, sending her closer to my side.

"Mom, can Allie and I take our plates on the deck?"

"Sure, honey," Mrs. Baylor said.

Mia nudged my arm, my cue to stand and follow her.

Their voices from inside abruptly cut off as the French door shut behind me.

Mia exhaled loudly. "So happy she said yes. I didn't want to start the trip staring at his face."

"It will be hard to get away from him the whole time. I mean he is in the same house for the week."

She shrugged. "Look at this view. God it's so amazing. Best house yet."

Sand dunes surrounded the back part of the house. It was equipped with a pool, shimmering from the remaining sunlight. Beyond the dunes was the roar of the waves, crashing over and over on the shoreline. I itched to go out and see the water.

"Want to take a walk by the ocean tonight?"

"Hmm. Maybe."

That meant probably not in Mia speak. Well, either way, I was going.

"Is that a hot tub down there?" Mia asked.

I looked in the direction she pointed. "Yep. And a diving board too."

"That could be fun."

I laughed. "When have you ever used either?"

She shrugged. "I could change that this week."

"You could, but you won't."

She rolled her eyes. "Hurry up and finish, I want to check out the pool."

"Do you want to go in?"

"No, just see what we're working with."

"Okay, well then I'm done."

She turned to stare inside at the table.

Only Hunter remained.

Mia stood and opened the door for me, then we headed down.

I grabbed my flip flops and pushed the screen door open to the back patio by the pool. Several lounge chairs were placed around the edge. The hot tub was bigger than it had appeared to be from the top balcony. It could have easily fit all six of us if we decided to get in together.

"This will do nicely," Mia said.

"You and I both know we will be at the beach more than at the pool."

"True, but still a nice one. You remember that one year where the pool's tiles started peeling off into the bottom?"

I laughed. "Yes! Ugh that had creeped me out."

"Me too." Mia kicked off both sandals, then sat by the edge, letting her feet dangle into the water.

I followed suit, smacking at a few bugs as they descended on us from the sunset. "So, will you walk out to the beach with me?"

"Do you really want me to go?"

That was her way of saying, I'll go if I must, but I don't

really want to. "No, it's fine. I'll take my phone and a flashlight."

She nodded but shifted her attention back to her phone.

I grabbed the flashlight from inside the door and used the back pathway to head toward the shoreline. Sand slipped between my toes and flip flops. After almost sliding down the dune, the sand evened out and I could see the waves crashing on the shoreline, the bright white illuminated from the moonlight taking over the sky.

No one walked by that I could see, just me alone with the sound of the water rushing through my ears. This was my perfect moment. My thoughts seemed larger at the beach, and made it feel like anything could happen.

After a few moments of letting the waves crashing lull me, I slipped my flip flops off and headed for the water. The first wave that rushed over my feet, surprised me as the warm water soothed me further. The night air dipped from its earlier heat, seeming to soak into the ocean water.

Someone cleared their throat behind me.

I startled and turned, shining a flashlight on them. "You decided to come—"

Hunter's green eyes illuminated brighter than any precious gemstone in the flashlight's beam, which is when I realized I should move it away from his face.

"Oh. I thought you were Mia."

"Just me. I'm sorry, I scared you."

"It's fine." I looked behind him, shining the light toward the beach house. "You're out here alone?"

"Yeah, Richard wanted to sleep."

"Oh. Okay."

"You came out to the shore without Mia? That's dangerous in the dark."

"So did you."

"And?"

"And what? I'm some defenseless girl who needs a chaperone?"

"That's not what I meant."

I retreated to my flip flops and plopped into the sand. I kept my gaze on Hunter's back as he stared into the water. Of all the places on the beach, why did he have to stand at this one? This was my escape from my feelings, and I hated that the other part of me was secretly excited that we were here ... alone. What did I expect to happen? I was his sister's best friend. Some useless sophomore. This was just a convenient spot, directly in front of the house.

I stood and slipped my feet into my flip flops. "I'm heading back. Have a good night."

"Duncan, wait. I didn't mean to crash your walk and then insult you."

"No harm done, Hunter. I should head back anyway."

"I can walk with you."

I waved the flashlight, sending it haphazardly across his chest. "I'll be fine. Enjoy the view." I turned to walk back.

I would be lucky if I could sleep picturing what could have happened on that beach. What I wished would happen. If only we were different people, and it wasn't forbidden.

* * *

I woke up early the next day not wanting to waste any second down by the water and tired of fighting sleep picturing different endings for my night. If we played it right, we could have several hours at the beach before lunch, then ride the four wheelers in the afternoon before dinner. It would be the perfect day to start our vacation.

Mia snored from the other side of the room.

I tiptoed to the bathroom and shut the door. My bathroom bag sat on the left side of the vanity. I had to rummage around to find my moisturizer with sunscreen for my face. I wouldn't waste time with makeup for the beach, but moisturizer with sunscreen was important if I would be outside in the sun all day. I brushed my teeth and adjusted my pajama top and athletic shorts before leaving the room. After breakfast I would get dressed for the beach. I hated sitting in a bathing suit if I was inside, it felt uncomfortable.

The top floor of the house bubbled with breakfast smells like bacon and French toast. Mrs. Baylor of course had woken up before me and was already cooking breakfast for everyone. When I was younger, I had always waited for Mia to get up before I went to eat, but then I realized I could be waiting for hours, especially as we got older. Mia liked her sleep, and I didn't want to starve.

Mrs. Baylor smiled as she flipped the French toast. Another round of sizzles sparked as the raw side of the toast cooked. "Good morning, Allie. Sleep well?"

"Yes, Mrs. Baylor, but I'm ready for the beach!"

"I'd sure hope so. Is Mia stirring yet?"

"Nope. It'll take a bomb; you know how she is."

"That girl! She'll sleep the day away."

"I'll make sure she gets up before that. We have plans to maximize all the beach time possible."

"Good. She can sleep when we're home."

"Exactly."

Mr. Baylor strolled from their master bedroom to the kitchen and kissed Mrs. Baylor on the forehead. "This smells delicious, sweetie."

"Oh no. You don't get extra bacon. Your egg whites and spinach omelet is ready and keeping warm in the microwave."

Mr. Baylor groaned. "We're on vacation. I can't have bacon?"

"Nope, you know your doctor told you no. You need to go

easier on your body. All that fatty and greasy food isn't good for someone your age."

Mr. Baylor crossed his arms. "Well, what are you eating?"

"I already had oatmeal. The French toast and bacon are for the kids."

Mr. Baylor harrumphed and trudged to the table with his plate. "Allie, have extra bacon for me since I can't."

I giggled. "You got it, Mr. Baylor."

The sound of feet thudding up the stairs echoed around the kitchen. Those feet were way too loud to be Mia, it could only be ...

Hunter.

His brown hair was shaggy on the top without his styling gel, while the sides were shaved down. It was messy, but still hot.

I gulped as he noticed the food and smiled wide. "Mom, this looks so good. I could smell it from my room."

"It's ready when you're ready for it. Is Richard up yet?"

Hunter shook his head. "I doubt it'll be soon. He was fidgety most of the night."

Mrs. Baylor frowned. "Was he uncomfortable?"

"I don't know. I didn't ask." Hunter pulled the stool next to me out from under the counter and hopped up. His mouth seemed to water as he eyed the food. His gaze flitted to me.

My cheeks warmed and I averted my gaze. I couldn't let him know I was staring at him. It was bad enough I couldn't resist his looks in my mind, but for anyone to know the truth would be a hundred times worse.

"Mornin', Duncan."

"Hey, Hunter."

Mrs. Baylor scooped the last four pieces of French toast on the plate and set it between us. She handed us our plate and then gathered syrup, butter, and honey which she placed by Mr. Baylor.

Hunter hopped from the stool, creating a thud as his feet hit the floor. His athletic shorts swiped by my calf as he moved to the other side of the counter to pile food onto his plate. Hunter's emerald gaze rose to meet mine. "Are we good from last night?"

"Yeah, of course."

"Okay. Did you want to get food first? You were here before me."

"No, it's fine. There's plenty for us both."

He didn't respond, but instead piled four pieces of French toast and four pieces of bacon onto his plate before dousing it in honey and butter.

"Allie honey, help yourself. You don't want to let it get cold," Mrs. Baylor said.

I walked to the other side of the counter. I had nowhere near the same appetite that Hunter did, but I couldn't resist bacon. God how I wished Mia was awake. Without her at the table, I'd have to talk to Hunter and her parents by myself, which in and of itself wasn't horrible, but it made it so much harder to manage my façade when I was forced to interact with him in front of others at such a close range. At least the previous night it had been dark enough to hide my reactions. In broad daylight, I could easily give myself away.

I chose the chair at the other side of Mr. Baylor, farther away from Hunter. As soon as I sat, Mr. Baylor stood with his empty plate and took it to the kitchen. My jaw clenched.

The buffer Mr. Baylor would have provided was now absent.

Great, just great.

"John! It's time to get dressed. The kids will all be up soon, and we need to be ready to head to the beach. Don't want to waste this lovely weather," Mrs. Baylor shouted.

Mr. Baylor pouted as he trudged to the bedroom. She left absolutely no room for him to sneak food.

The sound of a fork scraping the plate brought my attention back to the table. Hunter and I now sat *alone*. What was the universe thinking?

"You and Mia have any plans for today?" Hunter asked.

I shrugged. "Go to the beach mostly, probably play volleyball to practice for tryouts."

"Ah. Always attached to that volleyball of yours."

"Have to be if I want to make the team. We aren't freshmen anymore. We don't get a special team that ensures we'll make it."

Hunter snorted. "I've seen you two play and I've seen the other girls on the team, I think you'll both be fine."

I tucked a stray brown hair behind my ear. "Well, thank you, but I still plan to practice every minute I can."

"Now, that I believe." Hunter finished cutting his French toast and took a bite.

When he looked up, I stared back at my plate. I could do this. I just had to eat, putting one bite of food in my mouth after the other. If I didn't have a lull in eating, it wouldn't be weird if I didn't talk.

"Nice pajamas," Hunter said.

The comment shifted my attention. I wore a T-shirt from middle school and athletic shorts. I didn't usually think twice about my pajamas but was suddenly aware of how much smaller this shirt was. I tugged at the hem. "It's comfy."

He chuckled. "I'll say, the color isn't even the same anymore. Didn't that used to be like a burgundy to match school colors?"

"Yeah, and?"

"It's like a pale pink."

"Is there a rule against how long you can wear a T-shirt?"

"No, was just pointing out it looked well-worn."

I pursed my lips. I didn't understand what his angle was. Was this small talk? I took a few more bites, as he polished off half of his food. "And what are you and Richard doing today?"

"Boogie boarding, might try to skim board, depends on the waves."

That sounded about right. The Baylors had tried to get me to do the same over the years, but my talent for both never progressed, although I never really tried either.

I shifted my fork around the plate, gathering syrup on the piece of French toast. "You never said why you had taken a walk alone last night."

Hunter's gaze flitted up to meet mine. He held my gaze, until I broke it first. "Wanted to see the beach. Seemed silly to drive all that way and not see it."

"Yeah. I thought so too."

Hunter smiled, then tossed his fork on the plate, stood, and pushed in his chair. "See you later, Duncan." He placed his dirty dishes in the sink before thudding back down the stairs.

I sighed and focused on my breakfast. With no one to talk to, I finished my food quickly, placed my dishes on top of Hunter's and then wrapped up two pieces of bacon in a paper towel before heading back to my room.

No doubt, Mia would still be swaddled in her sheets, oblivious to the time.

The door creaked as I closed it. Sure enough, Mia laid wrapped in her blankets, mouth agape, eyes closed.

I took the bacon and waved it several times over her face. "Wake up, sleepyhead."

Mia shifted and then peeked open one eye. "Is that bacon I smell?"

I giggled. "Of course. Your mom made bacon and French toast. Hurry up and go get some before it's all gone. Then we can go outside, or I'm leaving your butt here."

Mia growled. "You wouldn't."

I arched my eyebrow. "I wouldn't?"

Mia tossed the blanket to the side and snatched the bacon from my hand. "Okay, yes you would, but that'd be so rude."

"Well, get up. It's vacation. No time to waste with *sleeping.*"

She held up her hands in surrender. "Fine. I'm getting up."

I sat on my bed and popped my headphones in as I scrolled through my phone. Mia shut herself in the bathroom for a few minutes, before disappearing upstairs. I took the time to check my texts. Nothing from my parents, but I knew they'd want to know what I was up to, even if they didn't initiate it themselves first.

Hey, you two, getting ready for the beach soon. Miss you both.

I hit Send and switched to my social media apps. Most were pictures of people tanning by the pool or the occasional beach picture, but what grabbed my attention was from Brittany Jennings.

Brittany was a sophomore just like Mia and me, but she was god awful. She lived to torture me and call me names. She started playing volleyball just because I decided to tryout and what's worse is she had a natural talent I couldn't ever stop being jealous of.

Instead of beach pictures or sitting by the pool looking gorgeous, Brittany wore her tightest spandex shorts and an old club volleyball jersey in a video of her spiking the volleyball using one of the many machines her parents had bought for her to practice.

Did I mention Brittany was next level rich? Her dad had invented some dating app and it went viral so fast the money came rolling in faster than they could spend it. Brittany, of course, used it to enhance her popularity.

I absolutely couldn't stand her. If anyone was competition for the limited openings on the team, it would be Brittany.

I glowered at the screen and my nostrils flared. Mia and I had to outdo her this year.

Mia burst in the room carrying another piece of bacon in her hand, with the other half sticking from her mouth. She stopped suddenly when she saw me. "What's with you?"

I shoved the phone toward her. "Freaking Brittany. Look at the setup she has to practice. We must make sure we condition this week too."

"Allie, relax. You take her too seriously. She doesn't deserve all that energy. You're the best setter I know."

I folded my arms. "So? What if she moves to setter just to edge me out?"

Mia rolled her eyes. "Not likely. Setter isn't flashy enough for her. She doesn't appreciate the subtle control that comes as a setter. She needs people to fawn over her and, unless you're a hitter, that's not happening."

"I can't stand her."

"Fair enough, but you and I have our positions on lock." She patted my knee. "Let's get dressed and head to the beach."

A half-smile escaped and grew as I thought about what she said. "Ugh, okay. I have to stop letting her get to me."

Mia cheered. "That's the spirit!"

As usual Mia was right, but I couldn't help it. Brittany got under my skin, and I had no idea how to let that go.

I pulled my suitcase out from under the bed. I had over-packed as normal, but I knew exactly what I wanted to wear for our first beach day. Over the years, Mia and I had devised a system for packing for Outer Banks. There would always be several nights we needed a nice dinner outfit, the during the day beach wear, four-wheeler wear, and then pajamas. If there weren't enough bathing suits for almost every day of the trip, then we packed wrong.

I passed over my one piece and searched through the silky and soft fabrics for my white and teal striped two-piece bikini. A small piece of the teal fabric peeked through the rest of my clothes, until I was able to pull out both pieces of the bathing suit. Next I needed my white coverup, baseball cap, and sunglasses for when we played volleyball on the beach.

Mia strolled from the bathroom decked out in her beige bikini and a black floppy hat. "I'm ready for my photoshoot."

I laughed. "You're a mess but love that whole look. New bathing suit?"

"Yep. Mom took me shopping and treated me to a few new suits."

"Nice. They look good."

"Let's hope they do their job."

My nose wrinkled. "Their *job*?"

Mia stared at me blankly. "To catch the attention of some hot local or tourist guys. Allie, please tell me you haven't forgotten about our pact to find something spicy to ogle?"

I gulped. It wasn't so much that I had forgotten, as much as I already had issues avoiding the spicy specimen of male attractiveness that resided down the hall—Hunter's body. "Of course not, Mia. I just didn't realize we were starting today."

Mia fanned herself with her hand. "Gotta start early. Who knows who will see us playing sand volleyball."

"If you say so. Personally, I won't look like a great catch all sweaty and gross from the sun."

"With your body? Yes, you will. Guys love a little cushion, and you have a cushiony derriere."

My eyebrows flew up. "Mia!"

Mia cackled. "It's a compliment."

"It sounds like a way to say my ass is huge."

"Never."

"Mm-hmm." I tossed a pillow at her side. "Hurry up. I'm dying to get in the water and go swimming."

She waved me off and I headed for the bathroom, my clothes scooped in my arms. I quickly changed and double checked nothing hung out inappropriately from my bathing suit before deciding I looked okay. Unlike Mia, my bathing suits were from the previous year, and while I loved them, I had grown since last summer. Not in height, but I guess it could be said that I filled them out a little more than before.

Mia whistled as I stepped from the bathroom. "You look hot."

"Cut it out. Seriously."

Mia giggled. "I don't know why you get so shy about your body. We are fit from sports. You have curves, but it's a sporty curve and girl you need to rock it instead of hiding it."

"Hush before I wear my cover up the whole time today."

She rolled her eyes and picked up her sunglasses. We were both finally ready and I couldn't wait.

I grabbed my small tote bag, filled it with my phone, sunscreen, and a towel, then followed Mia down the stairs to the backyard pathway for the beach. If it had been my parents, I would have had to wait for them to lug everything we owned down to the beach and give them a detailed description of what we planned. But the Baylors were laid back. It didn't matter that they might still be in the beach house. They would join us on the beach eventually and we were free to head out on foot whenever we wanted.

Mia opened the gate leading to the planked pathway. Tall beach grass tickled my arm as we moseyed down the path until it reached the top of the dune and the ocean stretched before us.

I breathed deeply, taking in the salty scent of the ocean and the noise of birds flying in the distance barely audible over the incessant crashing of the waves. The view was ten times better in the daylight.

Mia had stopped walking and perched her hand at her

brow line to survey the beach below us. I could see two small people-dots, but no canopy or beach stairs, which meant only Hunter and Richard were in the water so far.

Mr. and Mrs. Baylor would set up a fort for the beach. Well, maybe not a fort, but it was certainly impressive. They brought chairs for each of us, coolers filled with water and sodas, and alcoholic beverages for them. They usually had a portable radio and would set up camp underneath their pop-up canopy.

Mia continued walking down to the beach. I slipped off my sandals to scrunch my toes in the sand, although it quickly became hot as we got to the bottom of the dune. I scurried toward the spot I last saw Hunter and Richard. My green polka dotted towel covered the sand as I hurried to spread it out then found relief for my feet when it was flat.

I peeled off the coverup, my hat, and sunglasses. My brown hair tumbled over my shoulders, and I swished it around, hoping to detangle a few of the spots before getting in the water.

I knew the salty water and wind would tangle my hair faster than I could undo the damage, but that's what detangler was for, wasn't it?

"You ready?" I asked.

Mia nodded and sprinted toward the water.

"No fair, you cheater!"

She stuck out her tongue and launched into the waves.

The sudden transition from the hot sand to the cooler wet sand was one of my favorite sensations. I stopped and let the waves wash over my toes and up to my ankle before receding. I closed my eyes and let the cyclic motion calm me before I got in farther.

Mia screeched as a wave crashed on her head. When she stood up from the wave several feet closer to me than before, her hair was stuck to the one side of her face and wrapped around like a turban.

I stifled a giggle. "Did it sneak up on you?"

"Yeah, I was trying to listen to Hunter and Richard. They were discussing some girl and then *wham* the wave caught me in the side of the head."

I scrunched my nose. "Why are you trying to listen to their conversation about girls? Since when do you care?"

"I don't, but I haven't heard Hunter talk about anyone in a while."

At the mention of Hunter's name my heart fluttered and then my stomach dropped. Was he interested in someone? He hadn't had a girlfriend in over a year and while that made it harder to ignore my attraction, it also wouldn't feel great that he would never see me like that. He was a senior and I was a sophomore, we couldn't have been in more of a different world than if we tried.

Mia treaded through the waves until she was even with the boys from the shore. She allowed herself to somewhat float, with her head raised above higher than the rest of her body, looking for waves.

We should have brought the air mattress. It was the perfect day for riding in the waves. One time Hunter, Mia, and I had ridden the wave all the way in from fifty feet out. We were so proud of ourselves. It was one of my favorite memories with the Baylors. But at this point, no one would want to go back for it. So instead, I relaxed into the waves and let the summer sun wrap me in warmth, while the ocean cooled my body. My eyes closed and I relished the sounds of the waves. Nothing was better than this.

Chapter Four

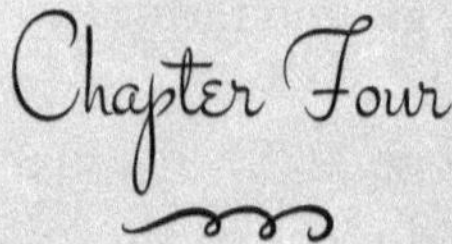

The water glistened off my skin as I laid on my beach towel, my coverup over my face. We spent what felt like hours in the ocean until Mia's parents lured us all back to the house with the promise of lunch.

The walk itself was enough to need a quick dip, which is exactly what I did. Mia laid next to me on her towel, tossing sand up in the air.

"Tell me again why we can't go on the four wheelers yet?" Mia whined.

"Because. You saw that video with Brittany, we must practice every day. The four-wheelers can be our reward for a good workout."

"Ugh, I so hate you right now."

I peered at her from underneath the coverup. "You do not. You secretly enjoy these workouts as much as I do. You love volleyball too. You are the best libero we have. I don't know anyone who can protect the back row the way you do."

"Had. We aren't on the freshmen team anymore. I may have been the smallest one last year, but I'm certainly not this year."

"You and I both know that size isn't the only factor in a libero. You're scrappy. You dig up stuff I've never seen before. It's quite inspiring."

"Whatever. If you're forcing me to do this workout, then get up." She chucked the volleyball at me, and it hit my stomach.

"Rude!"

"Well, let's go hot shot."

I growled toward Mia as I shook the sand off my towel and my legs. I grabbed my hat and trailed after her. It was probably a good thing to not be fully dry as we played in the hot afternoon sun.

Mr. Baylor sat under the canopy resting, while Mrs. Baylor hadn't pried her eyes away from the next steamy romance novel she was reading. She always had some nonfiction dust jacket over the cover, but I knew better. She *only* read steamy romance novels. Mia and I had snooped at what she was reading one year. We had thought it was a biography on Roald Dahl, an author we had read that previous year. But it certainly wasn't about Roald Dahl. I had learned words I never expected to in thirty seconds. We had slammed the book shut and hid it in her towel before she came back. We never did discuss it again, and we never snooped on what she was reading after that.

Hunter and Richard were now using boogie boards and skim boards to play in the waves. Hunter seemed to be a pro compared to Richard. Richard had fallen and eaten sand at least three times by my count, while Hunter's perfectly chiseled chest never fell once.

Focus, Allie.

Mia had walked at least fifteen feet from me and was bumping the ball to herself in short little spurts. Her control was envious. I was an all-around talented player, but spiking was always my weakness. I had never gotten my timing down to be a good spiker, nor could I manage enough strength in my upper body to have any hard hits. My strength resided in my hands. I could set a ball in my sleep. I could also anticipate where hits would go and working with Mia, we were unstoppable. But the libero and setter never received the recognition. Hitters were the power players, and everyone focused on how far to the corner and backrow they could hit. Not if someone could set the ball perfectly above the hitter's hand in time for their swing.

"I'm ready," I shouted.

Mia smirked and tossed the ball into the air, then spiked it hard. She might have been petite, but she was feisty.

I dug into the sand, retrieving it and passing it back to her. We gathered a rhythm as she bumped it to me, and I set it back to her. Occasionally, one of us would spike it, but we worked on our control. Light feathery touches for my set that soared up high and lobbed over to her, while she focused on bumping it back to me high enough to set, but also make me work for it.

"Looking good, ladies," Mrs. Baylor called.

I averted my gaze to see Mrs. Baylor standing under the canopy with two thumbs up.

Hunter and Richard used their towels to dry off as they looked our way. Hunter's gaze focused on our practice and the attention made me uncomfortable. I missed the ball as it flew past my face toward the canopy.

"Allie! Get your head into it. We had a record going."

I shrugged her off and jogged toward the ball, but Hunter had already grabbed it and held it out for me.

"You guys are getting better. I knew you stood a chance."

I smiled and dipped my gaze under my hat as the heat crawled over my cheeks. "That's the goal." Without looking I reached for the ball and our hands brushed each other as Hunter handed it over.

The touch was light, barely noticeable. But I felt it to my core. The feeling of his hand touching mine was enough to make my skin go cold, even in this summer heat.

But for all the reaction I felt, I knew Hunter had probably not even noticed. He had turned before the ball was truly in my possession and walked back toward Richard under the canopy.

What did I expect? Even if he wasn't off limits, did I really expect someone like him to notice someone like me? I wasn't in his league, and I knew it.

Two teenage boys walked past us closer to the house side. Mia eyed them and then gestured to me to throw the ball. We bumped it back and forth a few more times, but she stopped trying so hard when they had walked past. They were the only boys we had seen all day, except for Hunter and Richard.

Mia waited for me as I tossed the ball from hand to hand. "Wanna go on the four wheelers now?"

Mia cocked her brow. "Are you finally allowing it?"

She could use a pick-me-up. "Why not?"

Mia grinned from ear to ear and bounced in the sand. We bolted over to our towels, shoved our things in the bag, shouted a quick goodbye, and sprinted up the sand dune and back to the house. We tossed our bags by the pool table in the game room, shoved our feet in our sneakers by the door, and raced to the four wheelers.

The Baylors had two utility four wheelers. They were larger than some and came with bars in the back, which made it a whole lot easier for two passengers to hold on. Technically we weren't allowed to drive them, definitely not on the beach, but no one really stopped us before and this year we were the closest to sixteen we could be without being old enough. We had discussed it on the way down, if we got caught we lied about our birthdays, it wouldn't be hard to change it by one year.

One four-wheeler was an electric-blue and the other was race-car-red. Mia's favorite to drive was the red one, which is the one she picked. She took two helmets off the shelf and tossed one to me. Then she grabbed the key off the hook and skipped to the four-wheeler.

"I have been dying to drive this."

I rolled my eyes. "You ride them all the time."

Mia puffed out her bottom lip. "Not with you and not on the sand."

"Well, hurry up then you're wasting time."

She pulled the helmet on and hopped up. Once she adjusted, I hopped up behind her. The four-wheeler roared to life and Mia accelerated down the sandy path. The sun was lower in the sky, but we had several hours before nightfall. It took the edge off the heat and as we flew down the path, the wind in our face, I had forgotten the warmth from the day.

One hand rested on Mia's side while the other hand clung to the bar behind me. Hair whipped around the helmet and my face as we went. I inhaled deeply enjoying the salty scent and the view.

Mia was right, this was the perfect place to ride the four wheelers. Nowhere else really compared. Mia braked and then passed an earbud to me. She skipped through her songs, clicked play on her phone, and then started back up.

It was impossible to hear someone on the four-wheeler, but it was our tradition to listen to music as we drove around the back sandy roads in the Outer Banks. The playlist rocked all our current favorites.

The ambience made my thoughts drift to Hunter. I wondered what they were doing back at the house. Every year things got harder to avoid my feelings for him, but this year was the worst. Maybe if I just made it through this week, I'd be home free. Would he really go on the next trip after he graduated? Even if he did, it wouldn't be the same.

That was it. That's all I had to do. I had to make it through this trip and then I'd be golden. Sure, we ran into each other at home and sometimes in the hallways at school, but the closest I ever came to him was on this vacation. His social life never matched with mine and to be honest his social life completely shadowed mine. He was a senior after all.

Chapter Five

The next day was a disappointment. Not only did it rain, but the water pelted the house like a monsoon. The thunder and lightning shook the house and lit up the dark gray sky. It was impossible to even go in our pool. The Baylors were relaxed about most things but risking our lives in a thunderstorm was not on the agenda.

I slouched against the sofa. "This sucks."

Mia's head bowed onto her hands. "Right? One perfect day and then *rain*."

Mrs. Baylor chuckled. "Relax ladies. It's only for one day. We can do plenty. I think there are some board games around here."

Mia held in a groan. "Board games, Mom? We aren't ten anymore."

Mr. Baylor cocked an eyebrow. "Are you saying you aren't cool enough to play games anymore? Or are you scared you'll lose?"

"I'm not scared of anything!"

"Well, then prove it," Mr. Baylor said.

"What's the game?" I asked.

Mr. Baylor scrounged around the cabinet in the main upstairs room. He finally pulled out Monopoly and set it on the kitchen table.

I did groan this time. "Monopoly? Do we think that's really a good idea? Think of how competitive everyone is!"

Hunter bounded up the stairs with Richard in tow. He eyed the board game and smirked. "Monopoly? Are you all insane?"

Mia made chicken noises at Hunter. "Someone scared?"

Hunter plopped in a seat at the table. "Never. Who's willing to play against me?"

Mia eyed me carefully and then winked. "Allie and I will play."

My mouth fell open. "Oh great, pull me into it. When I get pummeled by someone, you bet you'll hear an I told you so."

Mia grinned. "That's fine if you play. But Hunter is the one who will lose, not me."

Richard sat across from Hunter. Mia shoved me into the chair next to Richard and she sat next to Hunter.

Hunter peered at his parents on the couch. "Are you two playing?"

Mrs. Baylor shook her head.

"Of course, I am," Mr. Baylor said. "Someone has to keep you kids honest."

Mia and Hunter both huffed.

"Dad, you're the one who cheats. If we cheat it's because we learned it from you," Hunter said.

Mr. Baylor sat at the head of the table. Hunter chose the car, while Mia chose the shoe. Richard chose the iron, and Mr. Baylor chose the thimble. I chose the dog and we finished setting up the game.

Mr. Baylor rubbed his hands together. "Let's roll to figure out who goes first."

We each took a turn rolling the dice, and of course, Hunter had the highest roll.

Hunter smirked. "You all sure you really want to play the master? It's not too late to back down."

Mia glared at her brother. "So cocky. It'll be so sweet when you're begging me to stay in the game."

Hunter huffed. "Please, when's the last time you won against me?"

Mr. Baylor chuckled. "Now, now, save the trash talk for when you have hotels and are bleeding us dry."

Hunter rubbed his hands together, blew over the dice, and released them onto the table. "Yes! Doubles."

"Seriously?" Mia whined. "*How* do you get that lucky? It's ridiculous."

Richard smirked. "He's a golden boy."

I stifled a laugh.

Mia's cheeks reddened. She would not take this well.

Richard was right. Hunter always managed to have luck on his side. When Mia and I were in fifth grade, Hunter had won his middle school's lottery drawing. He was able to go to the local Rosewood College's basketball game and shoot free throws with the players. I had never seen him so excited and Mia so mad in my life.

Situation after situation, Hunter ended up on top. It was a part of his charm.

Mr. Baylor tapped the side of his lemonade glass with his hand. "What do you say we go somewhere for dinner tonight to get out of the house?"

Mrs. Baylor raised her hand from the couch. "I'm in. We could go to the shops and look around too."

"I'm in," Mia said.

Hunter and Richard nodded as we continued our turns.

"Perfect. We could leave once the game is over."

"Well, that won't take long," Hunter said.

Mia rolled her eyes. "Says you."

"You two are terrible, can't you just play the game?" I asked.

"No," they said in unison.

I stifled a giggle. They were both so much alike it was crazy. A fact they refused to admit. I supposed they were closer than some siblings, but their rivalry still caused strife every now and then. Their competitive spirit was what ruined any hope I had of ever being with Hunter. They saw everything as a competition, and if Hunter dated me, Mia would see it as a loss, even though it was absurd. She couldn't *lose* her best friend to her brother ... not that Hunter was even interested in me. Either way, it would never happen.

Two hours later and the only two players left in the game were Hunter and me. How I managed to still be in was beyond me. Mr. Baylor and Richard were out within the same turn of each other. Mia held on, but it ended when she landed on my hotel.

Mia glared over the rim of her cup. "Hunter just lose already. I'm hungry and Allie will obviously win."

Hunter's brow furrowed. "I don't just *lose*, Mia. I still have a chance to win."

"We could finish the game later."

"What? No way!" Mia said.

"Sorry, Allie, but Mia's right. You must finish the game. Those are the rules," Mr. Baylor said.

I rolled my eyes. "That's silly."

"The winner gets bragging rights; you can't defer that until later. Then it's like playing a whole new game. It has to end now." Hunter rolled the dice. He landed on six, which gave him a chance card.

I sucked in a breath as he looked at the card.

His hand slammed down on the table, causing our game pieces to jump a little. "Freaking jail."

I giggled. "Again?"

His eyes narrowed. "Yes, again." He flipped the card over, flicked his wrist, and let the card fly from the table.

Mia smirked. "That's a record for you, big brother. Maybe Allie is your kryptonite."

My eyebrows rose and my pulse quickened. I knew she meant only in terms of Monopoly, but my mind wandered. What if I was his kryptonite? What would it be like to make Hunter Baylor melt with adoration and lust? I couldn't imagine me ever evoking that in someone, let alone in Hunter, but the thought was nice.

Hunter grunted his response.

Mr. Baylor chuckled. "Jail isn't a bad thing at the end. It at least saves you from ending up on your opponent's properties."

"Yeah, but not when you get so close to the last property you need to collect them all and you get launched around the board again," Hunter said.

"True, son, very true."

My roll provided me the opportunity of adding a house on my third orange property, effectively having a house on each of my properties, while Hunter only had houses on two properties. This was in my favor.

Hunter snatched the dice from the board, held them in his hand while he whispered over them, then launched them at the game. "Yes! Doubles. I'm out baby!"

Mia huffed. "How...?" she pinched the bridge of her nose. "You know what never mind. I need to stop bothering to ask that question."

Richard clapped Hunter on the back. "Way to go man! There's that golden boy streak."

Hunter rolled double fours but ignored what property

that landed him on—Tennessee Avenue—my property. The rent was one-hundred-eighty dollars, and the last time I checked he only had one hundred. This was it, the end of the game.

Hunter's eyes widened. "Dammit! That puts me on your property. I don't have the rent." His jaw tightened as he looked up into my gaze. "You won this time, Duncan."

Mia launched from the chair, the force knocking it over. "Wahoo! We won! We won!"

"You didn't win, Mia. Duncan did," Hunter said through gritted teeth.

"She's my best friend, so I win through proxy."

"Not even close." Hunter combed his fingers through his hair. "I'm getting changed. I wanted to go get food anyway." He turned and walked down the stairs, Richard in tow.

Mia wrapped me in a bear hug. "You beat Hunter. I am *so* reminding him of this loss for at least the next month."

I shook my head. "You two are too competitive. It was a board game."

"And we won!"

"Well, unwrap yourself from me so I can get changed. I'm famished."

Mia released me, but her grin grew. "Whatever you say. You can have whatever you want tonight because you beat him, my treat."

I wiggled my eyebrows. "I will definitely take that offer, no backsies."

Mia crossed her fingers over her chest. "Never, you've earned it."

I quickly changed my outfit from the sweats and baggy T-shirt to my favorite jean skirt, flowy shirt, and brown wedged sandals. The sandals were not the best choice in the rain, but I didn't care. They paired perfectly with this outfit, and I had been dying to wear it. I knocked on the bathroom door. "Mia, I'll be upstairs. You coming?"

"In a minute," Mia said.

Yeah, right.

Mia was never ready in a minute. She was notoriously late, but at least I knew to expect it.

The upstairs was vacant. I plopped on the sofa as I waited for the Baylors to be ready to go. My phone beeped with a new notification. I had a new comment on the photo I posted of Mia and me posing in front of the beach house.

I scowled reading the comment. *Great house guys. It's almost as big as the one we rented a few years ago. Enjoy! Xoxo Brittany*

My nails dug into my palm as I tightened my fist. Why did she have to comment at all? She acted like things were great between us, but I knew that every word she typed was chosen to send a perfectly passive aggressive message to us both.

"Woah, why do you look so tense? You won Monopoly; shouldn't you be elated?"

Hunter's voice sent a shiver down my spine. "It's nothing."

He sat opposite me on the couch. "Your face says otherwise. That and your knuckles are white. Something's obviously wrong."

I closed the app. "It's just a stupid comment from someone who doesn't matter."

His eyebrow rose. "If you say so, Duncan."

I released the tension in my hands and focused on Hunter. He had gone with army-green colored shorts and a pale blue button up shirt that he left open to reveal a plain white T-shirt. The longer part of his light brown hair was gelled on the top of his head to reveal the closely shaved sides.

I took shallow breaths and hoped I regained the ability to breathe deeply, but he looked amazing without even trying.

With a smile plastered to my face, I stood and walked to the kitchen. I needed water and I needed it now.

Hunter tapped his foot on the floor. "God, why is everyone so slow? I swear none of them know how to be prompt."

I giggled. "You know how they are more than I do. It's just how your family is."

"Well, it drives me crazy. I hate being late. I mean honestly how long does it take to get ready. You got changed and you look good, why does it take everyone else ten times as long? Even Richard is a freaking slow poke."

My breath caught. Did I just hear him right? Did he just say I looked good?

Hunter's body moved closer to my right shoulder.

The heat radiated from him. The hair on my arms stood straight up.

Breathe, Allie. Breathe.

Hunter elbowed my arm. "At least I can always count on you." He winked and left the room.

My mind went blank. I couldn't process anything. Two compliments in less than five minutes and my brain was actually mush. Mush, like you see on those silly high school TV shows where the girl just goes straight stupid around someone. How was it possible that he could influence me like that? Not to mention, what did he mean by his comments?

Did I look good like in a sisterly way? Or a friend way? Or did I look good like someone he would take to the dance?

"Earth to Allie! Grab me a water would ya?" Mia shouted.

I jolted. "What ... Oh yeah, sure. Sorry."

Mia's eyebrows drew together. "What was that about? You were totally zoned out."

"I was thinking about Brittany's comment. Did you see what she wrote?"

Mia rolled her eyes. "No. I didn't read it because I don't

care. Who cares about her? You let her get to you too much. She's not worth it."

A twinge of guilt radiated from my stomach. I hated lying to Mia, but other than my feelings for her brother, I was always honest with her. It wasn't like I lied about everything. It was just a small omission. Barely even a lie.

Mr. and Mrs. Baylor exited their master bedroom.

"Are we all ready?" Mrs. Baylor asked.

"Yep," Mia said.

"Good, let's get in the car. Hunter you ready?" Mr. Baylor shouted.

Hunter peered upstairs from the bottom of the steps. "I am. Richard is almost ready. But I'll drive us there, so we'll be right behind you."

"Make sure to lock up, okay?"

Hunter nodded as he caught the keys launched toward his face.

My shoulders slouched at the thought. I hated that he could drive. It meant the time that he had to spend with me was lessened just because he wasn't forced to be in the same vehicle. And let's be honest, those were my favorite moments. I could relax because the proximity was not of my own creation and therefore, Mia never questioned it.

Mia wrapped her arm over my shoulder and pulled me toward the stairs. "Stop pouting over her comment. You don't want to put frown lines all over your face for when we check out what the outlets have to offer."

"Huh? The outlets won't care if I have frown lines. It's a bunch of stores with clothes."

Mia's smiled turned devilish. "Who said anything about the clothes caring? I'm talking about the *boys* we can meet at the outlets."

I rolled my eyes. "You can't be serious. Your parents are with us, Mia."

"So? You know they'll go one way and let us wander. We're old enough now, Allie. Besides, are you really going to tell me that you wore *those* sandals while it's raining? Those are boy catching sandals."

"This just sounds like trouble."

Mia winked. "Sounds like *fun*."

Chapter Six

The outlets were teeming with people. Everyone had the same idea to enjoy shopping and tourist areas while it poured.

As usual, Mia was right. Her parents let us wander off on our own if we promised to stay together and text her mom our general location if we went to different sides of the outlets. Mia, of course, jumped at the chance and now pulled me in ten different directions, unsure of which way she wanted to go.

"Mia, you're pulling my arm off. I can follow you if you just decide which direction to go."

"I know, but this is more fun, and I know that you won't lose me."

"That's crazy. You know that right?"

She shrugged and launched toward a map.

"What are you looking for?"

"Do you remember that one store that sold beach stuff? Like boogie boards and gear?"

"Vaguely."

"Well, I'm trying to find it."

My nose scrunched and my brows knitted. "For what? Did you suddenly develop an affinity for boogie boarding?"

"No silly. But *boys* love that crap."

It quickly dawned on me that this was the beginning of her mission to hunt down eligible high school boys that she wanted to shamelessly flirt with. At home Mia didn't bother, but on vacation it was like she dialed up the flirtation tenfold. I never understood it, but the lure of never seeing them again, made her love the interaction.

"Mia, I don't want to spend this whole time looking for guys. I want to see what designs they have for a new OBX shirt and go to that bookstore."

Mia audibly moaned. "You are seriously boring. You have plenty of books and like ten thousand OBX T-shirts. We always do those trips before we leave, why waste a chance tonight on something that's inevitable?"

"I don't find it boring or a waste. So, promise me that we will go to *two* stores at the most to hunt for guys and then we go to our places and look. Who knows, maybe we'll see them at those stores too."

Mia placed her finger in her opened mouth and pretended to gag. "If we find a guy at some bookstore then he'll be boring. I want adventure this year. How cool would it be to meet someone and then hang out on the beach together?"

"The coolest." My comment dripped with sarcasm, but Mia didn't seem to notice or seem to care. In reality, I had two reasons to not want to do this—adventure was not my scene and Hunter Baylor. How could I flirt with someone when they paled in comparison to Hunter?

I had a problem. I knew I had a problem, and yet, I couldn't break the cycle. Hunter had seeped his way into every cell of my being, and I had no idea how to remove him. Or if I even wanted to.

Mia's finger smacked the map board. "There it is. Let's

go." Without warning, she yanked my arm and launched us into the crowd toward the southern part of the outlets and down a flight of stairs.

Parents glared as Mia nearly ran over a few toddlers and narrowly missed an elderly couple. "Mia, slow down. The store won't get up and walk away."

"I don't want anyone to leave. We might miss them."

"You don't even know if anyone is there."

"Well, that's why we have to hurry, isn't it?"Mia released my arm and opened the door. "Now let's find a place to look and be natural."

"Be natural? You aren't even being natural now."

She flipped her hair over her shoulder. "Of course, I am."

I sighed and shook my head. There was no point in fighting it. At least she had agreed to only two stores, then I could get lost in my love of books and the smell of paperbacks.

Mia prowled around the room, peering over racks and shelves. She looked ridiculous. Thankfully, no one else could see her. The store was dead. No one besides the workers were there.

Mia's bottom lip puffed out. "Well, this place sucks. No one is here."

I crossed my arms. "Told ya so."

She scowled. "Well, I have one more chance before your precious bookstore."

"Lead on."

At a much slower pace, Mia wandered down the pathways peering into stores to see how many people were there. Most customers seemed to be families with smaller children, or couples in their twenties. We had yet to see a group of teenage boys in any store.

"Are you ready to go to our places now? This isn't working. Besides, you owe me for winning Monopoly. You told me anything I wanted."

Mia scuffed her shoe against the ground. "Fine." She smoothed her hand over her tank top and adjusted her shorts. "This outfit will be wasted on absolutely *no one*."

I feigned hurt. "No one? Do I not count? Can you not wear outfits for me?"

Mia half smiled. "Fine. I'll rephrase. It needs to be appreciated by the male species and we're fresh out."

I linked my arm with hers and tapped her hand. "Better, now let's go look at books."

"You're lucky you know too much about me, or I'd have to drop you as a friend. You are such a nerd, how is it possible we're friends?"

I laughed. "You love me. Now navigate us back to the bookstore."

Mia nodded and effortlessly led us back to our normal section of stores.

The bell above the door rang as we entered. Quiet instrumental music played over the speakers.

"Allie Duncan!"

I turned on my heel and came face to face with my favorite person in OBX. "Mrs. Wagner! How are you?"

Mia stifled a giggle and mouthed over Mrs. Wagner's shoulder, *You're such a nerd*.

"I'm wonderful. It's so good to see you. I have a new selection of that author you love. Come, I put the display over here."

"You spoil me."

She waved me off. Mrs. Wagner was the kindest lady and to make it even better, her love of books was bigger than mine. I had spent so much time in this store over the years that she grew to recognize me. Every August I could count on her presenting me with a few options I hadn't seen at home. She was a special lady.

The display in question was at the back of the store on a

circular table with a pyramid apparatus in the middle. It reminded me of a Christmas tree, but instead of branches, it had books.

"If you need anything, let me know," Mrs. Wagner said as she squeezed my shoulders.

"Thank you."

Mia used her finger to push up her nose. "Brown noser."

"She's a sweet woman, don't make fun of her."

"Oh, I'm not making fun of her. I'm making fun of you. You peruse. I know how you are. I'll be in the magazine section reading all the latest teen celebrity gossip. Come find me when you've pulled yourself from the book world."

Mia sauntered away, leaving me in peace with my stack of books to delve over. The display was full of books from a local author. She had published her own novels and wasn't found in many large bookstores, but every time I came to OBX, I added to my collection.

I searched the titles looking for ones I hadn't read yet. The newest titles were at the top of the display. I lifted on my tiptoes to reach the book, but I just wasn't tall enough, even with my wedged sandals.

I harrumphed. "Well, now what?"

A hand steadied on my shoulder, warmth seeping through my shirt into my skin. My gaze traveled up the hand to see the face of who it belonged to—Hunter.

"Is it this one, Duncan?"

I nodded.

Hunter reached effortlessly to the top of the display and pulled the book from the shelf. He didn't even have to stand on his toes to do it. He handed me the book and gave me his best smile. The one he did naturally. The one I loved the most.

"Thank you." I looked around him to see where Richard was. "I'm surprised to see you in here."

Hunter shrugged. "I always come in here."

My eyebrows rose. "What? No, you don't. I would have seen you."

Hunter chuckled. "Doubtful. You're always so engrossed over a stack of books, I doubt if you would see a whale swim through the aisles, let alone me."

My cheeks flamed. "I'm not that oblivious."

"I wouldn't say you're oblivious. I would say you're focused."

"I guess focused is better, but I can't believe you come in here and I've never noticed."

"I can't give away all of my secrets, even to you, Duncan." Hunter winked, tapped my arm, then strode to a different section of the store.

My feet were frozen, my jaw slackened, and my lungs sucked in air that never seemed to reach far enough. Tingles shivered down my arm from his touch. I was overreacting. He was my best friend's brother. He saw me struggling and helped. It meant nothing. His secret comment meant nothing, and yet, the flutters in my stomach wouldn't stop.

Against my better judgement, I strode to the aisle he disappeared down. "What do you mean by that?"

He turned on his heels, clearly surprised I had followed him. "I can't keep my title of being mysterious if someone knows everything about me."

I giggled. "Oh. Well, what do *you* come in here for?"

He shrugged, as he trailed a finger down the shelf of books. "This and that. Nothing specific. Sometimes books in psychology. Sometimes historical nonfiction. Just depends on my mood."

My brow knitted. In all the years I had known him, I had never seen him with a book. Not even a cursory glance. When did he read and where did he keep them all?

"What are you thinking about?"

I startled, realizing he was studying my gaze. "Who says I was?"

"Your eyes are squinted, which you do when you're focusing on some thought train."

Did I really do that? "Oh. I was thinking I didn't know you read. I've never seen you with a book."

An amused grin plastered across his face. "Like I said. Got to keep some secrets."

"Well, I'll leave you alone to find your book." I turned when his hand reached for mine. I spun around and glanced at his hand holding mine, until his fingers slipped away.

"Let me know if you need help with another high book, Duncan."

I arched an eyebrow.

He shifted his weight from foot to foot.

Was he nervous? Why would he be nervous?

"You did beat me, so just this once, think of it as perks of the winner."

I smiled. "Okay, thanks." This time he let me go back to the stack of books, more confused than ever before.

Chapter Seven

The next day was beautiful with not a cloud in the sky and temperatures in the high eighties. I was thankful to not be stuck inside again. It was bad enough that I couldn't stop thinking about my interaction with Hunter in the bookstore.

It took everything I had to convince myself it was normal behavior, and even then, my wall had cracks riddled throughout.

"We need a game plan," Mia said.

"For what? We're on vacation."

"I know that, but we're behind after yesterday's rain fiasco. Before we know it, we'll be leaving and I for one don't want to have anything on our list that we haven't checked off."

I rolled my eyes. "Mia, what could possibly be on your list? Go to the beach, ride the four wheelers? We've done both already."

"Yes, but there's a trail I want to check out today and we must make sure we manage to get the four wheelers without the boys interrupting. They'll be itching to take a ride today too. I know how Hunter is."

"Why are you so competitive about it? There's enough gas for everyone."

Mia slouched into the couch cushion. "Because I like to win."

"Well, what's the plan then?"

Mia grinned. "We beach until ten thirty, then have an early lunch, and take the four wheelers out, come back and go in the pool, then get ready for dinner."

"Isn't that what we do every day?"

"Yes, but it's sooner."

I stifled a laugh. "Sure." I checked the time on my phone. "Shouldn't we be walking to the beach like *now* if you want that plan to work?"

"Precisely. So, get ready."

My bathing suit and cover up sat on my bed. Mia was getting ready faster than she normally did, but I knew I would still manage to be done before her. I carted my clothes to the bathroom. Today's bathing suit was a Hawaiian print of navy blue and white flowers. My cover up was gray and honestly looked more like a dress than a cover up. However, it would work perfectly for when we went to the four wheelers. I could be comfortable and cool.

As expected, Mia was not finished getting ready when I exited the bathroom. "I'll be waiting by the backdoor, Mia. Hurry up would ya?"

Mia grumbled.

I grabbed my beach bag from the bed and sauntered toward the door for the backyard. Once outside, I stared into the crystal blue water of the pool. The heat from the sun warmed my cool skin. I loved the feeling after being so cold from the air conditioner and then going outside. It was a perfect five minutes or so as my body thawed before the true humidity of the day set in. Most people thought I was crazy, but it was unlike any feeling in the world.

"Duncan, what are you doing?" Hunter shouted.

I startled. "Waiting on your sister."

Hunter chuckled. "That will take forever. I saw her upstairs still in pjs."

I growled. "She was just in a bathing suit when I was in there."

"Not anymore."

Richard exited the house and stood next to Hunter. He eyed me by the pool. "Why are we all standing around?"

Hunter squinted as he turned to face Richard. "I'm waiting on you, which apparently is the theme for today."

"What? I'm ready."

"You are now." Hunter walked past, a hint of his shampoo filtered into my nostrils. "See you at the beach, Duncan."

I watched as they both left.

The sliding door opened, and Mia finally stepped out. "Sorry, I had to change my bathing suit."

"Mm-hmm. The boys beat us to the beach."

"Crap!" Mia shuffled past me and bounded up the dune to the other side.

From the top of the dune, I could see them already in the water with boogie boards. The waves were perfect for it today. The ocean was still rough, preparing for another afternoon storm.

We set up our towels near where the boys had, then ran into the water to cool down. I didn't boogie board, never had. I tried once. Mia had been determined to get me on one when we were younger. I didn't do badly, but I liked to float. Give me an air mattress or a floatie and I would sit in the water and soak up the sun. I would also rather read a book on the sand than romp around in the water.

Mia was the opposite. She had to be doing something always. She would sunbathe too, but not longer than ten minutes.

The water was nice, not too cold, not too hot, but once my body dipped a few degrees, I climbed out and headed back to my towel. Mia stayed in the water, diving into the waves and pushing the boys off the boogie boards so she could try. I dug my newly purchased novel from my bag, laid out on my towel and became consumed by the pages. The day couldn't get better than this.

* * *

"Wake up, sleepyhead," Mia said as she nudged my foot.

Somehow, I managed to nod off as I read my book. I peeked open my eyes to see Mia looming over me. "Is it lunch already?"

"Yep." Mia grimaced as she looked me up and down. "Girl, you didn't use sunscreen did you?"

"What? No."

Mia giggled. "You're going to be hurting later. Not to mention you have a lot of work cut out for you to even that up."

I looked down to see what Mia meant. As far as I could tell my arms looked a little pink, but nothing to warrant her comments. "I think I'll be fine."

"I was in the water for over an hour. You've barely moved in that time. You're going to be a lobster, but only on the front."

"I will not. Are we going to get food or not? I don't want to wreck your perfect plan for the four wheelers." I stuffed my book in my bag and pulled my cover up over my head.

"I'm waiting on you."

"Well, lead on."

Mia wasted no time hurrying up the pathway back to the house.

I surveyed the beach. The boys were still paddling away on the boogie boards, at least they wouldn't bother us.

The sand burned the edges of my feet as it slipped between my flip flops. My skin felt taut as the wind blew over my arms. Was Mia right? Did I actually get burned and couldn't tell yet? I certainly would find out when the sun went down, but to head it off, I would use some lotion with aloe before I went on the four wheelers. If I had burnt it would help, if I didn't it would still be good for my skin.

Mia held open the door as I walked through the doorway. The cool air sent shivers down my arms as my body adjusted to the air.

"Gotta get something quick so we can beat the boys to the four wheelers. Sandwiches work for you?"

I shrugged. "Whatever you want."

"Good."

We headed upstairs and I sat at the counter as Mia got out the ingredients to make us sandwiches. Surprisingly to most, she could cook. I didn't know how she knew what she was doing, but she always made surprising combinations that turned out to explode with flavor. She always just seemed to know, even when we were little. I never did find out if someone had taught her, or she just worked it out for herself.

"So, where's this trail you want to take?"

"Near the back by the bay. I want to see if those hills are still there from last year."

My eyebrows rose. "The ones that had mud like ankle deep after the rain?"

Mia grinned. "That's the one."

"You're going to get us so muddy, aren't you?"

Mia slathered the bread with mayo as she winked. "Maybe."

I sighed. "How fun." Mia didn't mind getting covered head to toe in mud, and it wasn't that I cared about being dirty, so much as the smell and trying remove it from my hair. Maybe if my hair was short it wouldn't be such a pain, but mid-way down my back required a ton of shampoo to get it clean. I would have to pile it on top of my head and make sure it all managed to stay inside my helmet before we went.

Mia slapped the plate down in front of me. "Madam, your chicken salad sandwich with walnuts, apples, cranberries, and extra mayo awaits you."

I giggled. "Why thank you, Chef Mia."

Mia bowed, grabbed her plate, and sat next to me. "Now, hurry up."

I saluted her and dug in. Just like usual, she had made a good sandwich. Each of the elements complimented each other, elevating the chicken salad. I know, it wasn't like filet mignon, but some chicken salads could be super bland.

I was only halfway done the first half, when I looked over to Mia's progress.

Mia rubbed her hands together quickly and then hopped down from her spot.

"Are you seriously done already? Did you inhale it?"

Mia's eyebrows knitted. "I took my time."

"Yeah right, maybe for a cheetah. You scarfed that down. I'm barely halfway done."

"Well, get busy eating. I'll be down by the four wheelers getting our gear together and all. Don't forget to put on your sneakers."

I nodded and stuffed the sandwich into my mouth. It wasn't pretty, but it got the job done. I took a long gulp of water, set my plate in the dishwasher, and headed to our room. After I used the lotion and changed my shoes, I jogged to the front of the house where the four wheelers were parked.

Adrenaline coursed through my body as I readied myself to go on the four-wheeler. There was nothing like riding them at OBX to relax and excite me. No matter how many times we rode them on this trip, it always felt like the first time.

Mia had both helmets on the seat as she rooted through a bag by the back door.

"All set."

Mia startled. "Jeez. A little warning would be nice. Did you tip toe out here?"

"No. You're just so absorbed in what you're doing you couldn't hear me."

"If you say so." Mia checked the gas gauge on the red four-wheeler and hopped up, securing her helmet at the same time. She tossed me the helmet I always used.

I secured the straps when the pounding of sneakers echoed.

Oh crap. I heard them before I could physically see them.

I didn't have to see Mia to know she tensed as Richard and Hunter bounded our way.

Hunter spoke first. "Woah, woah, woah. What are you two doing?"

Mia straightened her spine and glared at him. "Allie and I are taking a ride."

Hunter crossed his arms. "False. We're going on a ride."

"We were here first, Hunter. I already checked everything. Allie and I are going." Mia jerked her head toward me, then eyed the seat behind her.

I knew it was her code for telling me to get on and get on quick, but my body betrayed me. Between the tension in the air and being this close to Hunter, I couldn't move.

Mia repeated the gesture again, but this time Hunter saw it all.

"Duncan, don't you even think about it."

"You can't order her around, Hunter. She's my best friend."

"I can do whatever I want. I'm older than you both and Richard and I are going on a ride."

Richard stood behind Hunter nodding as his arms were crossed.

I stifled a laugh. Richard looked more like a bodyguard than someone invested in going on an actual ride.

"Go after we get back. We won't use all the gas."

Hunter shook his head. "No can do. Mom and Dad want us home early so we can get ready for dinner. Which means by the time you two get back, we all have to get ready."

Mia sighed. "I'm not getting off the four-wheeler. Allie and I can ride this one. You two ride that one."

Hunter scoffed. "You can't be serious. We both don't fit on one."

Mia giggled. "Not our problem, is it Allie?"

I held my hands up in defense. "Don't drag me into this. This is for you two to figure out."

Hunter smiled devilishly as he eyed me.

I squirmed from the look he gave me. It was like he was staring into my soul or at least past my defenses and I certainly didn't like that.

"Well, if you two insist on going on the four wheelers, how about we all go?"

"That's what I've been saying," Mia said.

He held up a finger. "But with a slight change."

My stomach dropped. What was Hunter about to propose?

"What change?" Mia asked.

"You ride with us."

Mia crossed her arms. "What? No. I want to drive the four-wheeler. And I'm not driving with you, Hunter."

My heart raced and my face flushed. Was what I thought really about to happen? Would he ...?

"Of course, you aren't riding with me, Mia. You ride with

Richard. You two can figure out who's driving. Duncan can ride with me."

Mia leaned close so I could only hear her. "What do you think? Are you okay with that?"

Hunter eyed us both.

"I-I'll do whatever you want to do, Mia. It's up to you. I know how much you hate Richard."

Mia huffed. "Fine."

Hunter hooted as he took the key from the hook and hopped up on the blue four-wheeler.

Richard's posture slumped. "Aw man. They'll slow us down, Hunter."

"Slow you down? As if, Richard. You're ruining *our* plans. I'm driving," Mia said with a stern expression.

"The hell you are, Mia. You're not even sixteen yet."

"So what? You're a guest."

They bickered back and forth like an old married couple trying to decide where to go for dinner. I wanted to be on Mia's side. I wanted to stick up for her as she battled it out. But all my brain could process was that I would be sitting behind Hunter on a four-wheeler. I would have to hold onto him as we flew down the trails. My arms would be wrapped around his body. Closer than I had ever been before.

My body felt hot and cold all at once. I didn't know if I would throw up or run a marathon.

"Duncan, are you coming?"

My gaze snapped back to Hunter's face. He had already secured his helmet and started the four-wheeler. I looked over to Mia, who now sat behind Richard, scowling at him from behind. Apparently, she had lost their argument.

"Yeah, sorry."

I walked as slowly as I could to the four-wheeler without drawing attention to myself. How did I get up? Did I put my hand on his shoulder and swing my leg over, like I did with Mia? Or did I avoid touching him too much and use the bars?

My head spun from all the thoughts.

Hunter managed to answer my dilemma for me when he proffered his hand.

I accepted as he held it sturdy for me to lift myself up and onto the four-wheeler. He released my hand as quickly as he had grabbed it, leaving tingles.

He waited for me to wrap my arms around him before he accelerated.

"Hold on tight, Duncan. I don't want you to fall off."

I nodded, then realized he couldn't see my face. "Okay."

What was happening? My brain cells misfired as they processed how close I was to him. My legs touched the outside of his as we were pushed together from the acceleration. I could feel his muscles under my fingertips. I knew he had abs. They were obvious when he had no shirt on, but feeling the pure muscle was different than seeing it. If he was uncomfortable, I certainly couldn't sense it. Although my senses were a tad busy.

"You okay back there?" Hunter asked. "You're quiet."

"Yep."

Hunter chuckled.

The movement moved through me, making it more than just a laugh. How did I tell him that I was quiet because I was losing my mind that we were this close? How did I say to him that the speed wasn't a problem, it was that I was dangerously close to spilling my guts? Something that would end badly, for so many reasons, but especially because it would be unrequited and that was the absolute *worst*.

I was so distracted that it took me longer than it should have to realized we stopped. "What's wrong?"

"Waiting for Richard and Mia to catch up. They're far behind us."

I quickly let go and shifted to look behind us. Sure enough, they looked like a little red dot. Why were they so far behind?

"Woah. You're not kidding."

"Yeah. So, what do you think of the ride so far?"

I nearly choked. "It's fine."

"Just fine? These are some of the best trails OBX has to offer. Fine is not a great description."

"Okay. The trails are awesome. Is that better?"

"I suppose, but if the trails are awesome, then what made it fine?" Hunter visibly hunched and then sighed. "Must be me."

My eyes widened. "What? Why would you say that?"

"Well, has to be. There's nothing else that would influence it."

"I-I. No."

Hunter chuckled. "Relax, Duncan. I'm messing with you. I know we messed up your plans with Mia. I just wanted to check you weren't freaked out from how fast we were going."

"Honestly, I didn't notice."

"Oh, well—"

The roar of the other four-wheeler drowned him out.

They pulled next to us, and my jaw dropped. The once red four-wheeler was caked in brown, sticky mud. Mia's face was covered as was Richard's and Mia was shouting as they stopped. This wouldn't be good.

Chapter Eight

"You are *such* a bonehead!" Mia shouted. She scraped off mud from her arms and climbed from the four-wheeler. "I can't believe you did that."

Hunter's eyes widened. "Dude, what did you do?"

Mia threw her hands to the sky. "What didn't he do?" She paced. "First, he stayed too close to the two of you, so the dust from your four-wheeler, nearly choked us. Then he decided to go off the trail you were taking and jump a mud puddle. He jumped it the first time and got so cocky he tried to do it again. The second time, we landed in the puddle and then got stuck while he spun tires. He ignored my shouting as the mud went everywhere. Then he almost lost you."

Richard shrugged.

Hunter stifled a laugh.

Mia glared between them. "It's *not* funny." She pointed at Richard and squinted. "I am not riding back with you. I will drive. I no longer trust your moronic ideas."

Hunter's hand hovered over Richard's back to congratulate him, until he thought better of it from the mud. Instead, he clapped then got back on the four-wheeler. "You'll dry off as we ride, and Mia I'll spray you down with a hose when we get back. It's not a big deal. You've gotten muddier before."

She growled. "I don't care about the mud. I care that he's an idiot."

My eyebrows rose. Mia was beyond mad. I smiled weakly in her direction, but she was too busy scowling at Richard to notice. At least I wouldn't have to hear her speech for the next forty-five minutes as we continued the ride. No doubt Richard would wish that he had lost his hearing by the time their adventure was over.

Hunter settled into the seat, brushing my legs as he did. I doubted he had even felt the touch, but I did. Every single time, I felt the spark that lit my skin and nerves on fire.

Hunter leaned sideways and closer to my face. "Hold on, Duncan. It's about to get faster than before."

My insides clenched as I scooted closer to him and held on.

He revved the four-wheeler and sped off, leaving Mia gesturing wildly as Richard climbed onto the four-wheeler. I released my laugh since she could no longer set her wrath on me. It was funny, even if she couldn't admit to it now.

"What's so funny?" Hunter shouted over the engine.

"Don't you dare tell Mia, but I can't help but to laugh. They looked wrecked."

Hunter chuckled with me. "Yes, they did. She's going to rip him a new one."

"You know it. You think he will be able to hear when she gets done?"

"Not a chance."

I laughed harder.

"There's the Duncan I know." Hunter revved the four-wheeler more and sped up. The wind blew over us, whipping through my clothes as we cruised down the trail. I unclenched my body the best I could, without losing my grip and falling off. Now that some of the shock had worn off, I could enjoy the feeling of flying down a dirt path on the four-wheeler, without the incessant buzzing in my head from his touch.

The sun dipped behind a cloud, providing a small relief from the blazing heat. The skin on my shoulders and arms felt stiff. I had a feeling Mia would end up being right about my sunburn.

Hunter veered from the trail and stopped before a large dune. "Want to take it on the beach?"

My eyebrows rose. "Can you?"

"Unlike Mia, I'm over sixteen, so legally I can. She won't be able to follow though. Or at least she shouldn't."

I gripped his shirt. "Okay, let's do it."

"Look at you, Duncan. You keep surprising me." Hunter peeled off and up the small space between the two dunes and over to the other side.

The ocean spanned as far as I could see in front of us. The salty air strengthened the closer we got to the water, and I breathed in deeply. Nothing could compete with the ocean air. I lived for it every summer and it always ended too quickly. The water sprayed up our legs as Hunter rode close to the shore. He veered back up on the beach and rode the four-wheeler in the ruts of a pickup.

Houses zipped by as we rode past, until the one we were renting this time came into focus. Hunter turned toward the sandy road that led close to the house. Before I knew it, we had pulled back into the house's driveway and Hunter parked the four-wheeler.

I released my grip as he hopped down and took off his helmet. "That was fun, Duncan."

I nodded.

"Who's the better driver? Mia or me?"

"Oh no you don't. I'm not answering that. I wouldn't

answer that if I had a gun to my head. You two are too competitive. I had fun and that's all you get."

"Party pooper. You don't have to admit it, you know the answer is me."

I climbed off the four-wheeler and released the chin strap on my helmet ignoring his comment. "How long do you think it'll take for them to end up back here?"

"Who knows. Depends on which way Mia went. It's shorter to go on the beach."

Hunter outstretched his hand.

I stared at it like it was a foreign object. What did he want? Was he going to hold my hand? That couldn't be it. He never did that.

He cleared his throat and chuckled. "I can take your helmet."

His comment pulled me from the cycle of thoughts swimming around my brain. "Oh, sure. Thanks."

He took both helmets and set them on the shelf, along with the key. I watched as his back was toward me. His muscles rippled under his shirt the more he stretched and moved, cleaning up from the ride.

I shook my head. I needed to put space between us. Without the helmet, I didn't have anything to shield my face from the obvious feelings written across it. I climbed the outside staircase and waited for Mia to pull up on her four-wheeler. It was safer being farther away from Hunter *and* Mia would see me as soon as she arrived.

I should have started getting ready for dinner but knowing Mia, she'd want me to wait. Not to mention, she would want the shower after being caked in mud. How she planned to get inside without leaving a trail was a whole other predicament she would need to figure out.

A door shut below the staircase, Hunter must have finally gone in. I exhaled deeply, encouraging my muscles to unclench from the ride. If I kept it up, I'd end up with a tension headache or worse. I needed to relax.

My eyelids flitted closed. I straightened my spine and focused on long deep breaths. After three ten counts, a distant roar of an engine prickled my ears.

Finally.

I stood and watched as Mia drove onto the house's sandy driveway and stopped. I had hoped that the ride back would cool Mia off, but based on her flailing arms and stomping, that hadn't happened.

I actually felt bad for Richard. That was a long time to listen to someone complain over a mud puddle. Was it really that Mia was so mad about his driving skills or that she hadn't been able to drive without him on the four-wheeler? I mean, had she not planned to go in the puddles?

I waved Mia up the staircase when she finally met my gaze.

Her feet slapped the stairs with a large thud as she ascended. "That was the *worst* four-wheeler ride I have ever experienced." She waved me on as she continued up the stairs. "I need a shower, then I'll tell you everything."

My eyes widened. "Did something else happen?"

Mia huffed. "You don't know the half of it."

* * *

The half of it was still a mystery. By the time Mia and I had both gotten a shower and ready for dinner, there was no time for her to tell me what had happened before her mother brought us to the table.

After a tense dinner, we were finally alone in our room. "So, what happened?"

Mia huffed and rolled her eyes. "He's so arrogant. He thinks he knows everything just because he's older than me. I've been riding four wheelers longer than Hunter and him have been friends. Does that matter? No! I'm just Hunter's little sister."

"Okay ..."

"When I drove, I told him to just sit there and don't fall off. He couldn't shut up. He kept saying to pull over to let him drive. He said he didn't do anything wrong; he just had a little fun."

"Well, I mean, no one was hurt, Mia."

She threw her hands up. "This time. He was reckless, Allie. I know I can be daring at times, but I'm never stupid, and I certainly don't do those things with other riders. He doesn't even know me. He has no way of knowing if I would have been frightened by what he did and he didn't bother to ask."

"Okay, you're right. That's not smart, but I don't know, it's not as bad as I expected. You made it sound like he was a killer or something, Mia."

"I might have over exaggerated a little."

"Ya think?"

"Well, he irks me, Allie. I can't stand his arrogance. I truly don't understand how he's friends with Hunter. There's too much ego for them both to fit in one room."

I giggled. "Do you feel better now?"

Mia scuffed her foot against the carpet. "I guess." She growled. "Why does he get under my skin so much?"

That was what I wanted to know. Mia never let anyone bother her. She was always my voice of reason when it came to Brittany, what was it about Richard that set her off?

"I don't know, but let's not let it ruin the night, okay?"

"Okay. What do you have in mind?"

"Hmm. How about the game room?"

Mia half shrugged. "What if the boys are in there?"

"Then let them be in there. You never let that stop you before."

Mia smirked. "Very true. Okay, let's go!" Mia sprinted from the room without looking back.

I shook my head, gathered my phone off the bed and followed her down the flight of stairs. As she had figured, the boys were in the game room, huddled over the pool table.

Mia stared at them while Hunter lined up his shot. "Who's winning?"

Hunter shot the cue ball into a striped ball. It ricocheted off the back and eventually into the pocket. He grinned as he rested on his pool stick. "Me, of course."

Richard rolled his eyes. "You're barely winning, dude. I've still got you right where I want you."

Hunter chuckled. "Sure, you do. Whatever helps you sleep at night."

I plopped down on the sofa a few feet away from the pool table.

Mia eyed the table, then sat beside me. "We could play foosball while we wait for the pool table."

"Sure, if that's what you want."

Mia squinted at me. "Is that a challenge?"

I lightly shoved her shoulder. "Maybe."

She gasped and hopped over to the table.

I laughed. "There she is."

"What?"

"Nothing." My plan had worked. Mia had released the tension from our earlier ride. Now I had to put my money where my mouth was. Mia was competitive, but I had always had a knack for foosball. The building where my parents worked had a game floor and I was able to visit when I was younger. People took it easy on me and would teach me tricks. I had gotten good, but that was a few years ago. Volleyball was the only real sport I practiced anymore.

Mia stood on the side with the green players, while I stood with the blue. I let her go first with no fight. My chances were slim that I would win the chance contest anyway.

"So, we only have a few days left before we leave. We need to strategize our last visit to the outlets."

I groaned. "Mia, why are you pushing it so much?"

Mia used her player to shoot at my goal, I barely blocked it, and she lined up again. "I want to meet cute beach boys. Why are you so against it? You don't have a boyfriend and no one at school you've been tracking. I don't understand why you aren't more for it."

"I'm not interested in following around guys I'll never see again. Besides, I'm more focused on volleyball tryouts than meeting someone."

"Yes! Pay up," Hunter shouted.

The noise jolted me. I wasn't completely lying. I was worried about volleyball, but I also couldn't imagine anyone living up to Hunter. And that would probably keep me alone, but it was true.

The distinct sound of the foosball scoring on my goal, followed by Mia's chants, echoed in my ears. "You two are literally the same."

Mia grimaced. "What? No! He's so much worse."

I shook my head. "You are so competitive you two can't see how similar you are. It's okay. I give up. You won."

Mia crossed her arms. "What happened to the overconfidence of five minutes ago?"

"It was a façade. I wanted to distract you from your hatred."

Mia smiled. "Aww, it worked, but I also won fair and square."

"Of course."

Hunter and Richard walked past, sending whiffs of Hunter's cologne, Ralph Lauren Red Rush, my way. He laughed, so carefree as he messed with Richard. I refocused my attention on the foosball game, but I couldn't help feeling his touch on my fingers as I remembered our drive earlier. I didn't think I'd ever forget this day, and on some level, I didn't want to.

"Ready to play pool now?" Mia asked.

"Uh, I guess? You know I suck at pool."

Mia waved me off as she skipped to the table.

I waited and watched as she racked the balls, then lined up her first shot. Just as she took her first shot, the boys returned, sodas in hand.

A few of the balls got close to the pocket, but only a striped ball went it.

I concentrated on Mia's next shot, even though the stares from the boys had set my neck hairs on alert.

Mia missed her next ball, letting it be my turn.

Richard snorted.

Mia swiveled as she glared in his direction. "What's so funny?"

"Nothing, just should have made that shot."

Hunter sent a warning glance to Richard, but he didn't seem to notice.

"Oh, is that so?" Mia asked.

Richard smirked. "It is. I bet I could easily beat you."

Hunter grimaced.

Clearly, Richard hadn't learned yet how competitive Mia really was.

I glanced between them both, their stances exuded stubbornness.

"Care to put your money where your mouth is?" Mia asked.

Richard outstretched his hand. "Ready if you are."

My eyebrows rose.

"Good. Re-rack them."

Hunter moved closer to the table, near where they stood.

"Richard, maybe you should let them be. Duncan was about to take her turn."

"Allie doesn't care. Do you?" Mia's gaze snapped to mine.

I wouldn't step between that. Mia had been challenged, there wasn't anything I could say to change that. "Not at all."

Richard smirked.

Hunter shook his head and sat.

I passed over the pool stick and sat at the other end of the sofa, putting space between Hunter and me.

Mia's expression turned rigid. She couldn't see past defeating Richard and wiping his smug expression from his face.

"This will end badly," Hunter said.

"Mm-hmm. It's like a train wreck. I can't help but to stare."

Hunter chuckled. "Who's your bet on?"

"Oh no. I'm not going there."

Hunter leaned a little closer. "Why not?"

I narrowed my gaze. "You know why. My official stance should be Mia, but heaven help us all if Richard wins."

"He won't."

I stared into his gaze, trying to understand. "You aren't rooting for Richard?"

He shrugged a shoulder. "It's not that I'm not, but I've seen Mia play and I've beaten Richard plenty of times on this trip. I don't think he can stay focused enough to win."

"Oh."

"Why didn't you want to play?"

"I would have, but I could already tell Mia had settled on her decision. You Baylors don't back down to a challenge."

He clapped his hand to my exposed back. "That's for sure."

I inhaled sharply. He hadn't touched my skin that hard,

but Mia had been right. My skin was burnt, and the four wheelers added to it.

"Oh, Duncan. My bad, I forgot about your sunburn."

I held my eyes closed, hoping the sting would subside. "It's fine. I should go put aloe on it anyway." I stood and walked to the stairs. I had gone up a few steps when I realized I wasn't alone. I turned and came face to face with Hunter. "Uh-uhm. What are you doing?"

"I was making sure you're okay. That was a stupid thing to do."

"I'm fine. You'll miss their game."

"They haven't even gotten half their balls in the pocket yet. I won't miss much."

"Oh. Well, I'm only putting aloe on a little of it. I'll have Mia put the rest on before bed."

My stomach clenched from the proximity. I could barely think with him being so close to my face. If I shifted just a few inches in front, our lips could touch.

"I can help you. I feel bad anyway. I know what that feels like."

Did he? Was he offering to put lotion on me?

I turned because words were too hard to form. I headed for my bedroom's bathroom, hoping my speed wouldn't allow him to catch up, but he was right there when I had paused.

I put some of the aloe in my hand, rubbed them together, then spread it on my arms. I avoided his gaze because I didn't know what to make of it. All I knew was that he hovered in the doorway.

When I attempted to do my back, with little success in the middle, he moved closer.

"It's no big deal. You obviously can't reach. Just let me help?"

He felt bad. That was all. I was his little sister's friend. My feelings for him were clouding the situation, but it was nothing.

I handed him the bottle and gathered my hair to the front.

He moved behind me and slowly spread the aloe, careful not to press too hard with his fingers. My skin was at war between the aloe cooling off my sunburn and his touch heating it back up. My breath hitched as his hands covered my back.

It almost seemed like his right hand lingered on my back before he had removed it and then gave me the bottle.

Maybe I had just imagined the hesitation.

I smiled as I faced him. "Thanks."

He tucked his hands in his front pockets. "No worries. I should head back downstairs to see who's in the lead."

I nodded and watched as he left the room, leaving me more confused than ever.

Chapter Nine

The next morning was another perfect day. After breakfast, Mia and I headed down to the beach, air mattress in tow.

"Look at these waves. These are the best they've looked so far this week," Mia said.

"Are you sure? Last year we ended up halfway down the beach!"

Mia laughed. "Yeah, but it was a good story. We haven't forgotten it have we?"

"Well, no."

"See?" She shifted the mattress again. "Help me carry it into the water."

I huffed. Half the time I felt beat up by the thing. Big waves meant more energy to keep it steady. "Where are the boys?"

"I think they took an early four-wheeler ride."

I giggled. "Didn't want to lose it to us again?"

"Who knows? Allie, which way are you leading us?"

I stopped and looked around. We were at least forty feet farther to the left than we should be. We would already shift down the shoreline to the left. We had to start way to the right so the current would carry us back toward the house. "Oops, my bad."

Mia shuffled the mattress in her hands, turned us to the right and picked up the pace.

"You'll tire us out before we even get into the water."

"I'm trying to let us float for a while."

I huffed. After what felt like a century. We stopped. I looked toward our left, and sure enough, the beach house seemed like a little speck in the distance.

"Your parents know we're out here right?"

Mia shrugged. "More than likely." She stared at my expression. "Are you worried?"

"No."

"Yes. We'll be down by the house soon enough. Come on, let's get it in the water. I'm sweating to death out here."

"Okay. Okay."

We lifted the air mattress and headed for the water. Small waves crashed into my shins as we waded out deeper and deeper. When the water was around our waist, we stopped and lifted on top of the mattress.

"I forgot how exhausting this is," Mia said.

"That's because Hunter is usually helping us. I don't think we've ever taken the mattress out by ourselves before."

"Stupid Richard."

I squinted at her. "What's the deal with him? I mean before you went on that four-wheeler ride, he hadn't really done anything to you. Why does he irk you so much?"

Mia shifted onto her stomach and away from me. "I don't know, it's just the vibe I get from him. He stares at my chest sometimes. I don't know. I can't explain it."

"Well, your boobs are bigger than most, but okay. I mean maybe he won't be so insufferable now that you beat him at the pool game yesterday."

She snorted. "Unlikely." She turned to gaze at the waves. "Are we going to ride these waves in or what?"

I nodded. "Point one out and I'll kick as hard as I can."

She smiled and adjusted her sunglasses. "Here it comes."

At the same time, we kicked as hard as we could and propelled ourselves on the air mattress toward the shore. The wave carried us farther until we were where the waves broke.

"Hold on tight," Mia shouted.

I gripped the mattress and prepared for a rough ride. As expected, the front of the air mattress was sucked under, causing me to get sucked down with it. I felt as the rest of the mattress rolled over me, pushing me farther into the sand. The bottoms of my bathing suit felt twisted as I tried to sit up and catch my breath.

My head broke from the water, and I sucked in deep breaths. Before I stood, I shifted my bathing suit back to where it should be as I surveyed the beach for Mia and the air mattress.

Mia's head broke free from the waves, and she stumbled as she tried to stand.

But the air mattress wasn't next to her.

I looked farther to our left and sure enough, the current was pushing it back and forth down the beach.

"Mia!" I shouted. "The air mattress."

She screamed and half trudged, half ran through the water to catch up to it. She caught up to it first, with me right behind her. We lifted it from the water and brought it ashore before collapsing onto it to steady our breath.

We glanced at each other and burst out laughing.

"You should see your hair," Mia said. "It's all twisted around your face."

I laughed harder. "Yeah, well nice run up the beach. You looked like you had toddlers strapped to your ankles."

We devolved into a fit of laughter.

When we finally calmed down, we looked around.

"Is that the house down there?" Mia asked.

I squinted. "Maybe." I stood and outstretched my hand for her to grab onto. When she lifted herself up, we exhaled loudly. "This will be a long walk back."

"Yep. Let's rest it over our heads so we're at least shielded from the sun. Then we can walk in the shallow part of the water, so our feet don't burn."

I followed her lead, lifting the air mattress above my shoulders and resting it on my head. The weight stiffened my neck, but it would be easier to carry, then lugging it awkwardly by our side the whole way back.

I breathed heavily as we carried it back toward the house. We stayed silent, using all our breath to complete the task. I needed a large drink, my throat felt coated in sand and salt.

After what felt like an hour, we reached the pop-up canopy signaling Mia's parents.

Mia dropped the mattress and sprinted to the cooler, where she grabbed two waters and tossed me one.

Mrs. Baylor tipped her sunglasses to look over them. "Where were you two?"

Mia pointed as she chugged the water.

"Wipeout and the waves carried us that way."

Mrs. Baylor laughed. "Well, be safe." Then she adjusted her sunglasses and focused on the book splayed across her lap.

Mr. Baylor hadn't even noticed our arrival while he fiddled with a radio. Static was all I could hear come through the speakers.

Mia crumpled the bottle. "You ready to go back out?"

I still hadn't even finished half of my bottle. "In a minute. I'll get a stomachache drinking my water that fast."

"Fine. I'm taking a dip. Bring the mattress when you're done."

I nodded, but she had already turned to run into the

waves. I took a few more sips, then put my bottle back in the cooler for later. I trudged over to the air mattress and lugged it toward the beach.

A shadow loomed over my arm.

I turned to see Hunter's green eyes reflecting the sun. His smile so white it was hard to look directly at it.

"Are you and Mia using the mattress by yourselves?" Hunter asked.

I nodded.

"Did you want help to bring it out?"

"Sure."

He lifted the back end and followed me toward the shore.

Mia waded in as we got closer.

"Are you joining us with the mattress?" Mia asked.

Hunter looked toward Richard. "What do you think? Want to chance it?"

Richard looked between Hunter and the mattress. "I guess. What exactly do you do?"

Mia laughed. "You stay on."

"That's not even a challenge," Richard said.

Hunter chuckled.

Mia took a corner of the mattress and placed it into the water.

Hunter and I let it slip from our arms as it floated on the waves.

Mia placed her hand on my shoulder. "Ask Allie, it's not as easy as it looks."

I shook my head.

"Wipeout today already?"

Mia laughed. "It rolled over her."

My cheeks heated. Of course, it was true, but I felt like an idiot.

Hunter studied my expression. "You okay?" He nudged

Mia's arm. "You two should be careful. What if it knocked one of you out and no one else was around?"

"We're fine, Hunter. Allie was fine. We both came back up and then retrieved the mattress." She pushed the mattress over a small wave. "Are we going or what?"

Hunter helped grab the one corner and I pushed the other as Mia headed out. Richard waded through the water but didn't help. Hopefully, he helped once we were all on the water.

"Allie, hop on first," Mia said once we reached waist deep.

"Why me?"

"Duncan, go ahead. Once Mia is on, Richard you'll get on next."

I didn't understand why I had to go first but did as I was told. Mia hopped up next to me, which only minorly helped how awkward I felt with Hunter and Richard staring at us while they got on.

I desperately wanted my coverup in that moment, but it was way too late to get it.

Richard hopped on next to Mia, which pushed her closer to me as he flopped on.

Hunter true to his word, joined next to me, his legs and arms brushing past mine, sending goosebumps over my skin.

Thankfully, he had no chance to see them, because as soon as he landed, he was focused on the waves.

All our feet hung off the back so we could kick when a big enough wave came.

"I think you should drive us to the outlets and out for ice cream tonight, Hunter," Mia said.

My eyes widened.

"I'm not your chauffeur. It's summer. Once we head back it'll be bad enough that I must drive you everywhere."

"Oh, come on, like you two wouldn't want to go to the outlets? It'd be fun for you too."

Richard peered over us to look at Hunter. "She has a point man. Weren't we heading there today or tomorrow anyway?"

Hunter glared at Richard. "Yeah, you and me. Not all four of us."

"Then don't take us. I'll just ask Mom," Mia said.

My stomach unclenched. If Hunter didn't drive, I didn't have to be close enough to him to deal with these feelings. It was bad enough that almost every day this trip something had happened to leave my walls shaky.

"Good. Now get ready, here comes a wave," Hunter said.

Clearly, he didn't want to take us. Why didn't my heart believe the proof that I was equal to his little sister. Nothing more.

Mia elbowed Richard. "Peddle your feet, dimwit."

"Hey, who are you calling dimwit?" Richard asked.

"You, obviously. It only works if we all move at once," Mia shouted back.

I groaned. "Can we just be civil and work together?"

They mumbled something, but the air mattress moved a lot more in sync afterward.

A wave picked us up, and this time we each held on successfully as we were pushed over the breaking waves and onto the shore.

Richard hopped off first, pumping his fist in the air. "Woohoo!"

Mia rolled her eyes, even though it was a fun ride in.

I still didn't believe her explanation. She had never just had a *vibe* about someone. Something must have happened that she still didn't want to tell me about.

"Up for another round?" Hunter asked.

We all nodded and plodded after him as he lifted the air mattress by himself, ready to ride the waves back in.

* * *

Mrs. Baylor did not agree to drive us to the outlets. When we arrived back from the beach to shower, she told us she had a headache and Mr. Baylor didn't want to leave her. So instead of having the safety of Mrs. Baylor to clear my thoughts, I would be in close confines with Hunter. It was bad enough that things kept happening each day while we were on the trip. One night alone wasn't too much to ask in my opinion.

"Now you have to drive us," Mia gloated.

Hunter raised an eyebrow. "I may have to drive you, but if you all aren't dressed and ready in ten minutes, I'm leaving without you." Hunter gazed at Richard. "That includes you, too."

"Me? I'm not slow."

Hunter huffed, while I pushed Mia out of the way. I could be ready in ten minutes no problem; they would be the ones who would have difficulty.

"Hey," Mia shouted right on my heels.

I decided comfort was the best method this time. I didn't need wedged sandals and a skirt, I wanted to roam around the aisles in comfortable clothes. I settled on my light-wash denim shorts, a burgundy cami, that I tucked into my shorts, and a navy-blue button up shirt that I left open. I slipped on a pair of flip flops, double checked my appearance in the mirror after adding eyeliner and mascara, then left the bedroom as clothes flew around the room while Mia decided on what to wear.

I skipped down the stairs and was surprised to find no one waiting at the door. I sat on the bottom steps and pulled out my phone to scroll through social media, when vibrations from someone coming down the stairs, reached me.

"I'm surprised—" I stopped when I realized it wasn't Mia.

"You really thought she'd be done in"—Hunter checked his watch—"five minutes?"

I shrugged, but he was right. That would have been a miracle if she had finished that early. I doubted she even had an outfit picked out, let alone on already. "I guess you're right."

"I am surprised *you* beat me though."

I stood as I took in his appearance. He had gelled his hair so that the longer hair up top had some body, compared to the shaved sides. He wore light gray cargo shorts and a light blue fitted T-shirt.

I averted my gaze, so he didn't recognize the blushing that had erupted over my cheeks. "Well, didn't want to be left behind."

Hunter chuckled. "I wouldn't have left you."

My eyebrow rose, but I didn't get a chance to respond, when Richard and Mia barreled down the stairs, pushing and shoving each other the whole way.

"I won!" Mia shouted as she jumped to the floor from the last stair.

Hunter rolled his eyes.

We followed him out and got in, boys up front, and us girls in the backseat of his convertible. Hunter had turned up the radio to avoid any conversations between Richard and Mia who continued to throw dirty glances toward each other. I on the other hand sank into the seat and closed my eyes, letting the vibrations from the radio radiate over me, releasing the tension in my shoulders and stomach as I anticipated the drive into town.

Before I knew it, Mia nudged my arm, and when I opened my eyes, we were parked in front of the outlets.

Hunter let us out his side of the car, then locked the doors. "Meet back at 8 or I leave you here."

Mia grabbed my arm and entwined it with hers at our elbow. "Ice cream or shirts and books first?"

I grinned. "Is it even a real question?"

Mia laughed. "Not with you. Fine, but only because I'll

need ice cream before we head home after looking for a new shirt."

We walked arm in arm toward the bookstore first. I wanted to grab two more books that I had seen from last time that went with the series I had finished on the beach. Then I wanted to grab my new Outer Banks swag, as Mia called it.

"Only one more day," I said. "How does it go so fast every year?"

Mia shrugged. "I swear someone shaves down each day without us noticing it. Like they shove the sand faster in the hourglass when no one is looking."

"I agree. It's not possible we have to leave in two days. It's a bummer your parents didn't come with us though."

Mia scrunched the bridge of her nose. "Why? Did you want a chaperone?"

I shook my head. "It's not that, usually we all go looking for shirts together."

"Oh, yeah, but they don't actually ever get new ones except occasionally."

"True."

The bookstore wasn't crowded, and I didn't see Mrs. Wagner, but I knew she'd find me at some point while I walked around. The store was setup the same since I had come in the other day. It took no time at all to find the two books I wanted. For fun, I floated down a couple aisles, peering at covers and titles, not sure what I expected to find. I liked the young adult romance books, and I was secure in the belief that those were the kinds of books that spoke to my soul. I didn't generally go looking in other sections, except for today.

Even without his presence in the store, I couldn't help to think of his influence. I found myself in the aisle marked Psychology. None of the titles seemed familiar, neither did the authors. I stopped when one author took up a large section of the shelf: Malcolm Gladwell. Out of the several titles, I pulled the one titled, *Outliers.*

It was a far cry from my normal reading material, but despite that, after reading the blurb, I placed it in my stack. Satisfied with my choices, I walked to the counter.

A young girl scanned each book, placed it in a bag, and stated my total.

"Where's Mrs. Wagner?" I asked.

The girl stared, then focused on putting through my purchase. "She's out."

"Oh, can you tell her Allie Duncan said hello?"

The girl raised an eyebrow then simply nodded as she handed me my bag.

Some customer service this one.

Mia waited for me outside the door. She had sat on a bench near the entrance, scrolling her phone oblivious to all those who walked by.

I crouched behind her left ear and shouted, "Boo!"

She practically threw the phone as she screamed and stood. Hand over chest she glared at me. "Allie! You scared the crap out of me. Don't do that."

I laughed. "You flew!"

"Not funny."

"I thought so." I outstretched my arm. "Ready to go get some shirts?"

She growled out a yes but didn't keep it against me for long.

"I thought you would have been scouring the streets for those cute boys. How will you do that with your nose in your phone?"

"Allie, have I taught you nothing? You can't make yourself seem desperate. If I look like I'm trolling that's not appealing. I must be nonchalant about it."

"Are you saying you were trying to catch someone's attention?"

She leaned close. "By the bookstore entrance, red shirt, black pants, blond hair."

I pushed my hair behind my ear as I carefully turned in that direction. Sure, enough someone matching her description was there and was staring at her. "Damn."

She smirked, then placed her arm around my elbow, as she led us away from him.

"How do you do that? And more importantly why don't you use it at home?"

She shrugged. "Haven't met anyone who is worth it I guess."

Was that really the reason? Or was it easier when you could be anyone you wanted in a different place?

The night was heavy with humidity. The more we walked the more my hair seemed to grow from the increased water vapor. Thankfully, the bookstore was a short two-minute walk from the store we bought our shirts. Unfortunately, as soon as we pushed open the door into the brightly lit place, Richard and Hunter were in perfect view.

Mia groaned. "I can't wait to be home and not worry about running into *him*."

I tapped her arm. "Only one more day. We've got this."

"Fine, but let's go this way before they see us."

Mia crouched a little lower, although we were already barely taller than the clothes racks, until we were on the opposite end of the store.

"The shirts are over there, though."

"And? We wait for them to move. The keychains and all are over here."

I sighed. "I'm not missing out on my shirts. If they don't move in like five minutes, I'm walking over there, even if you choose to hide here."

Mia pouted and puffed out her lip.

"What happened to the big bad Mia? Suck it up buttercup."

"Pfft."

I giggled. I knew she wasn't mad at me, and besides, I didn't want to go over there. Hunter's presence had already had its effects on me. Any more time with him this week and I was worried at what I might do.

Mia surveyed the keychains, as I glanced in their direction. They hadn't noticed us yet.

"What do you think about this one?" Mia asked.

It was a rose, with the words, I'll be your thorn. "For whom?"

"Me, duh!"

"Why?"

She shrugged and placed it back on the hook. "Because it was cute."

I raised an eyebrow. "One, you don't have anyone to fill either spot and two, thorns aren't a good thing."

"It's a metaphor, Allie. Of all people, I'd expect you to catch that."

"I do but doesn't fit you." I nudged her elbow. "What's going on with you lately?"

"Nothing. I just thought it was funny." She moved to the row of keychains and magnets showing Outer Banks, instead.

It didn't seem right to press her on it, but I didn't believe that story. I glanced in the direction the boys were standing, but they had disappeared. "Want to head over to the shirts?"

Mia glanced in that direction, too. "Where'd they go?"

I shrugged. "They aren't in here though, so?"

"Fine."

I smiled, even though she trudged behind me. My fingers hovered over the cotton fabrics. I probably shouldn't have been so excited to pick out a shirt, but it was my tradition.

Each trip, I bought a shirt to remember the rays of sunshine and the salty air.

Mia knew better at this point than to tease me about my process. I never liked to get the exact *same* one. There had to be variations, but I still only bought certain logos. I perused my choices. Some were gray shirts with varying colored logos. Others had black logos and varying colored shirts.

Mia leaned on my shoulder as she peered at the stack. "What will it be this year?"

"I think gray with turquoise logo."

"You don't have that combination yet?"

"Nope."

"Then let's buy it and go get ice cream!"

I giggled as she pouted, trying to do a sad puppy dog face. "Alright, alright. I'm going."

She tossed me a keychain. It said OBX lover. I smiled and held it with the new shirt. "Cute."

"I figured you'd like it."

"I'll add it to my house keys."

"Or car keys."

I rolled my eyes. "Because being able to drive in a *year* means I should buy one now?"

"Yep."

"What about you?"

She swung a black shirt with Outer Banks written in white over the middle. Then she held out her hand, letting me go first toward the cashier.

She bagged up my stuff, while I paid. Then I waited for Mia. "Are they boys getting ice cream too?"

Mia shrugged. "I guess if they're over there when we get there."

"Gotcha. How much longer do we have before we must return?"

She checked her phone. "Thirty minutes, plenty of time."

"You better hope the line is short."

"He better hope it is. I'm not leaving without ice cream." Mia walked toward the door, then held it open for me. We walked across the street toward the ice cream shop. It was a few minutes in the opposite direction, but closer to where Hunter had parked.

As we approached, the unmistakable figures of Hunter and Richard became clear at the front window of the ice cream place.

"Well, guess that answers my question."

Mia hadn't noticed them yet, until she raised her gaze to where I pointed. "Ugh. Did they have to be at this one? Now they'll ruin my sugar rush."

"As you say to me about Brittany, don't let them."

She glared at me but opened the door anyway.

A bell chimed overhead, an employee called, "Be with you in a minute."

Hunter and Richard turned to see who had entered when Richard's expression soured upon recognition.

Hunter's expression remained neutral. "Well, at least I won't have to go searching for either of you."

Mia stuck out her tongue and then studied the menu.

I tried to focus on the menu, as I shifted my bags from one arm to the other. I knew Hunter's gaze had settled on me, evidence of a conversation we hadn't finished.

When I decided on my usual—strawberry with chocolate syrup—I approached the counter.

The employee was barely older than me. A highschooler forced to work for the summer. He had sandy brown hair and black rimmed glasses.

"What can I get you?" he said.

Before I could speak, Hunter cut over next to me. "Probably the strawberry with chocolate syrup."

My eyes widened. He knew my order? I peered around him. What did Mia think of that?

Except she was too busy scowling at Richard to pay any attention to us.

"How'd you know?"

Hunter chuckled. "Allie, you always get the same thing. When you stop ordering that, then I'll be surprised."

The male employee stared at me. "Is that what you want?"

I nodded as he rang me up.

What did I do with that kind of information? Sure, it was reasonable to assume he had heard my order once or twice, but to keep that in his memory? Did it mean something?

Could he?

No.

What was I even thinking? I had already explained it, as did he. I had always ordered that. Nothing cute or romantic about it. Just basic facts of me. That was it.

Chapter Ten

I raised my face into the sunlight as I laid by the pool. "I can't believe tonight is it. This week has gone by faster than ever before."

"You're telling me."

I braved the sunshine to glance at Mia. "When we get home, we need to practice more for volleyball tryouts. We only have a week left. We barely played on the beach."

Mia rolled her eyes. "I still don't understand why you're stressing about it. You're the best setter I know."

"That might be true, but now it's not just the freshmen we have to compete against. We have to be the best out of basically the whole high school. You know they've had the same setter for three years. Sammie is a senior and is bound to get her spot. That leaves a backup, *maybe* a second backup."

Mia shrugged. "And so what? Allie, you're over thinking it." Mia splashed water on my legs. "Get in the pool and stop worrying."

I scowled. "I don't want in the pool. I'm evening out my tan."

"Then you better flip over cause you're going to be way too dark on the front and not the back."

Following her advice, I rolled over. I envied her confidence. Volleyball was so important to me. I didn't know what I would do if I didn't make the team, but Mia didn't sweat it. Liberos weren't an easy position to obtain, and she acted like she either didn't care one way or the other or she knew she had it.

The French door slid open and then shut. I squinted to see who had gone in or come out, when what felt like a tsunami hit me. "What the heck?" I asked as I stood, sopping wet.

Richard floated to the surface after doing a cannon ball, while Hunter stood near my chair chuckling.

I eyed him and he shrugged, then jumped in the pool himself, albeit more gracefully than Richard did.

Mia climbed from the pool and trudged to her towel.

"What you can't be in the same pool as me?" Richard asked.

Mia glared. "I prefer to relax in the pool, not be assaulted by water. So, no, I can't."

Richard shrugged. "Your loss. Sounds like a waste of the last day to me."

Mia settled her hands on her hips. "Why aren't you two at the beach anyway?"

"The water is too calm today. No fun if there are no waves. Figured we would see what you two were doing at the pool. Who knew you'd both be boring in the pool too," Hunter said.

Mia scowled. "Not boring—"

"Just relaxing, we get it," Richard said.

"I'm trying to tan, so please don't send tidal waves my way," I said.

"I can't make any promises," Hunter said, then winked.

Was he ...? Was that flirting? I shook my head.

Get a grip, Allie. Your best friend's brother wasn't flirting with you.

"Well, try really hard then."

Mia wrapped her towel around her body, then walked toward the door. "Allie, are you coming in?"

I shook my head. "You know I hate going in the house soaking wet. I'll be in after I dry off a bit."

"Suit yourself," Mia said as she slid the door open.

I readjusted my now damp towel and listened as the boys stayed in the pool.

"Your sister has such a stick up her butt."

"Well, you did get her covered in mud."

"Big whoop, Baylor. Can the princess not handle a little dirt?"

I resisted the urge to call him out. If they knew I could hear, what would they do?

Hunter chuckled. "It's not about that and you know it. Just lay off her a bit and she will forget eventually."

Yeah right, Mia held grudges until Hell froze over.

"You're lucky you didn't have to deal with her on that four-wheeler ride. I would have rather had Allie."

My eyebrows rose as I kept my neck flat and gaze toward the cement.

"Yeah, well that'll never happen."

Richard scoffed. "Why not?"

"Because I'm never riding with my sister on a four-wheeler, that's why. Besides, when do you expect to have a chance now that the vacation is almost over?"

"She goes to our high school, there's plenty of chances."

What was happening? Were they really discussing me like this? And what did it mean? Was Hunter just being protective of me or did he dismiss the idea because Richard could do better?

"Not likely dude. Allie isn't some girl you can use as a conquest. Got it?"

Okay, this was officially weird. I needed to get out of here.

Carefully I shifted on the chair and wrapped my towel around me. I shoved my flip flops on my feet and shuffled to the door, opening and closing it before I could hear anything else.

The air conditioner froze me as I still dripped water all over the floor. I really hated being this wet and going inside. I'd much rather be warmer and only slightly damp, but they ruined that. There was no way I wanted to stick around to hear the rest of that conversation.

I headed to the bedroom and found Mia sitting on her bed scrolling through her phone. Her hair was wrapped in a towel, and she wore comfy clothes.

She eyed my dripping appearance, her face scrunching up. "I thought you didn't want to walk through the house wet?"

"I changed my mind."

Mia dropped her phone and stared at me. "What happened?"

"Nothing. Just didn't want to be out there anymore."

She didn't look convinced, but she let it go. "I know I certainly didn't. I hope it takes a while before Richard is back at the house when we get home. I'd be fine if I never had to see his face again."

"I'm taking a shower." I snatched my bag off my bed and launched myself into the bathroom. I couldn't tell Mia what they said. Not only would it make no sense if I told her without her brother's input, but I didn't know how I felt about Richard's confession either. Not to mention I didn't want to send Mia into a rage about the comments he made regarding her. It was better I kept it to myself.

* * *

The next morning Mrs. Baylor lined us all up on the stairs to the front of the house to take our yearly group photo. The cars were already packed, and the house had been checked. The only thing keeping us here was this last task.

Mia elbowed Hunter. "Can you scoot over?"

He ignored her.

"Hunter seriously, please?"

He rolled his eyes but did move over, putting him that much closer to me.

I tried to ignore the brush of his skin on my arm, but the tingles spread with each interaction.

"Say cheese," Mrs. Baylor shouted. "Allie, move a little closer to the left."

I scooted a little closer, trying not to end up too much next to Hunter when his arm came around the side and moved me closer to the middle.

My smile faltered. How was I supposed to concentrate when his arm rested lazily over my shoulder? As if he did that all the time? As if it meant nothing?

Cut it out, Allie.

I needed to stop that. Hunter was off-limits, both because of Mia and he would never be interested. It was high time I focused on that reality and let go of my crush on him.

Mr. and Mrs. Baylor stuck both thumbs up and waved us down from the stairs. Mr. Baylor scooted closer to Hunter's convertible as they discussed something.

"You ready to drive back?" Mia asked.

I shook my head. "It's always bittersweet to leave Outer Banks. I wish we could visit the beach all the time."

"You and me both."

We piled into our designated spots in the backseat. Mr. and Mrs. Baylor got in shortly after us.

Mr. Baylor adjusted his mirrors, then glanced toward us. "Are we all ready to head home to Chesapeake Hills?"

We both grumbled.

Mrs. Baylor laughed. "Well, away we go anyway."

Mia picked up her phone and pointed to it, then her fingers moved across it like she was texting.

My phone vibrated in my hand with a message from Mia, *Seven peaceful hours without the brute.*

I giggled, *Seriously, why do you hate him so much?*

Why not? He's a big galoot and I can't stand to hear him at all.

Well, in that case then you certainly do get your wish.

What a bummer we had no luck with boys this summer.

Of course, that was her takeaway.

Are you spending the night tonight?

Probably not. I do need to go home and do laundry and actually see my parents.

Lame. :p

Whatever. You will survive without me for a night.

I might not, but whatever. Janet and Arnold can have you for a night. What about the next day?

Maybe. We aren't even back in Maryland yet. Why don't we see how things go once we're home?

Fine. I'm taking a nap. Mia shoved headphones in her ears, then stuck out her tongue at me as she listened to her playlist.

I couldn't help but to grin like an idiot. Who else had such a good best friend that after a week on vacation with their family, they still wanted to spend time together?

I needed to remember that. Our friendship was more important than any feelings I had for Hunter. Sure, he was dreamy, muscular, and well ... hot. Mia was there for me. That was always more important.

Chapter Eleven

True to my word, I went home once we had arrived back in Maryland. The Baylors had dropped me off, even though Mia stared out the window pouting until I walked through the threshold and shut the door.

My parents had been in the family room when I arrived. We had a simple meal, then went to bed. I had been exhausted from the drive anyway. Every stop on the way home, and granted there weren't many, my brain couldn't help trying to catch a glimpse of Hunter, and when it hadn't happened, I pouted, then yelled at myself internally for even trying to continue that line of thinking when I had sworn off my crush.

I stayed home that Sunday to spend the usually one day a week my parents wouldn't work with them, but when Monday morning had come around, I couldn't deny the urge to practice volleyball with Mia.

She had texted me earlier in the morning and begged me to at least come by and practice or sit by their pool. It didn't take long, before I changed into athletic shorts and a tank top, locked up and started walking to her house.

It was a rare day with little humidity, a treasure for August in Maryland. Most people were at work, their kids at daycares or inside soaking in the final hours of summer.

Mia had promised to take this final week seriously. One run on the trail and volleyball drills for at least an hour every day, maybe more if we weren't too tired from the scorching sun.

Standing in the driveway by the basketball net, Hunter dribbled a basketball, lost in the actions of his own movements. He faked to the right, then turned as he pretended to avoid a defense player before he shot and made a layup.

Of course, he was shirtless, and I nearly stopped dead. It didn't matter that I had seen him shirtless the entirety of the previous week. There was no appropriate amount of time that would desensitize my reaction to his bare abs and toned muscles.

He caught the rebound and walked back toward where he had started as he dribbled. He removed his AirPods. "Duncan, didn't get enough of us last week?"

My eyes widened.

Mia turned the corner and lobbed the volleyball at his head, which he ducked. "She came to practice with me obviously."

Hunter chuckled and replaced his AirPods, before starting the routine all over again.

"About time you showed up. I've been so bored."

I snorted. "Twenty-four hours, Mia. I mean, really, you need some hobbies."

She shrugged. "You ready to go in the back? I cleared more space next to the campfire for us to bump the ball around."

"Okay. Can we start with control drills first?"

She nodded as she walked around the back.

I dropped my house keys and phone on the sectional by the back door, then sprinted an appropriate distance from Mia and stretched.

"Do you really think this will be enough to get us spots on the team?"

Mia groaned. "Why is it so hard for you to accept how good you are?"

"I don't know, but I can't help it."

"Yes, we can do this. I know we can." She bumped the ball toward me.

We volleyed back and forth for several minutes, focusing on our techniques. Control drills were about keeping my fingers light and the ball high, for her it was about good form to take any spin off the ball, albeit I wasn't sending it to her too recklessly. We created an easy rhythm which allowed my attention to shift to the shirtless boy on the front driveway. Even from the backyard I could hear the steady *thump, thump, thump* of the basketball before he practiced free throws. He had a routine. Dribble it three times, then shoot—like a volleyball player about to serve the ball. It was sacred.

"Let's do some serves," Mia said as she held the volleyball, shaking me from my thoughts.

I stepped even farther away from her. With our new distance, I had a prime view of his shirtless workout, not to mention more time to stare at him.

Needless to say, the ban on my feelings for him was not going well.

* * *

The week passed quickly from the plethora of volleyball drills and running Mia and I had accomplished.

Today was the day and my stomach lurched at the slightest thought of tryouts. I didn't want to see Brittany and listen to her comments. I also wasn't thrilled that Hunter would drive us. My façade had been cracked and being around him was harder than normal.

Mia tossed me a water bottle. "Stop stressing. Your face is all contorted. It will get stuck like that if you don't relax."

I giggled. "I'm not stressing."

Mia gave me a knowing look. "Sure, you aren't. Want me to smash the volleyball into Brittany's face today?"

"No. Yes. No. I would love to see that, you know I would, but then coach would reconsider your position so, ultimately, no. Don't sabotage anything."

She slouched and puffed her bottom lip. "Fine, Ms. Debbie Downer. I wanted to see her face when the ball launched at her head."

"Me too."

Hunter strolled into the kitchen, twisting his lanyard around his fingers. "You two ready?"

"Yep," Mia said.

Hunter grabbed a soda from the fridge and strolled to his car. Mia followed closely behind, and I brought up the rear.

Mia took the seat up front, and I sat behind Hunter in the backseat. It was easier for Mia and me to chat as Hunter drove. Something we had done a million times since he could drive us. Yet here I sat with absolutely nothing to say.

My phone dinged and I checked the text message that scrolled across my screen, *Stop worrying*. The text was from Mia. I sent a sticking out your tongue emoji and shoved my phone in my drawstring bag. She was right. I was worried for nothing. I worried about Hunter and what to do now that the thoughts weren't walled up as much. I had known him forever and my feelings toward him were one sided. I needed to stop pretending he could potentially feel more than he did.

As for volleyball, I had trained and worked hard. If I didn't make the team, then someone else better than me deserved it and I needed to accept it. What would be would be.

Our high school gymnasium loomed in the distance. Many cars were parked out front and girls strolled to the gym doors. A sign decked out in purple and white—our school colors—was right next to the door.

I remembered my first day of school the year before. Rosewood High had seemed like a giant's school—the three-story stone foundation had been intimidating, compared to the middle school. An extremely animated Raider had greeted all of us.

Now looking at the school, it seemed big enough for all the activities, but it no longer scared me.

I gulped down my nerves as Hunter parked and Mia and I hopped out. Mia locked arms with me and the chirp of a locked car echoed in my ears. I turned to see Hunter following us.

"Are you coming in?" Mia asked.

Hunter nodded. "I'm not wasting gas while I wait for you, and it'll be cooler inside. Besides, Mom and Dad want updates about your tryouts. I can't do that if I don't go in."

Mia shrugged. "Whatever, just don't shout anything."

Hunter held his hands, palm out. "You won't even know I'm there."

Great, just great. As if I wasn't nervous enough, I now had an audience. What else would go wrong today?

* * *

The first part of our tryout was a one-mile run. We had to complete the mile in under ten minutes. Thanks to our incessant running trips this summer, that would be easy peasy for me. I hated running as a rule, but I had to do what I had to do to make the team.

After today we wouldn't be forced to run anyway. I had plenty of stamina for a game to bust my butt around the court. I took a large gulp of my water as I waited for Coach Sawyer to announce the next set of drills. Most likely Mia and I would be separated since we didn't try out for the same position. Coaches always wanted to work their setters and liberos differently.

"I am *so* nervous."

"Well, don't be, Allie. You'll do great. Your hands always have a light touch on the ball, and it soars up just at the right height. They'll see that."

"I sure hope so." I checked the bleachers. Hunter still sat in the same place scrolling through his phone. "You're not nervous?"

"Me? No." Mia grinned. "No one digs up a ball better than I can."

"True that. You've got those pancake hands!"

Mia giggled. "You're such a weirdo."

"What? You do. That ball last year was *on the ground* yet somehow you snuck your hand under there. It was impressive."

Mia bowed. "Well, thanks my dear." Mia's eyes widened. "Don't look now, but here comes Brittany. Put on your smile and stand up straight. Don't let her rattle you."

My stomach lurched. Why did Brittany have to bother me? Couldn't she keep her blond-haired-ponytail and perfect body away from me?

Brittany squealed as she got closer. "Mia. Allie! It's so good to see you. I've missed you this summer." She made kissy faces at us both before stepping back.

"Hey, Brittany," Mia said. "Killer run you completed. I could barely see you at the front."

Brittany's smile widened. "Thank you. I've been going hard with my trainer. She's a beast."

"Totally."

Brittany placed her hand on my arm. "Allie, you seem a little faster than last year. I'm surprised, you've never been one to practice your running. It'll certainly help you if you make the team."

Keep your face blank. Keep it blank. She's not worth it.

"Yep, it certainly will."

Mia glared at her from behind.

I stifled a giggle as she continued to make faces.

"Well, good luck both of you. I need to stretch before my spiking drills."

"Of course. Bye, Brittany," I said as I secretly wished for her to trip or get nailed in the face with a ball. It was one thing to be good. It was another to be so passive aggressive about your abilities. Why she felt she had to say anything to put someone down was beyond me. We all tried out for the same team. We needed to be cohesive, not secretly sabotaging one another—something Brittany failed to understand.

The whistle blew, our sign to head toward the middle of the court for more directions. Assistant coach Leslie stood at the middle of the huddle. "Listen up, ladies. There will be four stations. The first is libero, the second is setters, the third is for spiking, and the fourth is serves. Everyone will end up at all four stations. I know you all have your *positions,* but I want to see what you can do in all stations. Are we clear?"

Many of us nodded.

"Good. First station Baylor, Duncan, Jennings, Smith, and Wilson."

Brittany? Brittany was in my group? *Just perfect!*

Mia grabbed my shoulder and moved with me to our station. At least I had her to offset Brittany. The volleyball gods hated me, that was all there was to it.

Chapter Twelve

My suspicion had been correct. Brittany found ways to not necessarily sabotage me outright, but to at least shadow me at every turn. Even though her position shouldn't have competed with mine, somehow it did. Every time I set the ball the best I could, she somehow did it better. Spikers and setters should have worked together, but she never received that memo.

"Stop psyching yourself out," Mia whispered. "This is the last heat. Show them your wicked serve and stop letting her get under your skin. She won't be a setter. You have that spot."

I snorted. "It doesn't feel like I have it right now. Brittany is killing this tryout."

"So are you." Mia elbowed me hard then tossed the ball so I could serve.

Every coach stared as we had three shots to serve the ball and then move on. Three chances were all I had left to show the coaches I deserved to be on the team. I needed this.

I closed my eyes, breathed in deep, then released it. Walking up to the line, I smacked the ball three times as it rebounded from the floor. I twirled it twice in my hands.

Raised my left arm and arched my right arm behind my head. One breath in, then as I released, I tossed the ball in my left hand high enough in front of me and followed through with the other arm as I stepped forward with my opposite foot.

The motion somehow worked together and provided me with a decent first serve. It wasn't stellar, but at least it was over the net. Now I just had to do it two more times.

Mia passed another ball and nodded. Her expression was determined.

I didn't know what I would have done without her at this tryout. She helped me keep it together and it was in moments like this I knew how much I needed her. If I crossed the line with Hunter, I'd ruin that. Why would I ever want to do that?

So, what if he had perfect hair and a perfect smile. Mia was always there to cheer me on, and a girl needed her best friend.

I managed to serve the next two balls into the court and put a little spin on the final one. It wasn't a jump serve, but at least they were serves that could have earned points.

Mia was up next to serve. She powered each one into a specific spot on the court. I watched the expressions on the coaches as she served. At least from what I saw, they were impressed.

When our group had finally finished serving, we sauntered to our water bottles and waited. Brittany thankfully had her stuff on the other side of the gym, which meant I didn't have to listen to her obnoxious comments while we waited for the other groups to finish.

Mia sucked down her water. "I'll be right back. Need me to fill up your water?"

I shook my head and watched as she jogged toward the bathrooms to fill up her bottle.

Hunter stood and walked down the remaining bleachers until he stood next to me. "Nice tryout, Duncan."

I shrugged.

He gazed at my expression. "Yanno, it's customary to say thank you when someone gives you a compliment."

I nearly choked on my water. "I-I ..."

He chuckled. "You seriously can't be this humble."

"What do you mean?"

"Your sets were flawless today. I'd say you'd give Sammie a run for her money, senior or not. I certainly wouldn't want a sophomore at your level to show up for tryouts in basketball for my position." He swirled his lanyard around his finger and shrugged. "Tell Mia I'll be by the car. Come out when you're finished."

He didn't wait for me to respond, and honestly, I had no idea what I would have said to him anyway. I had no idea he thought I was that good. Did he really think I'd edge out Sammie?

Thankfully, I didn't have long to dwell on his comments before Mia was back and the coaches were thanking us for trying out. We would know if we made the team in exactly a week.

Seven days to torture myself with the possibility that I wouldn't play volleyball for my high school—my worst nightmare.

* * *

Hunter dropped me off at my house after tryouts on their way home. It probably was a bad idea to go home instead of to Mia's. She would distract me, which I desperately needed, but at the same time, I wanted to sit at home and think about things.

"Mom," I called as I dropped my bag off by the front door. I wound down the hallway to her office.

The light was off, and the room felt cold, like no one had inhabited it for several hours. I slumped in her armchair and surveyed their office. Papers were strewn across both their desks and books had pens shoved inside to use as bookmarks. Post-its stuck out at all angles, haphazardly placed.

My face scrunched as I tried to pry one book out from the pile. The cover and title were in English but seemed like Greek to me. Whatever it was, it was mega research, which meant that Mom or Dad was beginning another research project at work.

I was happy that they were so successful at their jobs and that their research made great strides in Biology, but it kept them away even more than usual. I would be on my own most of the time instead of having two parents waiting for me when I got home late. I doubted they would notice much of anything about me for a few months.

The desire to curl up into a ball and disappear was tempting. It wasn't that I wanted parents always in my business. In high school, it was actually nice not being interrogated all the time, but no one wanted to be left alone *all* the time.

I trudged up to my room and kicked off my sneakers. I needed a shower after my intense tryouts, plus it gave me something to do. My bedroom was equipped with a bathroom attached, which made it nice. I would never have to go downstairs if it wasn't for needing food.

The knob for the shower was icy cold as I reached to turn on the water. Someone had the air conditioner on full blast in the house. Dad never liked the house to be above seventy degrees, even if it was one hundred degrees outside or below thirty-two. Our house was a constant sixty-eight degrees—snow or sun.

Once the air warmed, I hopped in, washed my hair, and quickly got back out. I wrapped the towel around my midsection and then a smaller one around my hair. I moseyed over to my bed and checked my phone. I already missed a few texts from Mia, even though we had been together all morning.

Are you coming over for dinner? Dad is bringing home crabs. Last batch for the summer.

My stomach lurched at the thought. She knew I liked a good crab feast. I looked from the stack of English books for my summer reading to my phone. I really should have stayed home and finished them for school. We only had a week and a half until school started and I had yet to read anything. I knew I could read one book a day and be finished in three days, but I just had to sit and do it.

I sighed, who was I kidding? I knew I would go to her house. What else would have I for dinner? A peanut butter and jelly sandwich was nothing compared to fresh crabs.

I texted Mia back, *Sure. What time?*

Six. Why don't you spend the night? Last time this summer? We can put the projector screen up in the backyard and sleep in a tent like we used to.

My memories flooded with images from Mia and me in the summer when we were ten. She had been obsessed with some TV show where the main character spent nights out in a tent learning about nature and living off the land. I couldn't believe she had been obsessed with a show like that, but she had been. As a result, we spent every night I stayed over that summer in a tent, having bonfires, and sleeping in a sleeping bag. We hadn't done that in ages.

Okay. My parents are starting a new research project I think anyway.

Yes! See you then.

My phone bounced a few times after I tossed it onto my bed. My small tote was shoved in the corner of my room from the last time I had stayed at Mia's house. I pried it from between the bookshelf and my chair as I peered inside. Wadded up in a ball was a T-shirt and shorts and a few pairs of underwear I hadn't needed the last time I had stayed over. I tossed all the items of clothes into the hamper, just in case, and rummaged through my dresser drawers.

I settled on a long pair of pajamas since we were sleeping outside, a big volleyball T-shirt, and my denim shorts. Then I checked my closet for what to wear over. Since picking crabs was a messy endeavor, I didn't need anything fancy. I was sure to have Old Bay and pieces of the shell shoved in the nooks and crannies regardless. I settled on a plain light pink cotton dress. It was a good find from a thrift store and didn't matter if it stained a little, it was easy to clean.

I unfurled my hair from the towel and patted my ends, before scrunching the hair up toward my head. It helped to set a few curls before it totally air dried. I finger combed the rest and then headed downstairs. It was only four and while I could have easily headed to Mia's house now, I didn't want to just yet.

Instead of grabbing one of the three English books, I grabbed a new novel I had bought on vacation. The book's pages were intoxicating as that new book smell wafted into my nose. It was a scent unlike any other and impossible to dupli-cate. The only better smell was an older book with that dusty musk added to it.

I dropped my tote next to the sectional, then let the massive sized cushions swallow me whole as I dove into the book's rabbit hole—more lost with each word and page I continued to read.

Chapter Thirteen

My phone rang. "Hello?" I asked slightly annoyed to stop at a good part in my book. The female main character, Clarissa, had literally ran into her crush at the coffee shop, making her cup of coffee launch into her nose and creating an embarrassing coughing fit.

"Where are you?" Mia asked.

I pulled the phone away from my ear and checked the time—6:10.

Crap! I fumbled to put the phone back to my ear. "Oh my god. I'll be right over."

"Hurry up! Hunter invited *Richard*. You know how he eats. You'll miss the good seats."

"Bye," I said as I clicked End. I shoved my bookmark between the pages and launched myself off the sectional. I picked up my bag from the floor, shoved my book inside and then headed out the door, locking it as I closed the door.

I sprinted toward Mia's house, luckily the evening had brought cooler temperatures and I wasn't sweating by the time I walked up their front steps.

Mia opened the door before I had even knocked. "What happened to you?"

I gave her a knowing look.

She rolled her eyes. "You were reading that new book, weren't you?"

I shifted my gaze to the ground and nodded.

"Well, throw your bag on the stairs and come out back. The boys aren't here yet, but I want to sit before they claim the good spot by the box." Mia turned on her heels and booked toward the back door.

I sighed. I hadn't seen Richard since the OBX vacation, but Mia still didn't like him being anywhere near her, which only meant that tonight would be full of melodrama instead of us enjoying one of the last summer nights we had left.

The Baylor's backyard was like someone had transplanted it from an HGTV magazine. A few years back they had hired a landscaper to redo the almost one-acre backyard. There was a gazebo-patio combination as soon as you stepped out of the kitchen French doors. The gazebo spanned the length of a full-size table and chairs for outdoor meals.

Toward the back part of the fence was a small game area: corn hole, horseshoes, and a small net for Mia and me to practice volleyball. In the middle, was a large bonfire pit with sectionals surrounding it and then behind the fireplace was where we put the projector for nights like this.

I was envious of the setup. My own yard still had a swing set from when I was a toddler, and it hadn't exactly been well maintained over the years. The newest thing back there was my hammock and that had been a miracle to begin with. I had begged for a hammock for almost a year before they bought me one for my birthday.

"Hey, Allie. How were tryouts?" Mrs. Baylor asked as she spread the newspaper pages across the table to aid with the crab cleanup later. "I tried asking Mia and she told me nothing."

I giggled. "They were okay, Mrs. Baylor. We know in a week. Mia did great."

An arm elbowed me. "Duncan, did too," Hunter said as he passed by to set a few more newspapers on the outdoor table.

Mrs. Baylor's eyebrows rose. "Wonderful. You ladies will do great this year. I just know it."

I managed a smile even though my brain seemed frozen. Two compliments in one day were enough to fry my brain mechanisms. Although, I didn't have long to dwell on it because Mia burst through the backdoor and plopped down in the chair closest to the middle of the table. She waved me over. "Sit. I saw Richard in the kitchen. I want to be firmly placed in our spots before he comes out."

I listened and sat in the chair she pulled out for me.

Mr. Baylor pushed through the backdoor carrying a large box, followed by Hunter carrying an equally large box.

My eyes widened. "Wow."

Mia nodded, with a similar expression. "Must have wanted to go all out this year for the end of summer. Maybe because Hunter's a senior?"

"Maybe, but I'm not complaining." I licked my lips. "This will be so yummy."

The smell of butter and Old Bay wafted toward me as they dumped the crabs on the table and spread them out over the newspaper. I could feel the steam roll off their little orange bodies. Mia and I pulled a few towards us, then grabbed a butter knife, mallet, and paper towel before we pulled off the legs.

It was a tradition in Chesapeake Hills to teach your children young how to pick crabs. I learned by the time I was three how to pull the delicate and delicious meat from the claws and other legs. I knew to avoid the yellow stuff, aka poop, and to strip off the lungs before I even knew my ABCs completely.

"Allie, were your parents home? There's plenty here. They could come on over, it's been ages since I've seen your mom," Mrs. Baylor said as she unloaded several drinks on the table.

I shook my head as I pulled another leg from my crab. "I think they've started another research project. No one was home when I got there earlier."

"Oh, what a pity. Janet loves a good crab feast."

I smiled and continued to shove pieces of meat into my mouth and then pried more from the shell. Mrs. Baylor was right, my mom did love to pick crabs as much as I did, but she loved her research more.

Sometimes, I thought she even loved it more than me.

Mia nudged my elbow. "Can you pass me another paper towel, mine fell off my lap.

I eyed the roll and then my messy hands. "Uh ... it'll get messy by the time I get it over to you."

She shrugged. "I need something."

"Okay, if you insist."

I shook my hands over top of the crab shells, but it was no use. Old Bay would be lodged under my fingernails and in my skin for days, shaking it wouldn't release it in the slightest.

I reached for the paper towel, when a larger hand gently moved mine and did it instead. I followed the arm up to the face but knew who it was before I had even looked at those beautiful emerald eyes.

Hunter had a distinct birthmark on his wrist on the underside of his left hand. It was two small perfect circles that made what looked like a colon. He finished ripping the paper towel off the rest of the roll and proffered it to me.

"It's for Mia."

He tossed the paper towel in her direction and then sat

across from her, while Richard sat across from me, and then the weirdest thing happened. Richard *winked* at me, and I practically had heart failure right there at the table, with Old Bay stuck to my hands and my cheek from when I had an itch on my nose.

Things were off and I didn't know how to fix it.

* * *

Luckily, Richard and Hunter stayed to their conversation and ignored Mia and me while they picked crabs. Then Richard had gone home after gorging himself on more crabs than I could keep track of, but at least throughout the whole ordeal, Mia behaved.

Mia scrolled through her phone looking for the movie she wanted to play on the projector. When she found it, she clicked the icon and waited for the projector to whirr to life.

Unfortunately, as soon as she had hit play and it began to roll, I had to go to the bathroom. I crawled from the sleeping bag in my tent and stood. "I'll be right back. I have to pee."

Mia groaned. "The movie just started. You want me to pause it?"

"No. I'll be right back out, no worries."

Mia trained her gaze back on the screen as I walked toward the house. The French doors were still unlocked, thankfully, and I pushed it open and headed to the downstairs bathroom. The kitchen was dark, except the light under the microwave and a few lights along the wall.

The downstairs bathroom was small, just big enough for a toilet and sink to wash your hands, but it came in handy for times like this. Instead of running up the stairs when I really had to go, I could use this one.

I quickly did my business and washed my hands. I closed the door and walked back outside when I ran right into the back of Hunter. His cologne was a dead giveaway, even though it had faded by this point.

"I'm so sorry," I said trying to figure out where to put my hands. I half wanted to touch him to show my guilt, but then thought maybe it wasn't appropriate.

"No worries, Duncan. It's not like it hurt," Hunter said as he chuckled. He looked around the kitchen. "Where's Mia?"

"Outside."

He cocked his head to the side. "Outside? For what?"

"We're sleeping out there."

"Willingly?"

I nodded. "It's nice. We're watching a movie."

Hunter smiled, setting off that twinkle that made me weak. "Full of surprises, Duncan. Full of surprises." Then just like that, he disappeared again.

I had no idea what he had come down to the kitchen for, but he certainly didn't get it. And what did he mean about *full of surprises*? Between Richard's wink and Hunter's comments today, I couldn't keep my head from feeling dizzy and I didn't like feeling out of control.

Chapter Fourteen

Mia and I had finished our movie and promptly fell asleep. Tryouts were nothing like practicing. We had been tired from the adrenaline rush and so much activity. When I had woken up the next morning, I ate breakfast with Mia's parents, then went home. Hunter either hadn't been awake or didn't come down, which only made the uncomfortable feeling in the pit of my stomach grow.

The next few days I had focused on preparing for school. Mom had taken me to the store for school supplies, just like always. Then I switched off from reading the book I had started before going to Mia's and onto my schoolbooks.

The sofa in my parent's office was like a big vat of quicksand sucking me into its depths as I tried to make myself focus on *The Catcher and the Rye*. This was the last book I had to read for school in a few days and I was about halfway through, but today was the day I would find out if I made the volleyball team.

My concentration wasn't at an all-time high. I still had more than half of the book left to finish. And unlike books I liked to actually read for fun, the spacing on each page was not as large as I was used to.

It wasn't like I was a bad student; I merely noticed the difference. Hadn't anyone heard of larger spaces when they formatted books back then? Maybe if they changed the formatting, more teenagers would enjoy reading the classics ... then again, maybe not.

I focused my attention on the page I was reading, so much so that it felt like laser beams would shoot out of my eyes and set the page on fire, when a loud knock, followed by the door swinging open, startled me.

"What the heck?" I said as I strained to hear who that could have been. I checked the time on the clock in their office, it was too early for it to be my parents. Untwining my arms and legs from the couch that had sucked me into its depths, I peered around the corner once I was finally free.

Mia was barreling down the hallway and toward me at top speed.

My eyes widened. "Well, hello to you too."

Mia's expression was wild, like a feral dog let out of the wilderness in broad daylight. "What have you been doing? I called you like fifteen times and decided to walk from my house to yours because you weren't answering!"

My eyebrows knitted. "I didn't—" Sure enough as I looked at my phone, I had indeed missed fifteen calls from Mia. "Oh, it must have gotten turned on silent by accident. I was reading the books for summer reading and didn't notice."

"Well, what a wonderful day to be a complete hermit. The coach emailed everyone about tryouts." She shoved the phone in my face.

I pushed her hand back a tad and tried to make the squiggles on the screen make sense, but it only looked like her screensaver, which was a quote from Maya Angelou. Instead of trying to get to her email, I used my own phone to check my emails and opened the one from coach. I skimmed over the introduction until I saw the list of names at the bottom—and mine was the fourth from the top. "I-I made it?"

Mia beamed. "Hell yes you made it! So did I."

I looked farther down the list. "So did Brittany."

Mia rolled her eyes. "Who cares about that half twit? We made the team!" Mia grabbed my hands and pulled me up and down as she leapt.

By the time we stopped jumping my cheeks hurt from smiling so hard. I couldn't believe I had made the team. It was like a dream coming true.

Mia looked around. "Wanna come to my house for dinner?"

I shook my head. "Mom should be home soon, she grabbed food from the Italian place by Rosewood college. Plus, I want to tell them I made the team."

Mia shrugged. "Suit yourself. Mom is making your favorite ..."

"Chicken pot pie," we said at the same.

Mia nodded.

I groaned. "Of course. Well, can you see if I can get leftovers? I'd eat it all week, even if it is a day or so later."

Mia giggled. "It's not *that* good, but sure. I'll have Mom save you some."

"Thanks."

Mia shook her head. "You could just come over for a little while ..."

"Bye, Mia," I said as I shook my book at her. "I need to finish this. I'm not even halfway and school is coming soon."

"Psh, it'll still be there tomorrow. Ignore it for a few hours."

I nudged her down the hallway and eventually through the doorway outside. "Bye, Mia."

She turned away and waved behind her as she stalked away

back toward her house. She certainly knew how to be stubborn, but I did need to finish my book and I couldn't have every meal that week with the Baylors.

* * *

By the time Mom walked through the door, I had managed to finish three more chapters of my book.

The smells wafted toward me before I could even hear Mom enter the house. "I'm home sweetie. I hope you brought your appetite."

I stretched from my position on the couch and walked through the doorway in the partial wall that separated the main space from the kitchen and then hallway.

Mom was busy getting out plates from the cabinets and then unloaded each carton of food when her phone rang. She squinted at the caller ID. "Go ahead and make yourself a plate. I'll be right back." She pressed the phone to her ear. "This is Professor Duncan ..." Her voice trailed off as she shut herself in the office.

I sighed lifting the Styrofoam lids on each package trying to find my shrimp scampi. Of course, it was the last lid I checked. I poured the shrimp and pasta out onto the plate Mom had set out, then grabbed myself a soda and plopped back onto the couch.

Somehow, I managed to prop the book open and still eat while I waited. I couldn't say I was surprised. Mom had in fact started a new research project, some innovative way to clean the pollution from the Chesapeake Bay, or it would be if they managed to get it to work.

I knew her work was important, but I wanted to be the center for once. At the Baylors they all sat together and had meals. No phone calls. No interruptions. Even if they weren't with the kids the rest of the day, they at least ate meals together. I didn't know the last time I had spent more than ten minutes in the same room with both of my parents, let alone had an entire meal where all we did was talk about our days.

Dad wasn't even home yet and probably wouldn't be for another twenty minutes. All I wanted was to tell them I made the team, but now with Mom on the phone, that didn't even look feasible.

I twirled the pasta around my fork, then stabbed a shrimp before shoving it into my mouth. I supposed on the bright side at least I had more time to read for school.

My plate was almost empty by the time Mom escaped from her office. The sun basked our family room in amber light as it continued its inevitable descent until sunset.

I could hear Mom rummaging in the kitchen, until she joined me on the couch. She eyed my book and then loaded her own fork up. "Ah, *The Catcher and the Rye*, one of my favorites."

I withheld rolling my eyes. Of course, it was her favorite. It only added to her nerdiness.

"Did you get to the part where ..."

I looked up to see what happened and once again the blue light of her phone lit up her features as it sucked her into the cyberworld.

I cleared my throat. When that didn't work, I tried two more times, until finally, she put down her phone.

"Thanks for dinner."

"Of course, sweetie. I've missed you."

God, how I wished that were true. If it had been true, we would have said more than three sentences so far.

I nodded instead.

"How was your shrimp scampi? Did they get it right?"

"Yep, extra sauce, just how I like it."

Mom smiled. "Good."

"So, I found out some news today."

"Oh?" she asked in between bites of her food.

"I made the volleyball team."

"Oh, how wonderful, Allie. Your dad will be so happy for you."

I frowned as I noticed Mom's attention drifted back toward her phone. So much for an actual conversation. I finished my food, cleaned off my plate and loaded it in the dishwasher. "I-I have some work to finish."

"Okay, sweetie," Mom said without glancing up once.

And just like that, I was in my room—alone.

Chapter Fifteen

The skirt I chose for the first day of school had already gotten on my nerves and it hadn't even been fifteen minutes. For what felt like the hundredth time, I smoothed the edges and tugged it a little farther down.

I tried to keep it simple. A white T-shirt, blue with little white flowers on the skirt, and my white sneakers. It wasn't too provocative, but it wasn't my normal jeans and a T-shirt either. It was elevated, classier. I was a sophomore; I couldn't just show up looking frumpy or like a typical teenager from the clothing store's mannequin.

This would get me noticed and let me still be comfier. If only I could just stop adjusting my skirt.

My phone chirped from the bed. I knew who it was before I even looked. It would be Mia outside waiting in her brother's car for us to go to school. It was our ritual. We walked in together ... always. So ever since Hunter could drive, he picked me up too. It was standard, which was also partially the reason for swirling in my stomach. I wanted to look good in general but knowing what he thought mattered too.

My bag waited for me by the door, right where I left it when I got ready the night before. I slung one strap over my right shoulder and winced as the weight of all my new school supplies weighed it down. It would probably be the heaviest it could get all year. Nothing compared to the weight of having all your stuff at once.

Mia was leaning out the passenger window from the other side of the car waiting for me. "It's about time." Mia gave me an elevator look, then whistled. "Allie Duncan, shut the front door! You look hot."

My cheeks flamed, especially when Hunter, who had been fiddling with the radio peeled his eyes away to look at me. The look made me feel exposed, like suddenly this was a dream, and I was walking around naked.

I adjusted the strap of my bookbag. "Oh stop, Mia."

"Ow ow ow. I'm serious. The boys will be *drooling* over you. Why didn't you tell me you changed your outfit for today? Now I'll look awful next to you."

I giggled. "Mia, you couldn't look awful even if you tried. You could go in sweats and still be pretty. Now hush up and get back in the car."

Hunter chuckled, even as he tried to avoid looking in my direction.

This car ride already went from semi awkward and nerve wracking to full blown I-just-forgot-I-had-a-big-test-and-need-to-do-well nerve wracking.

The door slightly creaked as I opened it and sat, letting my four-hundred-pound bookbag crash against the floor.

Mia started talking as soon as I buckled up, but I had a tough time even listening when I kept catching Hunter's beautifully green eyes find mine in his rear-view mirror.

I knew that he was just being a good driver and watching the road, but I had no reason to constantly stare at those eyes.

I needed to pull it together. I wouldn't want someone staring at me while I was driving, so why would he?

Thankfully, school wasn't a far drive, or walk for that matter. In less than five minutes, we arrived in the school parking lot. Since Hunter was a senior he had first dibs on the front parking spots, letting him and the rest of his class escape the lot before the traffic really began.

On the one hand it would be nice when winter started and we had to freeze our butts off walking to the car, but for at least the first couple of months of school, Mia and I had practice almost every day.

I lugged my bookbag off the floor of his car and adjusted my outfit as I caught up with Mia. Hunter took a tad longer to walk away from his car, but I could feel his presence behind me.

I forced myself to listen to Mia.

"I don't like that we don't have the same lunch period this year. How will I catch up with you?"

I rolled my eyes. "Mia, I see you all day. We drive to school together, have volleyball together. We're always together. Maybe if you didn't take that cooking class, we would have lunch together."

Mia's shoulders slumped. "Fine." She linked her arm with mine. "But I'll miss you."

I giggled. "I'll miss you, too."

Hunter cleared his throat.

Mia turned at the sound. "Are you picking us up after practice today?"

"I guess. What time does it end?"

"Four."

He nodded and then headed in the opposite direction as we reached the doors to Rosewood High.

"Are you ready?" Mia asked.

"As ready as I can be."

She gripped my hand and pushed open the door. The hallways were full of students hugging and kissing—*yuck, with tongue*—as they welcomed each other back from the summer.

"My locker's this way," Mia pointed to the left.

"Mine's this way," I said and pointed to the right.

"Text me if you need to," she said and headed toward her locker.

I walked down the hallway toward my locker and homeroom. I didn't recognize many of the people I saw. I was either in the freshman hallway or upper classmen and I didn't know how I felt about that. I'd rather be near Mia. Our names weren't that far off, how could we possibly be so far away from each other.

Halfway down the hallway, I found my locker in all its purple glory. It was at least a top locker, so I didn't have to worry about anyone dropping anything on me.

I pulled the tiny paper from my bag with my locker combination and unlocked it, then unloaded most of my books except the first two classes. I would be close enough to my locker to grab more books afterward.

A familiar laugh pulled me from my thoughts about my schedule. I turned and only a few feet from my locker was Hunter on the opposite side of the hallway.

My mouth threatened to betray me as it opened wide and then I forced it shut.

I spun around before Hunter could see me. I leaned forward into my locker blocking my view and hopefully his. I grabbed what I needed for Geometry and English, then shut the door.

My hopes all crashed and burned when Hunter's emerald green eyes stared back at me from behind where my locker door had been. "Duncan, look at this. Same hallway this year, huh?"

I nodded and gulped, hoping he couldn't hear the sound as well as I could as it echoed in my ears.

He nudged my arm then waved at someone farther down. "See you later."

"Yeah ... see you." I managed to finally get out, but too late. He had already moved on catching up with his other friends.

My stomach finally unclenched, and I leaned against my locker door. The universe was laughing at me. Totally and completely laughing. It couldn't possibly find any other way to slowly torture me and my feelings.

It was finally lunchtime, and I was practically starving. I couldn't wait to get my hands on something from the lunchroom and then organize my planner. I already had a lot to do, and it was only the first day of school. With my volleyball practices and games, I needed to make sure that I kept up with my studies. My parents might be lost in their own research world, but they'd notice if I started getting grades lower than all A's.

The one upside to not having Mia at lunch with me was that I could use the time to do work and actually focus. Sure, I would probably sit with some girls from my classes too, but today it was all about organizing my planner.

The line for lunch wasn't too bad. I grabbed the raviolis and a small salad, then headed to a table near the back where I could concentrate and see out the window. A little sun always made me feel better. Unfortunately, it would soon get darker earlier and that usually affected me negatively. So, for now, I wanted to soak it all in.

I grabbed a few bites of my salad and opened my planner, then took out the syllabi I had so far and plugged-in dates of big tests, quizzes, projects, and finally homework. By the time

I was done, my weeks would be organized at least for my morning classes, then I would finish it later for the afternoon ones.

I crunched on a crouton when a lunch tray bumped my elbow. I slowly turned to find the owner of the lunch tray was Hunter. I froze midbite and tried to remember how to chew as I watched his expression shift to amused.

"Duncan, we meet again. Are you following me around?"

"I-I ... No. Of course not."

Hunter chuckled. "I'm kidding." He peered over to see what I was doing, his eyebrows knitting. "Are you spending lunch planning out your *homework*? Duncan, tsk tsk tsk. That won't help you at all this year. No one will approach you if you're doing work." He looked around me. "You should be sitting with friends, not by yourself."

My heart was going into shock. My rhythm was off. Surely this was a dream. There was no planet where Hunter Baylor sat next to me at lunch and gave me advice. All of this was wrong.

He cocked his head to the side. "Duncan? Are you there?"

I coughed and finished my crouton, slowly peering into those beautiful green eyes. "Yeah, of course. I just don't understand why you're sitting here instead of with your friends."

He chuckled. "I'm still planning to do that but had to check on my little sister's best friend. She would kill me if I didn't."

Suddenly it all clicked. Of course, he was over here on behalf of Mia. She must have known that we had lunch together and asked him to say hello. That's all it was, and I was an idiot for thinking it was anything else.

"Oh, of course. Well, check it off your list. You've completed your task." I averted my gaze back toward my planner and my ravioli's.

"And maybe, *I* wanted to check on you too. You seemed lost at your locker this morning."

If I had been eating, I would have choked. "Oh, I was just trying to figure out my schedule, that's all."

He eyed the paper in front of my planner, before he reached for it. "Let's see who you have. Oh, you have Mrs. Widows for Chemistry? Yikes. Watch out for her."

"Did you have her?"

"Nope. Richard did though."

My nose scrunched. I could imagine *most* teachers disliking him. He just looked like the type of person to never be prepared for class.

"What was that face about?"

"Huh? What do you mean?"

"Your nose scrunched like you smelled something bad."

Crap. Why was he paying attention to my expressions? "Oh, I was just thinking about having Mrs. Widows. I hope it's not as bad as you say."

I peered around the lunchroom. Many of the girls surrounding the table were watching us. This was bad. I didn't want people to talk. Nothing was happening between us, what if someone said something to Mia and she didn't believe me.

"Sure, Duncan."

"Well, I don't want to keep you." I motioned toward his lunch tray that he hadn't eaten anything from yet. Then I averted my gaze back to my planner. The longer he waited, the more I could feel the stares.

He eventually stood. "See you after school, Duncan."

I nodded and scheduled in my geometry work. I finished just in time for the bell to ring. I threw away my trash and headed to chemistry and then it would be history class with Mia. This day was already full of the universe mocking me. How would I avoid how I felt about Hunter if our schedules aligned so much?

* * *

After school we had volleyball practice ... our first one since making the team. To say I had been nervous was an understatement. For the first twenty minutes, I felt like an imposter somehow. The warmups, the drills, they all seemed like someone else should have been on that court instead of me.

The senior setter, Sammie seemed to flawlessly release the ball from her hands, and I watched as it soared to the hitters and they spiked it to the floor on the other side of the net. It truly was magical, but then it had been my turn to set during the drills.

The coaches were watching me closely, probably trying to determine if what they had decided was good or not. But as soon as my sneakers hit the setter's spot up by the net and the first ball was bumped to me, I zoned everything else out and focused on the ball and where I wanted it to go.

I boggled one or two, at least in my opinion, but then I got in the *flow* as Mia called it. I had always done it, at least I thought so, where I only had eyes for the ball and then my movements just sang with precision.

By the time we did a practice scrimmage with the freshman team, my nerves were replaced with excitement for the season. I couldn't wait for our first game this weekend, even if I wasn't the starting setter. I was excited to learn all I could from Sammie before she graduated.

Mia bounced the ball off my arm.

I rubbed the spot. "Ow. What was that for?"

"You were on planet Allie again. I was talking to you and yet, you had no understanding of anything. Where'd you go?"

"I went nowhere. I was thinking about practice. That's all."

"Well, stop stressing. You did great. Our scrimmage was

perfect for highlighting our talents. The coaches noticed. I could tell."

I rolled my eyes. "You think the coaches always notice even if they glance in our direction. I was good, but I don't mind learning from Sammie. She's earned her spot and I'll take notes from her."

"Please, your hands are better than hers. You could set around her in your sleep."

"Would you stop before someone hears you? I'm not trying to be that Sophomore who thinks she's better than she is."

"Fine, but I said what I said because it's true." Mia slung her gym bag over her shoulder and headed for the gym doors.

I grabbed both my bookbag and the bag that carried my outfit from school and followed her out.

The air was still warm, teasing me with its resemblance to the summer. In only a few short weeks, the mornings and evenings would be crisp with fresh fall air and warm days of eighty-degree weather would be replaced with scarves and coats. It was normal in Chesapeake Hills, and I quite enjoyed the seasons, but some seasons I wished lasted just a little bit longer.

I yanked at my spandex shorts for the hundredth time. New spandex always rode up and drove me crazy, but at least they were easy to play in. Mia was going on and on about something as we approached Hunter's car. He was sitting on the hood waiting for us and hopped down when we got closer.

God, he looked so hot. Why did he have to be so gorgeous? If he could have been just average looking it would have been easier to ignore him, but every ripple of his muscles and every twinkle from those emerald beauties did me in.

He tapped the hood as he walked around to the driver's side.

I loaded my things into the backseat and as I got in, I noticed a strawberry blonde, volleyball spiker staring at Hunter. What was Brittany doing watching him? And why did it make my stomach twist in ways I didn't think were possible?

<h1 style="text-align:center">Chapter Sixteen</h1>

There was something about the excitement of a volleyball game that changed everything when I entered a gym.

Today was our first game of the season. I didn't have many expectations. I was prepared obviously, but I didn't expect much playing time. Sure, Sammie would need a break at some point, especially if we went to the third set, but substituting for the main setter was different from *being* the main setter.

Either way, I was giddy at the prospect of our game. The stands were full, but from the moment I started warming up, I tuned it all out.

It was a special superpower. As soon as I was on the court in my uniform, I didn't pay attention to anyone in the stands. A celebrity could walk in, and I wouldn't even know they were there.

Mia had always been jealous of my ability to do that, but I never purposely did it. It just seemed to happen.

Mia elbowed me and then tossed me the ball. We all were warming up in pairs, bumping, setting, and spiking the ball occasionally when we had the chance. Soon we would get in hitting lines and then serving lines. Every warmup before a game went the same. It was on purpose to give each team a chance to do all the skills required of a game, but it also was the time I scouted out the other team. Learning who could spike to the corner of the court or who lost their spike's power by overcompensating and making it soar.

I had a knack for finding their strengths and weaknesses just from the warmups and using it for our team. This time though, I hadn't planned to openly speak up about what I saw. I would use it for Mia and me to help us shine, but I was brand new, I knew better than opening my mouth to players who were older and had more experience.

"You nervous?" Mia asked.

"Of course, but you know how it goes. Once it starts, it all fades away."

Mia snorted. "Maybe for you. My palms are sweaty. This is more than just playing on the freshmen team. A whole lot more eyeballs staring at us."

"Well, then pancake the crap out of the ball and crush it like I know you will."

She stuck out her tongue, then launched the ball at my head.

I managed to bump her wild attack and slow it down enough for her to get back under it. We shifted back and forth, showcasing our unique abilities. I focused on setting as much as I could, while she waited to the last possible second before bumping the ball. Liberos didn't have the easy passes, they had to scrape whatever they could off the floor, even if that meant they only had an inch to do it. And Mia did a damn good job.

A whistle blew, signaling it was time to transition into hitting lines. I stayed in the back of the court on our side to get a good look at the other team while I tried to return their spikes. Sammie parked herself at the top of the net, setting the ball to our team as they spiked it to the other side.

Both sides moved in a steady pattern, managing to avoid spiking the ball at the same time, until the other team sent the tallest girl to the net. She readied her stance and waited for her team's setter to put the ball where she needed it.

Her approach was impeccable. Her shoulders lined up with the sideline on our side and I waited and watched to see if she would indeed spike it down the line and be accurate.

I scooted toward the line and parked myself so that anything over my head would be out. The girl wound up and spiked the ball. It hovered in the air and then dropped a foot in front of me.

This girl would need to be blocked at all costs. She could hit. I found Mia on the side shagging a ball and gestured toward their spiker.

Her eyes were wide, which meant she had seen what I did too. She would have to watch the line closely when she was in the back—especially since it would be her position's responsibility to return it for our team.

One more whistle blow and we transitioned to serving. Mia had grabbed two and tossed me one. She threw the ball against the floor letting the bang echo as several players did their warmup routine before a serve.

Most players did something—a twirl, spiking the ball a few times against the floor, or a tossup and catch—Mia's was two spikes, a twirl, and then she reached back and hurled the ball to the other side landing inside the court every time. I served a few times and then the final whistle blew. We all jogged toward the bench and waited.

"Okay, listen up," Coach Leslie said. "Here is the starting lineup starting with the number one position: sixteen, twenty-eight, nineteen, four, two, and nine. Get your hands in here."

We all leaned forward and put our hands in the middle. We pushed down the group and waited to hear what to shout.

"On three let's go Raiders. One, two, three ..."

"Let's go Raiders," we shouted.

The starting team lined up against the serving line and waited for the whistle blow, which was when they would shake hands with the other players and then get in position.

Mia and I weren't in yet, which was fine. We jogged to the bench and sat. The whistle blew and the game began.

* * *

To my surprise, I ended up being put into the second game almost from the start. We won the first game with a substantial score of twenty-five to fourteen. Then after we switched sides, coach had Sammie sit and called me in. Mia had played close to the beginning once her *player* rotated into the backrow. So far, she only had the one player she subbed in for, which was fine for her.

I had just rotated to the front and unfortunately Brittany was one of my top row hitters this game. It was game point if no one screwed up the serve or any of the hits in between.

Mandy, a junior, served the ball and it arced into the backrow, where one of their players popped it up to their setter. I watched the net for a quick tip, but she sent the set to her hitter. Their hitter lined up a cross-the-court spike, but Mia dug it up and sent the ball soaring to me at the perfect height. Brittany was lined up and ready, so I took a breath, and let my feathery touch grasp the ball and ricochet from my hands toward Brittany.

Despite my annoyance of her as a person, she was decent at hitting and gave us a good shot. Brittany glanced at the other side, then went through her wind up, her hand connected with the ball a foot above the net and in between the other team's block.

They missed it and the spike dropped right behind the block before the setter could recover it.

The crowd that I had almost forgotten was there, roared. We just won the game and I had set the final point. My insides screamed at the excitement of that play. Our coach roared with delight. We just won our first game and I had helped.

Mia ran up behind me and smacked my leg. "Girl, that set was *beautiful*. Holy crap. You keep that up and coach won't just have you play a little."

I beamed. She was right, that had been a perfect set and I couldn't be happier with my first game. We all lined up to shake the other team's hands, then gathered our stuff from the bench.

I peered at the stands looking for Mrs. Baylor. "Mia, where's your mom? I don't see her."

Mia glanced at her phone, then frowned. "I guess she had to leave."

My heart dropped into my stomach as I slowly processed what that meant. "When?"

"By the second game I guess." She peered around me and nodded at someone in the crowd. "Hunter came by to pick us up though. He's over by the bottom."

I cringed. Had he seen me play? Had he seen my uniform? I jiggled my shorts down farther as I scanned the crowd. Spandex showed off more of my legs than usual, except when I wore a bathing suit.

I checked my reflection in my phone's screen, flattening some of my flyaway hair. It wasn't the best, but what else was I supposed to do on short notice?

My throat felt like it had constricted, cutting off my air supply.

Mia approached Hunter first. "Thanks for picking us up."

"Sure, you guys—"

Brittany cut him off when she squealed and grabbed my hand.

My brain continued to falter. I glared at Mia who stifled a giggle and shrugged.

"We won! Did you see my spike? I was amazing! Take that," she shouted too close to my ear.

Hunter's expression shifted into one I had only seen from a distance. He eyed Brittany giving her a full elevator look, then put on the charm. "That was a pretty nice point. You're the one who spiked it I presume?"

Brittany twirled a strand of her hair from her ponytail. "You know I was. No one else on our team looks *this* good in this uniform," she said and winked.

My stomach roiled at her comment. This was not happening. She was not flirting with Hunter, and he was *not* flirting back! This couldn't be real. I just needed to pinch myself and it would all be over.

Except with each successive pinch, it only got worse. I could barely understand the words leaving both of their mouths and Mia looked green.

"Of course, how could I make such a mistake?" Hunter asked.

Brittany moved close and grazed her finger over his chest. "Better not again," then she sashayed away.

Hunter chuckled and walked out the gymnasium doors.

I looked at Mia and back at Brittany, then did the vomit gesture. She nodded and cringed as we walked away. This was not good. Brittany could not sink her claws in Hunter. I absolutely forbade it. There was no way I would watch Brittany freaking Jennings go out with Hunter Baylor. I just wouldn't.

Chapter Seventeen

On the rare occasion I couldn't go to Mia's house after school, Mom brought me to her work. Why I couldn't just walk home baffled me. Alas, here I was sitting at the large table in Mom's office.

Dad had his office down the hallway but was on travel for a few days. Not that it was much different from usual. I barely ever saw them, especially since the research project had received grant approval.

Mom glanced at me. "Allie, don't you have homework?"

I paused the steady scrolling I was doing on social media. "Already did it. It's only the second week of school."

Mom waved me off. "I lose track. I give homework the first day."

"That's college, not high school."

"Same thing basically. It's good practice." She tapped her chin. "Maybe I need to have a chat with your school. They should be preparing you all more."

I groaned. "Please do not call school and convince them to give me more work."

"We'll see."

Hopefully, she would forget. If she concentrated on her research enough, I'd be home free. If not, I was sure to be a laughingstock and I didn't need that.

Mom diverted her attention to her computer right as my phone vibrated.

Mia had texted, *All done my dentist appointment. Are you surviving?*

Barely. I'm bored out of my mind.

Nothing to work on?

You know I finished it all. I wish we had practice tonight.

Well lucky enough for me, we didn't. Otherwise, I couldn't have gone to my appointment.

What are you doing now?

Mom wants to take me to look for a homecoming dress.

My eyes widened. *It's like three weeks away. Isn't that a bit early?*

Mom says it's actually late. This is sophomore year. We can't go in just anything, especially if we want to catch some male attention.

Which of course is all you want, I thought. I shouldn't have been so hard on her. I thought about what attention I was receiving too; the only difference was I had someone in mind. *I thought we were going to go together?*

We still can. Mom wants to take me to some upscale boutiques. You know I never like any of those outlandish designs that make me seem like I'm trying too hard. We will go to our normal places together. Maybe we can convince Hunter to drop us off at the mall.

My stomach lurched, even though this had happened a million times. This year just kept feeling different. I needed a killer dress to grab his attention instead of Brittany. I would die if he liked her instead of me.

Maybe. But don't pick anything. I haven't even begun looking.

Don't worry, girl. I got you.

That's what I'm worried about.

You know I only push you because you have a fit body, and you don't flaunt it. How will anyone know you play volleyball and work out if you wear clothes that are too *big?*

Well, at least I'll know why they're talking to me.

B-O-R-I-N-G. You need to live a little, Allie. High school only comes once. You really want to wait around to see if something magically happens in your love life, or do you want to put yourself out there and do something about it? Don't let others be in control.

I hated to admit she had a point. If I just waited around and hoped things would happen, I could be single for forever. Wasn't it true that men needed straightforward talk, that hints were too subtle? Was I being too subtle?

I thought back to how Brittany was with Hunter and while I didn't enjoy watching her flirt with him, she wasn't being subtle. She was straightforward and he responded.

Of course, I knew I couldn't do anything to get Hunter, but it didn't mean I had to be single for all of high school did it? I needed to change my game for homecoming. Mia was right.

* * *

For the next week, school and volleyball kept me busy. It was a miracle I had managed to even accomplish everything for school. Apparently, two weeks was the maximum time for minor amounts of homework, then everyone decided that gobs and gobs of work was more in tune with the school's philosophy. Regardless, tonight was the first time I had time for myself.

Mia was out with her mom on another adventure to a boutique several towns over. Mom had picked me up and dropped me off at home for once after practice instead of dragging me to her work. I finished my homework and now, I decided to use the trails in our neighborhood for a second workout of the day.

The trails started in our neighborhood then went through two other neighborhoods and a large section of one of Maryland's State parks and then looped back around. Depending on the level of intensity, a trail could be anywhere between three to seven miles, with opportunities of linking up to other trails to lengthen it as well.

I personally, never went on more than one trail. The blue trail was my favorite. It started about halfway between the Baylor's house and my house. Then it went for a mile or so into the wooded areas until it opened to a massive lake. The trail wrapped around the lake, continued farther into the woods on the other side, peeked from the woods to the C & D canal, then went back in. The views were amazing.

And who knew how long I could stand to go for a walk outside. Soon the weather would significantly shift leaving the mornings and nights too cold to enjoy a walk ... at least in my case.

I was never one for bundling up in eighteen layers, just so my toes and fingers and body didn't immediately freeze.

Practice was about cardio and strength. This walk was about enjoying the outdoors and my evening, while getting more steps in. I didn't plan to have a fast pace. In fact, I wasn't sure I wouldn't just get to the lake, sit at the bench for a while, then turn back around. I probably would only have enough time to do that anyway. The sun had already begun setting and I had just started walking.

My light zip up broke the slight breeze as I walked through the neighborhood. It didn't take long before I turned off the asphalt road and walked on the dirt path. My feet crunched the first set of leaves that had abandoned their trees. Fall was setting in before my eyes.

It always baffled me how quickly nature changed. One day you were walking around outside in shorts and a tank top, still roasting every cell in the blaring heat, then almost as suddenly, wrapped up in fuzzy blankets with socks and long sleeves hoping to retain your body heat.

A second set of crunching broke me from my thoughts. I turned to find Hunter Baylor jogging up the path, closing in on me. My pace faltered and I nearly fell but managed to catch my balance at the last second, keeping it my secret.

I focused on breathing in and out as if my crush wasn't getting closer with each breath. Soon he would catch up and realize who it was, and I had no defenses already intact to protect myself from my true feelings.

Overall, this was a bad scenario.

"Duncan?" Hunter asked. "Is that you?"

I turned back quickly, pretending I needed to look because I hadn't already seen him. "Yep," I shouted over my shoulder.

Next thing I knew, he jogged in place as he kept side by side with me. "I didn't know you ran."

I snorted. "I wouldn't call this running. I save that for practice."

He chuckled. "I suppose you're right. I just meant, I never imagined I would see you out here, especially without my sister in tow."

I shrugged. "We don't do *everything* together."

He gave me a look like he didn't believe that. "Are you planning to walk to the lake?"

I nodded.

He slowed his pace all the way down to mine. "I'll walk with you then."

It took all my self-control not to slacken my jaw and gape at him. Why would he want to walk with me?

"If that's okay?"

"Up to you," I said and tried to play it cool. I didn't want him to know just how nervous I was that he had decided to walk with me. For the life of me, I still couldn't understand why he would want to.

"How's practice going? I heard the team is still undefeated."

"Yeah, but it's still early."

"You have to be the only humble sophomore. Most would brag about being a part of the team that's undefeated, but you say it like you don't even believe how good you are."

"I guess. I don't want to jinx it."

"Maybe."

For the second time, I got the feeling he didn't believe me. Could he be that perceptive? I let the thought fall away. If he had been that perceptive, he would know how I felt about him and I was sure no one knew how I felt.

We walked farther, letting the sounds of nature echo in my ears. I wasn't entirely sure he hadn't already walked away, except for the steady sound of his breathing and the crunch of leaves under his feet.

The longer the silence continued, the more uncomfortable I felt. Was I supposed to ask him questions? Was I supposed to stay silent? I didn't know what sounded normal, so I kept my mouth shut, hoping that was the best option.

The trees thinned, opening to the beautiful lake before us. The sun reflected perfectly off the water, setting the water on fire in yellow and orange hues. One could even consider the scene romantic, had Hunter and I been dating.

"Want to sit?" he asked.

"Uh ... sure. Weren't you on a run though?"

He shrugged. "It doesn't hurt to slow down every once and a while."

My body tensed, every muscle and cell intensely aware of

how this had *never* happened with us before. He had never willingly in public decided to spend time with me. Sure, we had been forced to be in each other's company. When Mia went to sleep, or when I snuck down to her kitchen for a snack after she had long since passed out. But not one single time had *this* happened.

Hunter gestured toward the nearest bench and waited until I sat before he did. His body was so close to mine, I could smell the scent of his soap and that cologne. It was intoxicating. I had to force my brain to focus on the words that were now escaping from his lips.

"So do you like your team?"

"Sure. They're good. At least we all seem to work hard."

He leaned his elbows on his legs as he shifted his body forward. "That's good. It can be hard if everyone isn't taking it seriously."

"Have you ever had that happen with basketball?" Soon he would be in his season and volleyball would be over.

He nodded. "Not always and not usually for teams with school, but travel teams and teams when I was younger, I definitely found that to be the case."

"I'm sorry."

"For what? It's not like you did it."

He had a point, but I still couldn't stop myself from feeling bad for his experience.

He leaned back making us even on the bench.

I could practically feel his body heat radiating through my light zip up. I couldn't get used to being this close to him. It sent off alarms in my body and mind.

He cleared his throat. "So ... uh, what's the deal with Brittany?"

If I had thought I was unnerved before, this was an entirely new level. Had I heard him right? Brittany, the sophomore Brittany? "Brittany on my team?"

"Yeah. What's her deal?"

My eyes widened. "I'm not sure." Why was he asking me? Why didn't he ask Mia?

"Is she dating anyone?"

"I honestly don't know. Mia and I don't hang out with her outside of practice." This could not be happening. How was this happening?

He stroked his chin carefully.

I desperately wanted to ask why, but I was too scared of the answer. Instead, I pretended to look at the time on my phone. "Oh, man. I should go. I need to get home." I stood and practically bolted away from the bench. This was the worst-case scenario. How could he like *her*? Of all the girls he could choose from, and it was Brittany?

I sighed. I had been an idiot thinking I ever had a chance, even a remote chance. It couldn't get worse.

Chapter Eighteen

The next three weeks, I spent every minute either working on things for school, playing volleyball, or trying to find a decent dress. Mia had abandoned me for most trips, forcing me to wait until my mom could take me. She had gotten lucky or so she said by finding that second boutique. She purchased something *too amazing for words—* her words, not mine.

I just wanted a decent dress in my color wheel that wouldn't look ridiculous a few years down the road. If there was one thing Mom always warned me about, it was that homecoming dresses had a way of not aging gracefully. They were either timeless, which was what I always needed to shoot for, or they looked bad almost immediately.

Anyway, I managed to find a dress that worked with my skin type and deep brown eyes. Somehow the dress even managed to bring out flecks of gold in my usually dark eyes. Inadvertently, my dress reminded me of a certain someone's eyes. It wasn't intentional, but it was over now, so no way I could change it.

"Allie, are you almost ready?" Mom shouted from the bottom of the stairs.

"Almost. I have to grab my dress and then I'm all packed."

"You have five minutes. I have to get to my office hours."

I sighed. I would have thought Mom or Dad would be sad that they couldn't see their only child get ready for homecoming and get all spiffy and take a million pictures. Most teens had to fight their parents not to be chaperones. But not mine.

Dad was already at his office and Mom was on her way. So, like normal, I would be an honorary member of the Baylors. Mom would drop me off. I'd get ready with Mia, which was what I wanted anyway, then Mrs. Baylor would drop us off.

I had hoped Hunter would see me in my dress before the dance, but Mia told me he had some secret date, which I wouldn't lie, made my heart hurt a little. So, while I would probably see him, it wouldn't matter. How would I compete with some senior anyway?

Either way, he was no longer our chauffeur.

Mom stood true to her word. At exactly five minutes after her last announcement, she opened the door and tapped her foot waiting for me at the bottom of the stairs.

I lugged my duffel bag—full of accessories, makeup, and clothes for after the dance—over my shoulder, while I carried my emerald-green dress in my other hand.

Mia planned to curl my hair when I got to her house. I had told her to leave it straight because I hated curling my hair. It was too long being halfway down my back. I never bothered to do more than just let it air dry, which was why Mia had decided it was her duty as my best friend to curl it for me.

I couldn't wait until she realized it wasn't the same as curling her shoulder length strawberry blond hair.

"You're sure you have everything?"

"Yes, Mom. And if for some reason I didn't, our house isn't that far. I can always walk back."

"Alright, let's go then."

Mom waited for me to leave through the doorway before she shut and locked the door. "You'll send me photos?"

"Mrs. Baylor always does."

Mom smiled and hopped into her Chevy Malibu.

Our two-minute drive to Mia's was over in a flash. I unloaded and headed in. I didn't bother knocking. They all knew I was coming, and Mrs. Baylor told me to stop doing that years ago anyway. She said, *Allie, when someone is over as much as you, you don't need to knock. You're part of the family.*

It had made me feel good, but it sucked that it came from someone who wasn't my parents.

The house was eerily quiet, except for a few muffled noises from the kitchen. Mia was in her room getting ready. She had sent me videos on socials religiously for the past hour. I didn't know what else she possibly had to get ready that it would take that long.

As I approached Mia's door, the sound of music blaring got louder and louder. I was practically assaulted by the song as I opened the door. Another perk of the Baylor's house was that sound really didn't travel that well. Most of the rooms felt almost soundproof, which may have been done on purpose, but either way was drastically different from mine.

Mia sat at her vanity in the back corner of her room. She turned when she saw me in the reflection of the mirror. "Yay! You're finally here."

I smiled and tossed my duffel on her bed as I tiptoed around the piles of clothes all over her floor. "You really need to clean this room."

She waved me off. "Maybe tomorrow. Tonight, we have more important things to worry about."

"If you say so."

She frowned. "What's with the attitude? It's sophomore year and we are single. Let's have a blast."

"Okay," I said, but wasn't really feeling it. Hunter was who I wanted to catch and apparently someone had already done that. I just hoped it had nothing to do with our conversation on the trails.

Mia forced me to sit in front of the mirror. Her hand hovered over the curling iron. She had prepared for my arrival by plugging it in. According to her, it should be almost at the perfect temperature. "Okay, before I start, can you change into a tank top? It'll be easier to get it over your head once you're finished."

I nodded, grabbed my hoodie, and pulled it off. I already knew the drill. Mia had warned me five times to bring something easy to wear and remove for my hair makeover.

She smiled when she realized I had listened to her. She got to work sectioning my hair first, then taking small pieces and wrapping it around her curling wand. "Anybody in class I don't know about that you might be eyeing at the dance?"

"Uh ... no. Why would you even ask that?"

She shrugged. "You just haven't seemed all that interested lately. Your wardrobe changes have had its impact but it's like you don't even notice."

"I don't know. I don't see anything like that."

She grabbed another section. "Then you aren't paying attention. I've heard a couple of the guys on the football team throwing around your name."

My eyes widened. "What do you mean? Throwing around my name?"

She leaned in making direct eye contact with me. "I mean, they've taken notice of your new look."

I stared in disbelief. "In what way?"

"In all the ways. They talk about you, like they are just waiting for their moment."

"And how do you know this?"

"I have other friends, Allie. They heard it and told me."

"Mm-hmm. That sounds sketchy. I'll believe that when I see it."

She nudged my shoulder. "Well, you won't see it if you keep wearing that scowl and mopey look. Boys aren't attracted to that. They want confidence. So, find yours."

I rolled my eyes. "Just finish my hair already. I hate sitting here."

I didn't want the other guys' attention. I only wanted one guy's attention and that seemed impossible.

Mia had finally finished my hair, what felt like hours later. According to the clock on my phone it had only been forty minutes. I slid into the guest bedroom upstairs and pulled my dress out.

Mia was using her room to get in her dress too. She had created this half up, half down hairstyle, curling the parts that were down and braided a *sort-of crown* for the up half.

Neither of us had seen each other's dresses, which was out of the ordinary, considering we usually found them together.

My dress was cut just above my knees, with box pleats and an off the shoulder neckline. There were tiny rhinestones on the bodice to offset it from the skirt, but not too much that it would look like a disco ball.

Mom bought me black velvet ankle strap heels that I had to admit were gorgeous even though I resisted them at first. I wore diamond drop earrings and no necklace—simple, but elegant.

Mia and I walked out of the bedrooms at the same time.

My mouth fell open. Her dress was short like mine, but a skintight eggplant color. It had a sweetheart neckline and was simply stunning. She wore silver ankle strap heels and matching earrings.

"Woah," we both said at the same time, then giggled.

"You look amazing," I said.

"So do you. Wow, we are hot."

My cheeks flamed.

"You ready?"

"Let me just get my bag from your room."

"I'll meet you down there."

Mia headed down the stairs as I grabbed my bag. I could hear the click of her heels on the stairs and then silence.

My clutch purse would hold my phone and some cash in case I needed it. I never knew where we would go after the dance or who we would be with. I snagged my matching clutch and headed for the stairs, when the voice that floated up to me, stopped me dead in my tracks.

I knew that voice anywhere.

As fast as possible in heels, I ran down the stairs—more accurately, hobbled down them. The scene before me did nothing to calm the ratcheting of my heart in my chest.

Hunter stood in his black dress pants, white button up dress shirt, and teal tie, which perfectly matched his date— Brittany Jennings.

My body vibrated with too many emotions. He asked her to homecoming. How could he ask *her*? She was fake and she wouldn't care about him. She only cared about herself and what his social status would do for her. If she dated a senior, she'd be set for the rest of high school.

Mia was just as annoyed with Hunter's decision, which was something. At least my true feelings about the situation wouldn't have to be masked. I could blend in with what she was thinking too.

"Hunter ... can I talk to you for a minute?" Mia asked.

His brows drew together. "For what?"

She gestured toward the side.

He still hadn't seen me yet.

He exhaled loudly and walked over to Mia. They talked in hushed tones in the corner.

I walked down the remaining three stairs and was poised right next to Brittany. She averted her attention to me, looking me up and down. Her face twisted.

I couldn't figure out if that meant she liked my outfit and was mad she did, or she thought I looked awful.

"Allie, hi." She walked toward me and did some fake kiss on both cheeks thing before she leaned back. "I didn't know you'd be here."

I resisted the urge to roll my eyes. She was cordial, so I could be too. But all I really wanted to do was to kick her face in with my very pointy heel.

Luckily, Hunter and Mia stepped back toward Brittany at the same time.

Hunter's eyes widened as he caught a glimpse of me. "Duncan, wow. That's a nice dress on you."

My jaw slackened. Did he just compliment me? In front of his date and his sister? My gaze flitted toward Mia, but she was still too focused on Brittany standing in the foyer at the bottom of the stairs.

"Uh … thanks."

Hunter winked, but Brittany's expression looked murderous. I had a feeling she wouldn't let that go too soon.

Another set of heels echoed around the foyer. "Oh, you all look so beautiful," Mrs. Baylor cooed. "Let's get your photos. Mia and Allie, you two first."

I grimaced. I didn't want to stand up there in front of everyone. I wanted to melt into the floor, or at least just get in the car, too bad I didn't have those superpowers.

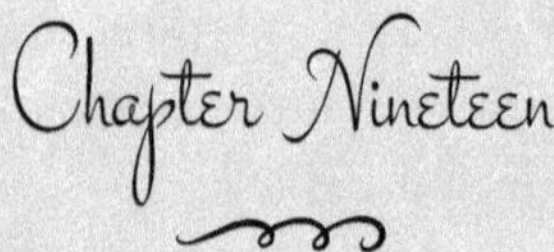

Thankfully, the photos were over with quickly and then Mia and I could escape to Mrs. Baylor's car.

"Can you believe he invited her to the dance? And then to our house?" Mia asked.

I shook my head because I knew words would betray my emotions.

"He literally couldn't pick anyone else? I swear he's such an idiot. Brittany showed him a little attention and he ran after it like a lovesick puppy."

I gulped.

"I'm sorry. You must hate this, too."

My eyes widened and I turned trying to figure out what she meant.

"You hate her more than I do."

I exhaled. "Yeah. Let's just forget about it."

She slapped my knee. "That's the spirit. They won't ruin the dance. We look hot and she can shove it."

"Yep," I whispered, just as Mrs. Baylor got in.

"All set, ladies. Here we go."

Mia woohooed really loud and then Mrs. Baylor turned up the music. At least we were headed to the dance.

As expected, cars lined the parking lot, like it was drop off in the morning. Girls and guys unloaded from the cars and trucks and precariously walked through the doorways which were littered with balloon arches. They were in our school colors, purple, black, and white. Mia's dress almost matched the purple balloons, but they were a shade or two lighter than Mia's eggplant dress.

Mrs. Baylor leaned toward the passenger side. "When should I come back and get you two?"

Mia looked between the two of us and shrugged. "Can we text you like ten minutes before?"

Mrs. Baylor frowned. "I suppose. When is the dance supposed to be over?"

"Like ten?"

"So, what if I get you girls at like ten-thirty?"

Mia's eyes widened. "Thirty minutes later than when it's over?"

"Would you prefer it was thirty minutes earlier?"

She shook her head.

"That's what I figured. See you ladies then."

We waited until she drove away before we went inside.

"That's peculiar," Mia said.

"Letting us stay later? I agree."

"Wonder what she's up to."

"I don't know, but let's head in. I just shaved and I don't want goosebumps all over my legs ruining the perfectly smooth feeling."

Mia giggled and shoved me lightly toward the door.

The hallway echoed with sounds of laughter and heels slapping the tile. I could feel the bass of the music from the gym, even from the front door.

Mr. Meyer sat at a fold out table in the middle of the hallway. It was also decorated with purple and white decorations like balloons and confetti, with a huge sign above his head saying, *Homecoming Dance, Let's go Raiders!*

He looked positively bored at the table. Mr. Meyer was my freshman year English teacher, and he was cool when he talked about the novels we read, but otherwise, he never seemed interested in anything ... well, cats. He loved cats.

"Good evening, Mr. Meyer," I said.

He squinted up at me, confusion at first, followed by sudden recognition. "Allie Duncan. Hello. Tickets?"

Mia and I handed our tickets over.

He ripped them in half and gave us the remainder. I kept mine in my clutch, but Mia tossed it the second we got past his table.

"That's a rough job. You have to come on your hours off to the dance and then they put you at the table all the way away from the music? Who'd he piss off?"

I shrugged. "Maybe he wanted to be out here."

"Allie, no one wants to be that alone."

I guess she had a point, but Mr. Meyer was a weird bird. And honestly, I think he would have preferred it out at the table than in the room with the rest of us. If he could have taught an empty room about his beloved novels and still get paid, I think he would, but I didn't tell Mia that.

The gym was transformed. The floor was covered in floor bubble wrap essentially. No spills or messes would damage the floor with that protective covering. Tables and chairs had been moved to the gym off toward the sides and a dance floor had been arranged surrounding the DJ's equipment.

Some pop song blared through the speakers as Mia pulled me toward the center of the dancefloor. If there was one thing Mia was good at, it was not caring what other people thought of her dancing. If she felt the beat, she went with it.

I on the other hand was not that person. I rarely danced

alone in my bedroom, let alone in the middle of the dance-floor. And yet, here I was.

Mia nudged my arm. "Come on, let loose. It'll be fun."

I sighed. "Mia, you know how I feel about dancing."

"I do, which is why …" she gestured toward me with her head as if she was watching someone else. "I figured you could use a partner."

Someone tapped me on the shoulder, and I could practically shoot laser beams from my eyes, because no matter who tapped my shoulder I knew it was Mia's doing.

When I turned I could see Bennett, a football player from our history class.

My mouth went dry. This couldn't be happening.

Bennett leaned close to my ear for his voice to carry over the music. "Want to dance?" he leaned back and stared in my eyes. He had light brown eyes, almost the opposite of my dark brown eyes. They were pretty, but they didn't have the same pull over me as those emerald eyes.

"I … uh. I don't really dance," I mumbled.

He grabbed my hand and laid it on his shoulder. "I'll lead, you just have to follow."

I gulped and stared at Mia wishing she would get me out of this instead of pushing me farther into his arms.

Mia completely clueless to how I felt, gave me a thumbs up, then turned and started shimmying with a few guys that I assumed were Bennett's friends.

Bennett wasn't a bad leader, although it had barely been a minute and I crushed his foot twice. But he didn't complain. If anything, he stared at me more with those lusty eyes of his.

I had barely talked to him before, but he seemed like he was enraptured by me, and I had no idea why.

When the song finally ended, I made some excuse to run to the bathroom and left Bennett in the middle of the floor.

The cool air from the hallway, relaxed my nerves a bit. I

did head to the bathroom, but not to go. Instead, I went and stared at my reflection. I was in some kind of nightmare. Somehow, the man of my dreams was with my enemy and Mia had convinced a football player to dance with me even though I couldn't imagine how that made me look like a good catch. Not with the puncture wounds to his toes.

I took a few deep breaths and headed back to the dance-floor. Mia was twirling around someone's finger, but it was too hard to tell whose from that distance. I tried to go around the opposite way from where I left Bennett, but he found me anyway.

He grazed my finger with his hand. "Want to sit for a minute?"

I nodded as he unexpectedly grabbed my hand and guided me through the crowd toward the first empty table. He pulled out my chair and waited for me to sit before he sat himself.

"I hope that dance was okay. I'm not usually a big dancer," he said.

My head cocked to the side. "You could have fooled me."

He chuckled. "I practiced that dance all week. It's the only dance I know unless you count the sprinkler."

I laughed. "That's two more dances than I know."

"You have a pretty laugh."

That made me nearly choke. I wasn't used to guys being so straightforward with me.

"I'm sorry," he said as he combed his fingers through his hair. "I'm not usually so forward either."

"Either that's a lie or I'm just bringing out all your surprises tonight."

"That's quite a possibility."

Well, this was getting awkward fast. I didn't expect this at all and to be honest, I didn't know what to do with the attention.

"So, you're on the volleyball team with Mia?"

I nodded.

"What position?"

"Setter."

"Cool, you're like the director of the court then."

"Yeah. Most people don't realize that."

He leaned in closer to my face, tugging on a loose curl that fell in front. "I'm not most people."

A shiver went down my spine, but it wasn't from Bennett. It was like an energy, setting me on fire from the inside. An energy I knew made no sense, until I turned and saw Hunter glaring at Bennett.

Why would he be mad at him? Did he know something about him I didn't?

I turned away to avoid seeing Brittany again. The image of her on his arm was enough for one night. I didn't want to see them dancing too.

Thankfully, Bennett didn't seem to notice. He started talking to me about football and how we had won the homecoming game. I didn't have the heart to tell him I hadn't gone, and that football wasn't really my sport.

Mia eventually filtered over to us and drug us both back to the dancefloor, which was fine because Hunter's stare was unnerving me more than I liked. I could feel his eyes on me, and it was worse than feeling invisible. I didn't know why he was staring. He had a date, he should pay attention to her, not me.

Luckily, a few line dances like the Cotton-Eye Joe and Electric Slide came on. Those I could do without feeling awkward and Bennett felt the same way. Everyone knew the line dances because in middle school it was part of the curriculum for gym class. No one escaped to high school without learning the Macarena, Fox Trot, and Electric Slide.

I was parched by the time we finished the third line dance. "I want a drink."

Bennett looked toward me. "I can get you something."

"No, I'll grab it. No worries. I'll be back."

He nodded and whispered something toward his friend. Mia eyed me and told me with her eyes that I better come back. I assured her I would and went to grab some punch.

The line was empty, so I ladled a few scoops into the plastic cup and sipped on the sweet red liquid.

"Well, well, well. Allie Duncan, all alone at the punch station."

I nearly choked from the familiar voice. It felt like every word was a carefully articulated to dig into my self-esteem and her winning spike was on its way.

"Brittany, hello again."

"*Brittany, hello again,*" she mocked in a high-pitched tone. "Who do I look like?"

"I-uh. What do you mean?"

This wasn't Brittany's normal style. She never outright insulted me, even if I knew we both had a mutual dislike.

"I mean, you act so innocent, and yet, you're so manipulative."

My eyebrows rose and my jaw slackened. "Brittany, I have no idea what you're saying." I looked around her for Hunter, but I couldn't see him anywhere. "Why don't you go back to your date?"

"*My date.* Funny you should mention *my* date."

I was seriously considering that maybe the punch was spiked because I was having difficulty keeping up with her comments.

"*Hunter* is *my* date and yet he's complimenting you and your dress. Why's that?"

So that's what this was about, his comment at the house. "Brittany, he's brought you. Why are you being ridiculous? He isn't with me, so what's a compliment matter?"

"Of course, he isn't with you. He would never stoop so low to be with *you*."

"Okay, well, if you're done, I'm leaving." I walked away, but she grabbed my arm before I went too far.

"You're not pretty, Allie. His compliment was because he pities you and it's about time you realize that. Mia had to practically promise Bennett and his friends money to dance with you tonight. Why don't you do the Baylors a favor and go home. They shouldn't have to carry such a burden like you."

I yanked my arm from her grasp and bolted from the gym. I refused to cry in front of Brittany. I dropped my punch cup in the trash by the gym doors and headed back down the long hallway to the doors outside, the sound of my heels echoing all around me. I didn't need to stay for this nonsense and honestly I didn't feel like doing much of anything at this point.

I pulled out my phone and texted Mia, *Headed to your house. Punch didn't sit well with my stomach. Have fun, see you later.*

I knew she wouldn't see it for a bit and by then I'd already be in her room. A walk to their house would help.

Determined, I set off in that direction. I felt a little bad for leaving Bennett, but Brittany's words swirled in my head. Was she right? Did Mia bribe them? I knew it was prearranged, but how much? What had she promised him?

I sighed.

Headlights swirled around me. I moved to the side of the road, but instead of going past me, it appeared to slow down.

My body tensed. This was it. I was insulted and now I would be kidnapped. What a night.

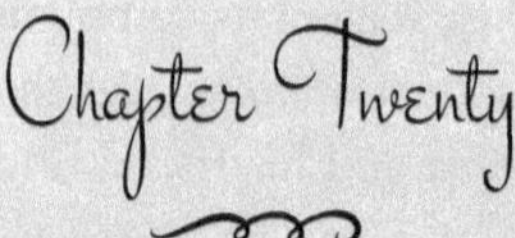

Chapter Twenty

I shut my eyes and held my breath, hoping that maybe I wouldn't be kidnapped, and that the car would disappear.

I could feel the vehicle come to a stop next to me and then heard the window go down. "Duncan, get in the car."

My eyes snapped open. It was Hunter. *What the hell?*

"Hunter?"

"Obviously, get in the car."

"Wh-what are you doing here?"

He peered around us. "Allie, please?"

He never called me Allie. Literally never. I gulped and walked around to the other side and hopped in the passenger seat. I was also never in this seat either. I was always relegated to the back seat. Mia always took the passenger seat unless Hunter had one of his friends, too.

I buckled up and looked behind me as he drove ahead. "Where's your date? And why aren't you back at the dance?"

"Our moms would kill me if they knew you walked back."

I crossed my arms. "Hunter, that doesn't answer my question. I'm not your responsibility. Why aren't you at the dance?"

He tinkered with the radio volume, lowering it, then raising it back up, until it was at the same volume it had been.

I took in his appearance. His tie was still perfect as was his shirt as it stayed tucked into his dress pants, but his energy felt different, almost nervous.

"I-I just wanted to leave."

"Nope. I don't believe you. There's no way it's a coincidence."

He arched his brow and gazed toward me. "What coincidence?"

"That your date would insult me, making me want to leave, then you magically appear in the road and know I'm walking? No way. I don't buy it."

Hunter blew out his breath. "You can't pretend to buy it?"

"No, because it makes no damn sense and tonight is full of moments that don't make sense." I turned to face the window. "Freaking spiked punch," I muttered.

Hunter chuckled.

"What is so damn funny?"

"You. The punch isn't spiked."

"You heard that?"

He nodded.

"Are you going to answer my questions?"

"I don't know."

"Fine."

We pulled into his family's empty driveway, and I bolted from the car. I threw open the door, took off my heels, and ran up to Mia's room. My heels clunked as they hit the floor. I plopped down on the edge of Mia's bed and let everything that just happened hit me.

I hadn't had time to cry on my walk before Hunter came

to save me and I didn't want to admit that Brittany's comments hurt, but I knew they did. They were my worst fears.

My hands cradled my head as tears trickled down my cheek. What would I tell Mia? She would take one look at me and know the punch didn't make me sick. How was I supposed to tell her Brittany's comments without it making her wonder why she brought up Hunter?

I guessed I could have just left that part out and only told her about Bennett. She may believe that.

I heard a light knock on the door and then Hunter peaked in. "Aww, man. Are you crying?"

I swiped at my eyes. "No," I said, but my voice trembled.

He came in, and I turned away.

He exhaled loudly as I felt the bed dip from his weight. "Jeez this room is a mess."

I glared at him.

"Right, not the point. Okay."

"Hunter, what is this? What are you doing?"

"It's my fault."

"What is?"

"Tonight. It's all my fault."

I crossed my arms. "How do you figure? Brittany is a big girl. She said what she said all on her own."

"I don't pity you, Allie."

My eyes widened. "You heard her?"

He lowered his gaze and nodded.

"How great." I rose from the bed.

"Allie, wait." His fingers grasped my wrist and tugged gently.

My brain exploded from the sensations of his touch. I didn't know what to focus on. The fact that one of the most embarrassing things I had ever been told was something he heard, or that he blamed himself somehow, or that he was now firmly gripping my arm to keep me from moving.

I tugged and he released me. "So, you heard, but it doesn't make it your fault."

"If I had paid attention to her, she wouldn't have come after you."

I crossed my arms. "Not true. Brittany has never liked me."

"Well, I didn't make things better."

"This is still making no sense, Hunter. I fail to see how you not paying attention to her makes it your fault. She said what she said. I just want to get changed and forget about tonight."

"You can't yet."

I groaned. "Why not?"

He pulled his phone from his pocket, scrolled for a minute or so and then placed it down as a slow song emitted from its speakers. "You can't let a dress like that go to waste already. It's not even nine o'clock yet." He outstretched his hand.

Was he serious? He wanted to dance with me? "I-I don't dance."

"That's not what it looked like to me."

My eyebrows rose. "You were watching me?"

He shrugged. "Just one dance."

My heart picked up tempo as it collided with the walls of my chest. Against all the warnings my body was setting off, I set my hand on his.

Unlike Bennett, Hunter didn't lay my hand on his shoulder. He held on to it as he set his other arm around my waist, pulling us closer together.

I could smell his cologne and feel his chest against me. This was overloading every circuit of my brain.

"Brittany was upset because I complimented you and couldn't take my eyes off you ever since I saw you in this dress. She tried to get my attention and all I could do was stare as that football player chatted you up on the dancefloor and at the tables."

Heat crawled up my neck. I knew he had watched me, but I didn't know it was about me. I had thought it was about Bennett, but maybe he saw something I couldn't. "Did I have something in my hair?"

He exhaled. "Jesus, Allie. I was jealous."

I leaned back to look up into his eyes. "Jealous? Over Bennett? Why?"

He bent his head, moving his mouth closer to mine. Something shifted in his gaze as he stopped dancing and held me close. "Because all I could think about were those perfect lips laughing at something he said and wanting it to be me."

"But—"

My voice was drowned out when his lips met mine. His kiss was better than I had ever imagined. His hands trailed up my back and entwined themselves in my hair as we leaned back, like a dip in a fancy dance.

Every wall I had ever built against my feelings for him melted. This was bad, like epically bad, and yet I couldn't pull myself away from his lips. Not even a centimeter.

He pulled away first, his eyes wide. My lip gloss was smeared above his top lip, evidence from our kiss.

My breath was heavy, as my brain tried to catch up with what just happened. Hunter Baylor had just kissed me.

Oh my God. We kissed. A real kiss, not one of my daydreams. I was dead. What would I tell Mia? She would kill us.

My phone chirped, shattering the perfect bubble our kiss created. "Oh god, Mia."

Dawning entered Hunter's expression. "Mia. *Shit.*"

Before I knew it, my hand reached toward his face as I rubbed off my lip gloss from his lip, which was a massive mistake. As soon as our skin touched, my body gravitated toward his.

Our bodies moved closer as our eyes locked. It took everything to force my hand between us as it splayed across his chest. "We-I, oh my god. What just happened?"

"I'm sorry, I thought ..." His gaze fell.

"Hunter, this can't happen again. Mia would kill me. And you're with Brittany. I don't want to be that girl."

His eyes found mine. "I'm not with Brittany. I told her to get lost after what she said to you. And for the record, Mia wouldn't bribe anyone to dance with you. It's not her style, not to mention she wouldn't need to bribe anyone. You're beautiful."

My cheeks flamed. "This can't be real."

"What do you mean?"

"Exactly what I said. This can't be real. You're a senior, I'm a sophomore. I'm your sister's best friend. Regardless of how I feel, this can't be happening."

"How you feel?"

Crap on a cracker. I did not just say that out loud.

If it was possible, my cheeks got even hotter than they already were. "Uh ... nothing." I tried to escape toward the bathroom.

"Oh no you don't. I admitted I was jealous. What feelings are you referring to?"

"Are you really going to make me say it?"

He smirked. "Yes."

"I like you. Okay? But you already knew that and besides, Mia *will* kill us both. This can't happen."

He spun me around, until I was barely inches from his face. "Then one more time, like a goodbye." This time, I half expected the kiss, but it didn't change the sparks that whizzed around my body. It was a G-rated kiss, no tongue, no groping, but it didn't matter. I felt drunk and dazed.

He pulled away, a satisfied grin on his face, then left Mia's room with me standing in the piles of clothes all over her floor.

My fingers hovered over my lips, still tingling from his touch. No matter how much time had passed, I would never believe this had happened. My insides warred with each other. The one half wanted to find him and kiss him again to make sure I hadn't imagined it. The other half was shouting that we needed to stay far, far apart.

I lifted my phone from my clutch. The chirp had been Mia texting me back, *Bennett asked about you. I told him you had a leg cramp and needed to go home. Feel better. I'll be home in a bit.*

My stomach twisted. Mia covered for me and here I was kissing her brother. I felt like the worst friend ever. I quickly changed into the pajamas I packed, took off my makeup, and twisted my hair into a messy bun. I would lay here and watch videos on my phone until she got back.

I wouldn't kiss her brother again. I wouldn't go in his room. I would be a good friend and I would never tell her it happened.

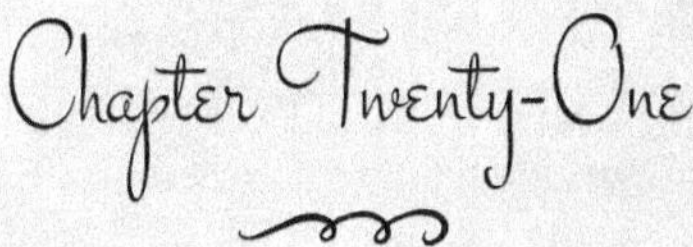

Chapter Twenty-One

By the time Mia arrived home, it was almost eleven. I knew because every painstaking moment that passed after the kiss felt excruciating. I still had to figure out what to tell her if anything at this point for the real reason I left.

If I told her anything, it would lead into Hunter driving me home, which would lead to him taking blame, none of which seemed like a topic of conversation I could manage currently. I knew if I got anywhere near the truth, my face would give away the biggest secret I would ever have to keep from my best friend and *that* never went over well.

Mia burst through her room door. "That was an amazing night." She tossed her bag and shoes to the floor and hopped on her bed, bouncing me, too. "I danced the night away."

"You did?"

She nodded. "Bennett's friend Jasper danced with me all night. He's a junior and has his own car. He is *so* dreamy." She sighed like she was content, and everything was perfect.

"So, what happened?"

She flipped on to her stomach to face me. "Well, I had met

him when Bennett had chatted with me about you. He ended up asking me to dance and then it just stayed that way all night."

"That's awesome, Mia."

She beamed. "He plays football, too. Oh, it was magical."

I giggled. "It was just one night, Mia."

"So? It was *amazing*." She slapped my hand. "It would have been better if you hadn't disappeared. Bennett was so disappointed."

"Wh—" I had tried to say, *what do you mean*? But Mia had already gotten off the bed and went to the bathroom. She came out a few minutes later, her hair up in a ponytail and her dress changed into pajamas.

"I'm starving. Let's go downstairs and make nachos."

Again, I wanted to protest, but she was already out of her room and going down the stairs before I could process what that meant. If I left this room and saw Hunter, I didn't know how I'd manage it.

On a good day, when I hadn't kissed him, I had a hard time looking into those gorgeous green eyes and strong jaw and not daydreaming about him. But this time was different.

I *had* kissed him. Like actually kissed him, and that image wouldn't leave my brain. It was like it was permanently glued to my retinas, burned into my mind for all eternity.

And if the image of what had happened wasn't enough, the taste of him on my lips was enough to totally derail me. So no, I didn't want to go downstairs and eat nachos, which would have to bake in the oven to get the perfect crisp and to make the cheese melt and increase the chances of me seeing Hunter.

But I couldn't say any of that to Mia. So, I trudged after her.

She was busy filling up a casserole dish with a layer of

chips, then cheese, then ground beef, then chicken strips, then started all over again.

My eyes widened. "Mia, holy crap. That's a lot of nachos."

"What? It will be so good and I'm starving. I danced all my dinner off. Plus, you'll help me, won't you?" She laid the bag of cheese on the counter and stared at me. "Or is your stomach upset still?"

I cringed inwardly. "Uh ... it's okay, I guess."

She rested her hands on her hips and eyed me warily. "Was it really the punch or did you pull a fast one on Bennett and bolt?"

"No. My stomach hurt, and I wasn't feeling myself."

She shrugged and picked the cheese back up, continuing to add layer after layer.

"I call dibs," a male's voice said.

I startled.

There he was standing a few feet behind me. Hunter had changed into a white T-shirt, the kind men wear under button up shirts, and basketball shorts, with black ankle socks.

And damn it if he didn't look hot *and* smug.

Mia crossed her arms. "I put in all the work to make it and you want dibs? Typical."

"Please, like it's hard to make nachos," Hunter said as he hopped up onto the stool in the kitchen.

"Well, then you can make your own."

"You've used up like half the ingredients, Mia. Just share. No way you're eating all that alone anyway."

"I'm not. Allie is too."

He cocked his head toward me. "Is she? Well, you *two* still can't polish all that off."

"Whatever," Mia said and waved him away.

But instead of moving, he kept himself right there. Only inches from me. It was absolutely maddening. He pulled out his phone and began to scroll, pretending to not pay attention to our conversation, but I could tell he was.

"Anyway, where were we? Oh yeah, I'm glad you're feeling better, Allie, but I have a confession."

My stomach sank.

"I gave Bennett your number."

My jaw slackened. "What? Why?"

She giggled like she had just told the funniest joke in the entire world. "You ran off and he thought you were coming back. I had to tell him something and he looked like a sad little puppy dog. So, I gave him your number."

I groaned. "Mia, why? You're not supposed to give random people my number." The hairs on the back of my neck stood up. I was extremely aware that Hunter was paying attention to every word of this conversation, even if he didn't outwardly look like it.

"He's not random, Allie. He danced with you a couple times tonight and don't think I didn't see you two laughing at that table. You liked him, even if you won't admit it."

I needed to die, right then and there. But when I could have used a freak lightning strike, the sky was clear and beautiful.

"I-I have no idea what you're talking about." I glanced at Hunter, which was a mistake. His expression told me he was curious about this whole situation, but it didn't matter. He and I couldn't happen and there was nothing with Bennett.

Mia opened the oven door and put on the timer, then wiped the counter from the bits of cheese and crumbs from the chips. When she finished cleaning up the mess, she diverted her attention to Hunter. "And don't think I forgot about *you*," she said as she elbowed him in the ribs.

"Ow," he said as he rubbed the spot. "What about me?"

"You brought Brittany to the house. Out of all your choices, you *had* to bring her?"

I gulped, if it was possible, this was an even worse topic of conversation than Bennett. I didn't want him to mention anything about what had happened. If he did and I hadn't said anything to Mia, she would think it was weird. We told each other everything and the last thing I wanted to do was hurt her any more than kissing her brother and lying about it.

He shrugged.

"Well, I don't want to see her again. Bad enough she's on our team, but she's rude."

"No need to get all worked up, I left her at the dance, too high maintenance. I don't have time for that."

I exhaled the breath I hadn't realized I was holding. He was so quick with his response even I believed it; except I knew the truth. He kicked her to the curb for me, and then we kissed.

Ugh, ugh, ugh. I needed to stop thinking about it.

"Good. I can't stand her and what's worse is she makes it her mission to pick on my best friend. She can't be trusted."

I cringed and took that as my exit to sit in the room that adjoined the kitchen. There was a large TV and a massive cream-colored sectional. I plopped onto the cushions and relished in the quieted tones of their conversation. I could still hear what they were saying, but it didn't feel like my emotions and reactions were on display. I could breathe again.

They changed the subject quickly, which was fine by me. I didn't want to be connected to any conversation right now.

My phone chirped, alerting me to a new text ... from Bennett. He said, *Hey Allie, this is Bennett. I hope it's okay I got your number from Mia. I was worried about you when you didn't come back to the dancefloor. Hope you feel better soon.*

It was actually sort of sweet. Most guys our age wouldn't have admitted to even caring that I didn't come back; it made them vulnerable. And I was sure that it was written in some handbook that being vulnerable was not a cool thing to do.

So, I had to give him points for that, at least it didn't seem like he would play games, which I did like.

He was nice to talk to. It wasn't like he had seemed like some ogre and overly aggressive, but he wasn't Hunter Baylor. He didn't have those beautiful green eyes that kidnapped my brain for too long. His body wasn't athletic, or at least not that I could tell in a dark gymnasium. He made me laugh so that was something, but how could I even attempt anything with Bennett when I felt so drawn to Hunter?

Except, I told Hunter we couldn't ever do anything again because of Mia. So why was I fighting the chance to spend time with someone who was sweet and funny, when Hunter was off limits? I mean didn't someone say it was easier to get over someone if you had someone else?

So that's what I needed to do. My feelings for Hunter were strong because they had never been contested, but here was my chance. Bennett was my age and at least seemed to be interested.

Which is why I texted him back, *Hey thanks. See you in school Monday.* Then added his number to my contacts.

Bennett deserved a chance, so that's what I would do.

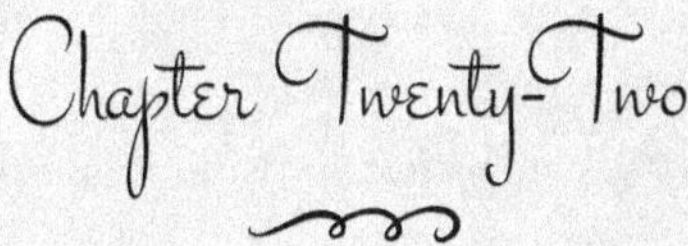

Chapter Twenty-Two

The next morning, I managed to get out of the Baylor's house and go home before anyone really woke up. Thankfully, this was a normal occurrence. Living so close to each other, Mia and I didn't take offense if we spent the night and ended up gone before we both awoke.

My parents sat at the kitchen table for once when I walked through the front door. Both had a cup of what I assumed was coffee for the time of day, and they were jointly reading a book that looked like a textbook.

"Hello," I said as I set my things on the floor.

They looked up, but it was Dad who spoke first. "Hey, Allie-girl. How was the dance?"

My stomach lurched. "It was fine. You know how dances are."

Mom snorted. "He wouldn't know, he was the kid in the corner of every school dance reading a comic book. I don't even think you went to prom, did you?"

Dad shook his head. "I still know how to boogie."

I rolled my eyes. "Please don't say *boogie*, Dad."

He did a little jig in his chair which was worse than using the word boogie.

Mom closed the book after she put in a bookmark. She turned her watch on her wrist and then looked at me. "If you get ready, we could head to brunch. That is if you don't mind us boogie-ing to the car."

"I'll get ready if you *both* stop using that word. It's embarrassing, for yourselves, not just me."

Mom giggled. "Okay, well go get dressed. I could use some bacon."

At least we agreed on food. Mom and I always usually ordered the same thing at restaurants. And if I knew Mom, she would order scrambled eggs, extra bacon, and a chicken quesadilla—the brunch special at our favorite restaurant in town, Hal's Diner. They had everything, and it was all amazing. There wasn't a meal I had ordered I didn't like.

I jogged up the stairs, combed through my hair after spraying some dry shampoo, then pulled on joggers and a crop top. I bounded down the stairs to put on my flip flops and I was ready to go.

"That was fast. Looks like someone is hungry."

I nodded. "Let's go."

They finished their cups and placed them in the sink. Then we all walked out the front door toward the driveway to get in the Malibu.

The drive to Hal's wasn't far, like most things in town. Our neighborhood was centrally located, and yet the trails behind the house made it feel like we were all alone in our neck of the woods. It was the perfect combination.

The parking lot was busy. Brunch was always popular for a Sunday at mid-morning. Many went to church and then ate at Hal's afterwards. We walked inside anyway, once my mom made up her mind on what she wanted to eat, that's what she ate. There was no talking her out of it.

Trust me, we had tried in the past. It never worked.

My dad went up to the hostess stand then turned. "Thirty-minute wait. What do you want to do, Janet?"

Mom sighed. "I want bacon."

He chuckled. "Three under Duncan."

The hostess put our name on the list, and we went back out to the patio tables and chairs to sit while we waited.

Mom stared at me. "Something's different with you."

My eyes widened. "What do you mean?"

"I don't know how to explain it. Something is different. Are you sure nothing happened at this dance? No boy kissed you, did they?"

My cheeks grew hot. How was it that she even knew something happened? I hadn't even thought about it since I got in the car, and yet she just *knew*. Isn't that just like parents to ignore all the boring moments in their child's life, but the second something exciting happens they notice.

"No, Mom. It was just a dance."

She eyed me a little longer, before she shrugged.

"Arnold, put down your phone," Mom said. "Enjoy the sunshine."

"Yes, dear."

I had to stifle a laugh. Mom was constantly on her phone, more so than Dad, but at least we were at brunch together.

"So, did you and Mia dance all night?"

"Now you know I don't really dance, Mom."

"Atta girl," Dad said and tried to fist bump me. He was so weird sometimes.

"Arnold, she's young. She should be dancing and having fun."

"Mia danced. I did the Electric Slide and the Cotton Eye Joe."

"With a boy?" Mom asked and wiggled her eyebrows.

"Janet, leave the girl alone. My word," Dad said.

"It's a line dance, Mom. You don't dance with one person in a line dance. It's a group thing."

"Duncan, party of three, Duncan party of three."

We all rose and headed toward the door.

The inside of Hal's had always been a bit eccentric. The best way to describe it was that he couldn't pick just one theme. So, each section in the diner was a different decade and the waitresses had tables based on the section and dressed accordingly. In the back was the twenties, with the flapper dress and tuxedos. Up a little ways but separated by the half wall was the fifties and the waitresses wore poodle skirts. In all, there was the twenties, fifties, sixties, seventies, eighties, and nineties.

To some people it might have had an identity crisis, but personally I thought it was unique. Who didn't want to see that many decades in one place? Today we were seated in the eighties, which my parents thought was perfect. They enjoyed going down memory lane, or so they said.

Mom smacked her lips together. "Mmm, mmm. I can practically taste the chicken quesadilla already."

Dad chuckled. "I guess I can assume you both are ordering the same thing as usual?"

"Why not?"

He jiggled his shoulders, like he was trying to do a dance. "Because, you must try new things. It's good for you. Otherwise, you get stuck in a rut and who wants that. Innovation doesn't come from ruts; it comes from unique ideas."

"Well, I like my rut just fine," Mom said. "And whose quote did you steal that from? Because if you bought it, you need a refund. That's just silly."

He chuckled. "I thought it was clever." He looked to me to agree. "Allie?"

"Nope. I'm with Mom on this one."

He pouted. "Fine."

The waitress came and took our order, some high school looking girl, then went back to the kitchen.

I stirred my orange juice, then took a few sips. "How's the research project going?"

Mom and Dad beamed. They loved discussing their project and they loved it even more when I took interest. Although I really didn't care, but it was nice to see them be passionate about something. I wanted that passion for myself, but I still had no clue what I wanted to do with my life yet.

I loved volleyball, but that wasn't an academic interest I could count on. For now, it kept me in shape and kept me busy. It looked good to be well rounded, but in truth, I had no idea what else to do.

Mia had cooking; my parents had their research. But every time I asked myself what I wanted, I heard absolute silence. The kind of silence sitting eerily still in the park or walking by a cemetery. As if any noise would disturb the cosmos, that's the kind of silence I heard. So, either the universe didn't know yet either or didn't want to tell me.

Mom kept discussing the project, even when the food came. I tried to listen, but she used the college level biology terms that I only half understood. I heard words I knew like cells, bacteria, and words that started with hydro, but other than that, I needed the layman's version and that was not on her explaining agenda today.

Dad was on the project too, but he let her discuss it while he ate his food. By the time we had all finished eating, I was sure she had told me the project's entire methodology, but it wasn't like I could repeat it. Biology didn't interest me; I knew at least that much.

But I still listened. I couldn't remember the last time the three of us had been together and with this being a rarity, I had learned to savor the moments, which is exactly what I did.

Chapter Twenty-Three

The week after homecoming had been harder than I had expected. Any time I saw Brittany in the hallways, she glared and not a I-hate-you-because-you're-wearing-that-cute-skirt glare, but a I-hate-your-guts-with-all-the-evil-in-my-heart-glare. Then if that wasn't bad enough, I managed to always be at my locker when Hunter was at his.

The winks, stares, and outright whistles were enough to keep a permanent shade of pink on my cheeks. I didn't understand why he didn't understand the words, *it can't happen*. It was three simple words. Was it really that hard to understand?

Or did he not care?

I shook my head. It didn't matter what he thought because I knew in my heart I couldn't date him, kiss him, or do anything *with* him without hurting my friendship with Mia. It was a no-go zone. Period, end of story.

And yet, as the last bell rang and I walked to my locker, the intense energy of someone, not just anyone, but Hunter, staring at me leaked into every cell of my body. I knew it before I turned and gazed into those green pools of gorgeousness that he was there.

"Duncan, are you riding home with us today?"

I nodded even though I knew he knew that answer. I wedged my head farther into my locker to avoid seeing his face again. I could tell, even from the other end of the hallway, that he kept looking in my direction. It unnerved me and not in a sexy kind of way.

Every time he looked at me like that, I thought about wavering on my stance. But I couldn't. I would give Bennett a chance. He knew that because he heard Mia ooh and ahh when she found my phone's messages from after the dance.

A locker door shut and then I could feel his presence next to me as every hair on my arm stood at attention. It was like he made my body react in a primal way. I could sense him without seeing him. A sixth sense. I didn't know if my body recognized his pheromones, or if that was just something they made up to let girls my age wait for that reaction to a guy before they *knew* how they felt.

Either way, I wasn't making it up. I was right 99% of the time and I was convinced that other 1% I was right too, but he had disappeared before I looked for him.

"Duncan, are you trying to avoid me?"

"N-no. Why would I?"

He inched closer to my ear, hidden behind my locker door when he said, "No reason."

The warm breath from his mouth sent shivers down my spine. And brought back our kiss to the forefront of my brain. This was totally unfair. Absolutely and utterly unfair.

I jerked my locker closed and looked around to see if Mia or anyone else had seen. "Would you cut that crap out?"

He smirked. "What? I didn't do anything." He tossed his bag over his shoulder and pushed his hands farther into his front pants pockets. "And anyway, I was thinking, we should be friends."

I stared at him like suddenly his hair was purple and he had a lip ring, although that was a bad thing to picture, because then I was thinking about his mouth and the heat crawled back up my cheeks as I remembered his mouth on mine.

He arched his eyebrow. "What are *you* thinking about? You just turned fifty shades of red there, Duncan."

I shoved his arm. "Your sister will be here any minute and you need to cut it out." I crossed my arms after gaining a little space between us. "And why friends? Don't you have plenty of those? Why would you want to be friends with a sophomore?"

"Is that a no?"

I exhaled loudly. "It's a sure. Knock yourself out."

He grinned, looking smug. "Awesome, well, as your friend, I feel compelled to tell you something."

"What's that?"

He tugged at the bottom of my shirt. "You need to stop wearing these."

"What? Why?" I looked at the hem of my shirt to see if there was something wrong. Had it frayed, and I hadn't noticed?

"Because it's driving me crazy."

I gasped, which made him chuckle. Then he walked toward the front doors, leaving me in his wake.

Thankfully, Mia jogged down the stairs by my locker. She looked around. "You okay?"

"Yep. Waiting to ditch this popsicle stand."

She squinted at me like I just said something gross. "That's a dad joke, don't repeat that." She linked arms with me. "I will agree that it's time to ditch though. Friday couldn't have come soon enough."

"You're telling me."

"Doing anything tonight? Want to sleep over?"

"Can't. I have some homework to work on since we have our game tomorrow. How about tomorrow?"

Mia sighed dramatically. "Fine, party pooper. But Saturday night, you're mine."

Hunter waited for us in the front seat of his car and like usual, he had his radio cranked up loud enough to make the hair on my head bounce. He lowered it only slightly when he saw us.

I crawled into the backseat on Mia's side, then focused on my phone. I knew if I looked up into the rearview mirror I would see him, and I didn't need any more reminders of what he had said only a few minutes ago.

While I scrolled, a text came through, *Hey, Allie.*

Bennett was of course the sender. He texted me more and more ever since the dance. It didn't matter that my final class had been with him and Mia in history, he still managed to text me like he hadn't seen me all day.

Hey, Bennett.
What are you doing?
Sitting in the parking lot, waiting to get out.
Me too. It seems worse today.
Yep.
What are you doing tomorrow?
I have my volleyball game.
Oh, right. Is that a home game?
I think so. I could check my schedule.
Already did. It's at our school's gym.
Nice, then yes.
Cool. Maybe I'll see you there?
Well, I'll definitely be there, so I guess it depends if you decide to go too.

He sent me a wink smiley face and I smirked. I guess I could expect to see him there. I wondered if Jasper would go for Mia's sake. She was still going on and on about him. She had gotten his number, although she still didn't tell me if she asked him, or he asked her. Either way, she texted him a good bit.

I leaned forward and sure enough she was texting someone now with a big ol' grin on her face. In one way, it was a good thing she was distracted, because she didn't see Hunter staring at me in the rearview mirror, just like I expected him to do.

I shoved my phone in my bag and forced my attention out the window. Soon I would be home and I could relax. His staring energy wouldn't find me all the way at my house.

Chapter Twenty-Four

I wasn't prepared to start in our volleyball game. We only had a few games left this season before playoffs and I figured Sammie would get all the playing time Coach would give her, but when she called my number instead of hers, I nearly fell over.

If it had been a surprise to Sammie, she didn't show it. She patted my shoulder. "Go get 'em, Allie. You've got this."

I smiled and mumbled thanks. Then we all put our hands in, did our cheer and lined up on the backline of the court. Brittany wasn't playing this game yet, either. Which was also surprising.

Mia lined up next to me. "What do you think that's about?"

I shrugged. "No clue. Weird though, right?"

"Absolutely."

We waited for the whistle to blow, and I took the opportunity to check the stands. Near the middle on our side was Bennett and sure enough, Jasper sat next to him. I didn't expect to see Hunter a few rows above him, sitting by himself leaning against the back wall.

"Why is Hunter still here?"

Mia averted her gaze to where I looked. "No idea."

Sure, he had drove us to the game, but he never usually stayed unless he had to pick us up too. And even then, he usually went back outside. As far as I knew, he didn't suddenly enjoy girls' volleyball any more than he normally did.

The whistle blew and I was forced to block it all out. It was game time. I was being given an opportunity to show what I had learned over the last several weeks of the season and there was no way I would waste it.

Not to mention, at this point in the season every game mattered. This team was near the top, if we beat them, not only would we mess up their record, but it gave us a better set up for play offs.

I started in the back, position six. Mia was next to me and was serving first. Luckily for us she earned seven points before the other team learned to handle her serve. Unluckily for us, by serve eight, the surprise was gone, and they no longer seemed clueless. They returned the ball right by the net, right in our hole.

Coach clapped loud from the sidelines. "That's alright, let's get it back."

I geared up for the serve. I was in the back middle and that meant it had an eighty percent chance of coming right to me. I got in my squat position, lightly touched the floor, and prepared to move.

As expected, the ball launched over to our side, floated a little and landed right near me. I had been ready, so I popped it up to our secondary setter on the court. They just did the first set until I could get to the front, then she set the ball to our spiker, and we earned the point.

We rotated and were up to serve. I stayed poised to move. As a setter, I was rotating and switching spots constantly the whole game. It was my job to be in my spot by the time the ball came back over and needed a second hit. It might not have been easy, but it kept things interesting. It also let me have eyes all over the court with different perspectives. All the other positions stayed in the same spots throughout the game, but I was able to move around a good bit.

On the next point, I dug a wayward bump from the net and managed to get it high enough for our spiker to hit the ball and score.

The stands erupted and for once, I heard my name shouted from the lips of a guy. Bennett had stood and cupped his hands over his mouth shouting, "Nice dig, Allie!"

I blushed. No one had cheered for me before. I glanced toward Hunter out of habit and immediately regretted it. He glared at Bennett's head like he had the ability to explode it just from staring.

Then he caught my gaze and his intensity flamed. I couldn't tell if he was mad at me or mad at Bennett. Either way, I didn't have time to dwell on it because it was the middle of the game.

We had a few volleys that felt like forever. We did three hits, they did three hits, and so it went on repeat, until we finally won the point. Once Mia was supposed to rotate to the front, Brittany subbed in. Now she was *right* next to me instead of Mia.

She never purposely upset the game, but her sneers and mumbled comments were plenty. She blamed me for Hunter's quick escape, even though she was the one who darted away. She also thought I was a two timer for having Bennett at the game too, as if I was dating them both.

I had to admit I was impressed she even thought I could manage both at the same time. Usually, I was considered to have no experience whatsoever, which was fair considering I'd never had a boyfriend.

And if it hadn't been for stupid middle school parties, my first kiss would have been after homecoming.

With only a few points left in the game, Sammie subbed in for me. She high-fived me as we waited for the refs to officially sub us in and out, but it felt good to be recognized for what I could do on the court.

Mia fist bumped me as I sat and sucked down water. Sammie served for me and never had to set because we took the game. Now it was one more and we would win completely. It was turning out to be a good day.

* * *

The second game we barely lost. The other team had finally woken up and realized they weren't playing to their potential. The third game was also a fight, but we won. Which if I was being honest, was more fun. Games where we smoked the other team were boring. We got to practice more as a team when we had to face another group that knew what they were doing, otherwise, we won without breaking a sweat.

After our final huddle, I sat by my bag to cool off. Sammie and I had played about fifty-fifty of the final game, and I had ended the second half, making me hot and sweaty.

Normally, I didn't care, except Bennett *and* Hunter were headed straight for me.

Bennett reached us first with Jasper.

Jasper wasn't how I remembered him from the dance. His hair was lighter than I thought, more blond than brown. His eyes were dark blue, like a stormy sky or the deep part of an ocean, and he was tall. Almost gargantuan tall, which looked funny as Mia stood near him.

"You two played amazing," Bennett said. "Allie, that dig in the first game was so cool. I had no idea you could play like that."

I averted my gaze to the floor. "Thanks. It's no big deal."

Mia elbowed me. "She's being humble." She placed her arm over my shoulder. "What are you two up to now?"

Bennett and Jasper exchanged glances, as if they had discussed this in case we asked.

"Thinking 'bout heading to Hal's later for dinner," Jasper said. His voice was gravellier than I had expected. "You two little ladies interested in joining us?"

My chest tensed because at that exact minute, Hunter had finished coming down the final two stairs, just behind them. He clearly heard their offer. He arched an eyebrow when Mia answered for us.

"Of course, we would. Right, Allie?"

Now being Mia's friend since well forever, I knew this was a rhetorical question. She didn't really want any other answer besides yes. It wasn't a debate or a discussion, it just was. So, I nodded, because what else was I supposed to do?

That clearly surprised Hunter who took that moment to clear his throat.

Bennett and Jasper turned and saw Hunter. Their expressions completely shifted to what I will name *bro mode*. They seemed starstruck, which was annoying, because of course they fawned over our star basketball player, Hunter.

"Dude, Hunter Baylor?" Bennett asked. They looked around him like he should be rolling with an entourage. "What are you doing here man?"

Hunter put on his star smile and wrapped his arm around Mia and even me. "Mia's my little sister. Doing my brotherly duties to pick up and drop off two of the star players."

I was dying. This was beyond embarrassing.

"Did I hear you two asking them to Hal's?"

Jasper's jaw ticked. "Yes, you did."

Mia glared at her brother and removed his arm. "Excuse

us, please." She yanked Hunter toward the other part of the bleachers, out of earshot.

I giggled because honestly, I had no idea how to react in a situation like this. "Those two are such jokesters."

Bennett exhaled like he had been worried. "He was joking?" He tapped Jasper on the shoulder. "Dude, he seemed deadly protective."

"Oh, no. That's just the game those two play."

Jasper and Bennett exchanged a glance I didn't understand and started laughing. "Wow, he was good," Bennett said.

"So, uh, will you tell Mia I'll be by to pick you two up around five?" Jasper asked.

"Sure."

"Cool. See you then."

Bennett waved, then walked off with Jasper, just as Mia and Hunter walked back.

Mia frowned. "Where'd they go?"

"They had to leave, but Jasper said he'd be by at five to pick us up."

Mia's expression immediately changed. "Oh perfect." She pulled out her phone and walked toward the gym doors. "You two coming?" But she didn't wait for us to respond. Instead, she kept going, as I collected my things.

Hunter hovered. I tried to ignore him, but it was becoming difficult. I shoved my kneepads into my bag along with my empty water container. I changed out of my sneakers, put on my flip flops and sweats, and slung the bag over my shoulder.

Hunter still stood there not saying anything, but also not looking away.

"What?"

He shrugged. "Nothing, I guess." Then he walked in the same direction Mia headed.

I double checked the bench one more time before walking

away, but not quick enough for Brittany to snag me before I left.

"Oh, Allie," she said and then laughed. "How cute."

I sighed. "What do you want, Brittany? I have to go."

"Oh, *nothing*."

I rolled my eyes, it was clearly nothing, but she decided to say it anyway. I walked a few feet when she started again.

"So naïve."

I pinched the bridge of my nose. "Would you like to explain your dissertation, or would you rather keep on being coy?"

She squinted like she wasn't entirely sure what I asked her, but continued. "Hunter sees you as a little project. When you stop being interesting, he will drop you."

"Wow, so he pities me and now I'm a project. You're really going all out to convince me."

She crossed her arms and narrowed her gaze. "You wait and see, but I'm right."

"Whatever, Brittany. I really don't care what you think."

I walked out before she could continue any longer with her ridiculous ideas. Even if she was right, it didn't matter. Hunter and I weren't dating, and we never would because I wouldn't do that to Mia. So, she was wasting her energy.

When I finally made it to the car, Mia stared. "Did you get lost?"

"No. Let's go."

Mia didn't push it, but Hunter gave me this look, like he was torn between asking me what happened and trying not to care. Either way, he stayed silent, which was fine by me.

Chapter Twenty-Five

The universe must have been looking out for me because Hunter left us alone all afternoon and then even while we got ready for this *double date*. I didn't know if I could really call it that. I didn't exactly have feelings for Bennett, I was just seeing what was there or could be there.

My heart was still too wrapped up in Hunter to fully release me toward someone else ... at least for now. Mia was on a date. Jasper had texted her all afternoon, ever since the game and she could not stop smiling every time her phone dinged.

I stared at the outfit I had chosen in the mirror. It was nothing special, just a pair of straight-leg jeans, my favorite pair of flip flops, although Mia kept telling me it was too cold for them at this point, and a flowy top, that I planned to cover a little with my favorite zip up. It was comfy and still cute, at least I thought so.

I sighed. "Are you sure I look okay?" I asked Mia for the fifth time.

"Yes, like I said the last time you asked me like a minute ago. Stop stressing."

"Okay." I twirled in her vanity chair until I faced her. "So, we really like Jasper?"

Mia's face got all goofy, like in those movies where the girl thinks about the guy. "Yes. Isn't he dreamy? That southern spark in his voice. Oh man."

I giggled. "You're crazy. And isn't he from here anyway?"

"No. He moved here for high school, but he used to live in Texas."

"Hmm." I had to admit, it made the gravelly part of his voice make more sense, but I didn't think the cowboy was enough to make me all goo goo ga ga.

She slapped my leg. "You ready? They should be here any minute. Jasper texted me to say he was almost here."

"He texted and drove?"

Mia rolled her eyes. "I don't know, but everyone does."

"That's not very safe."

She glared at me. "Is this really about his driving or about Bennett being in the car and your nerves have suddenly hit you?"

And that's why she was my best friend. I stuck out my tongue.

"That's what I thought."

The doorbell rang and Mia bolted down the stairs.

I took one last glance at my reflection, decided it had to be good enough and followed her down.

She had already let Bennett and Jasper into the house. They both appeared to have changed from earlier. Bennett wore dark jeans and a tan polo shirt with sneakers. Jasper definitely showed his roots. He had on a baseball hat, a tight T-shirt, and jeans that hugged his hips.

My eyes widened, maybe I had misspoken. Cowboy had a body under all those clothes. Mia's gaze met mine and I knew she was saying I told you so with her eyes. I stifled my giggle; I didn't want them thinking I was weird for not even saying hello before I burst out laughing.

Bennett watched every move I made. I could feel his eyes boring into me, but that's not what caused the prickling of the hair on the back of my neck. No. I knew who had caused that.

I spun around slowly, while I listened to Jasper and Mia chat about something he had texted her. Sure enough, I could see the edge of Hunter's face standing in the kitchen, leaning against the counter.

He was watching us. It made me squirmy, but in a good way. I liked knowing he possibly cared about what was happening. *Wait.* What was I thinking? I needed him to stop if I ever had a chance to get past him.

"Shall we go?" Bennett asked, pulling me from my thoughts.

I nodded and followed him out, Mia and Jasper taking up the rear. The boys led us to a big pickup truck, with a cab behind the driver's row of seats. So at least we would all fit, but from the looks of it, we would be squished in the back.

Bennett opened the passenger door, then opened the back row's door. "Mia, I'll sit back here with Allie. You can have up front."

Mia's eyebrows rose. I could hear her thoughts from where I stood. *Ooh, snuggle up next to him.*

And as much as I didn't want to do that, I couldn't get her voice out of my head. The images that floated through weren't with Bennett, but with Hunter. I needed to try harder to get him out of my head. Here I sat next to a boy who clearly liked me and did make me laugh but didn't focus on him long enough to really know anything.

"So, do you like going to Hal's?" Bennett asked.

"Yeah, my parents and I go there occasionally when they're not too busy."

"That's cool. My parents think it's too busy looking. They don't like all the decades."

I gasped. "But that's the best part."

He chuckled. "I've tried to tell them, believe me."

I smiled. Bennett's charm was infectious. When I knew Hunter wasn't in earshot, Bennett's eyes and his smile made me feel comfortable, like a warm blanket wrapped around me. But ... I guess a warm blanket wasn't exactly the most romantic way to describe how someone made you feel.

But I only just met Bennett. I couldn't expect to feel fireworks the same way Hunter's kiss had made me feel. I had known Hunter my whole life. I had years of time to learn his quirks and grow fond of him before a full-on crush emerged.

"So, what do your parents do?" he asked.

"Oh ... hmm?" I tried to focus on him. "They are, um, professors."

"Oh, cool. At Rosewood?"

"Yep."

"What do they teach?"

"Biology and some upper-level classes. They do research on the Chesapeake Bay."

His eyes widened. "That's really cool."

"Yeah."

He studied me, then moved an inch or two closer before he looked ahead. We pulled into Hal's parking lot, parked, and headed for the door.

Mia kept sending googly eyes toward me, but I couldn't figure it out if she was trying to say that to me or about Jasper.

Jasper tipped his hat toward Mia while he held the door for the rest of us. We were seated in the eighties again and the waitress's hair was teased out higher than the width of her face. It was impressive. I wondered what kind of hairspray she used to keep it in place.

"So, Jasper was telling me how he used to do the rodeo when he lived in Texas," Mia said giving me a death glare.

I was in trouble; my space cadet thoughts weren't going unnoticed. "Oh?"

Jasper spread out in the booth. "Yeah. Bull ridin' helluva rush. Nothin' like ridin' a bull."

"Sounds risky."

"That's the point."

I raised an eyebrow. He was so not who I expected Mia to fall for, but she couldn't stop staring at him. I couldn't get her to break eye contact for more than four seconds before her eyes roamed over his chest and arms again.

When the waitress came back to our table, I practically had to kick her under the table to get her to pay attention.

Bennett eyed me like he was unsure of how things were going. If I planned to get over Hunter, I had to take this seriously.

I turned toward Bennett. "How did you meet Jasper?"

"I met him at the football team tryouts."

"That's cool."

"Yeah, we hit it off pretty quickly."

"You have bull riding in common?"

Bennett chuckled. "No. I think he's crazy. I can't imagine putting myself in harm's way just to impress people by riding an animal, but we related about our families."

"Oh? Like how?" I asked as I took a sip of my soda.

"We are both the middle sibling. Something about being in the middle makes you invisible."

"That can't be true, can it?"

He nodded, then chuckled. "It is what it is. I use it to my advantage. You can't get in trouble if you aren't seen."

I frowned. "Yeah, but that's awfully lonely."

"You said that like you know how it is."

I never really spoke to anyone about stuff at home, Mia

knew bits, but most didn't know how I felt being left out. I tucked one leg under me and leaned against the edge of the table, swirling my straw through the soda. "I'm the only child. My parents are busy with their research. I guess you could say I have more unsupervised time than I really want."

Bennett rested his hand on my arm. "That sounds tough."

"Yeah—" My thoughts froze as if the conveyor belt of thought suddenly broke down and stopped moving forward. At the door was Hunter Baylor and Richard followed behind him.

What on earth was he doing here?

They sat in a booth in the sixties. Hunter sat himself in perfect view of me from his table.

I scowled. Was he serious? This was the exact opposite of what I had told him. Why did he even care? I was his sister's best friend. I was a sophomore. Brittany was right, I was *interesting* and when the chase faded, so would this.

His eyes locked on mine and despite my mind fighting every urge, I could feel the squirming of my insides. They lurched and twisted like on a rollercoaster. And that reaction made me even more mad.

I pretended to cough. "I, um ... I'm going to go to the bathroom."

Bennett scrunched his nose in confusion.

Mia looked away from Jasper's face to ask if I needed company with her eyes.

I shook my head and stood. I wasn't even surprised when the hair on my arms raised as Hunter approached me in the hallway headed toward the bathrooms. I could always feel him before I could see him, and this time was no different.

"Are you seriously out of your mind?" I asked as I whirled around to face him.

He smirked, which irritated me more.

"It's not funny, Hunter. Why are you here?"

"I don't trust that dude. So, I had to make sure everything was okay."

"Which dude?"

He glared toward the table. "Honestly, both."

I huffed and rolled my eyes. "They're harmless, but I'm not about to be. Neither will Mia if she sees you. Just go home."

His expression faltered for a second. "You don't want me here?"

My shoulders slumped and I rubbed my hands down my face. "How am I supposed to answer that question, Hunter? I don't understand any of this. It makes no sense to me."

He looked around, then nudged me closer to the wall before putting his arms to the left and right of my head and leaning toward me. "What doesn't make sense?"

My brain sputtered. Thoughts were difficult to form. I could smell the peppermint from the toothpaste he used and his cologne. Manly and yet very Hunter. I splayed my palm against his chest and pushed gently, to get him to move farther away. I gestured between us. "This. What is this? A few weeks ago, you were my best friend's brother, and I was just Mia's best friend. I had a crush on you, but that didn't equal anything real. You didn't like me, and I saw you, but it didn't make a difference. Now I don't understand."

He put his hands in his pockets. "Is that what you want?"

I groaned. "What I want? What does it matter? This isn't possible."

He nodded and walked away.

The knot that grew in my stomach as he walked away felt worse than seeing him did. I couldn't tell if I hurt him or he was upset or just didn't care, but this feeling sucked.

* * *

Surprisingly, he and Richard left shortly after our little conversation. When I sat back at the table, I focused on Bennett. He was sitting here with me, and I was being a jerk not giving this a proper chance. He made me laugh and feel comfortable. Wasn't that how everyone said the best relationships started? Wouldn't that mean we were on the right track?

"You ladies ready to hit the road?" Jasper asked.

Mia nodded and rested her hand briefly on his arm before she moved it back to her side. The brush had Jasper winking at her and then he followed us out of Hal's.

My stomach grumbled as I hopped into the back row of seats. I had barely touched my chicken fingers with how much my stomach churned. It was worse than enduring a hurricane on a little boat in the middle of the ocean, but now I was starving, and I couldn't just eat the leftovers in Jasper's truck. It'd be weird and who knew how long until they dropped us off. Jasper and Mia could barely stop staring at each other long enough to breathe let alone discuss their plans with us.

He pulled out of the parking lot and headed in the opposite direction of our neighborhood.

Bennett jiggled his knee as he glanced toward me. "When did you start playing volleyball?"

That had not been the question I expected him to ask me. "I played on a team starting in fourth grade. I played at home and around with my mom when I was younger, but only a little here and there. I honestly fell in love watching her play on teams. But she stopped playing because her research kept her crazy busy."

"That had to be cool playing the same sport as your mom … at least for a little while."

"Yeah, it was." Except, she hadn't played with me in so long I couldn't even remember the last time we bumped the ball around, but I didn't have time to dwell on it too much because a loud pop echoed through the truck, and we slowed down.

Mia looked me dead in the eye then back at Jasper. "What was that?"

"Tire blew." He smacked the steering wheel and hopped out.

I strained to look behind me but couldn't get a good look.

"Jasper's good with this kind of thing. It'll be fine," Bennett said.

Mia nodded, but the look in Bennett's eyes told me he wasn't confident in what he said, he just didn't want to freak us out.

I checked my phone, the screen said it was seven, which wasn't that late, but wasn't exactly early either. It would have been better if it wasn't dark already.

Jasper opened the door and leaned in. "Totally flat. No way to patch it. Gonna need a new one."

"So, what does that mean?"

He sighed. "It means we're stuck here. I don't have a spare tire and there's no way we're moving."

My stomach clenched. This was not good.

Mia gave me a look that said she completely agreed with how I felt. I pulled out my phone and texted her, *What should we do?*

Idk. I don't want Mom coming out here. She's cool but I'm not ready for her to meet Jasper.

So, what else can we do? My parents are at work. There's no way they can come pick us up.

I'll text Hunter. Maybe we will get lucky, and he'll be in the area.

Okay.

Except it wasn't okay. I knew he was in the area, and I didn't want to see him. Would he just show up like some knight on a white horse saving us after what I had said? Not to mention we'd all have to get in his car. Nice and cozy like. That sounded like a personal way to torture me. But what choice did I have? It wasn't like I could tell Mia, *Oh no, that's okay. He's in the area, but I told him to go away, and I don't want to see him now.*

Yeah, definitely not.

There was no way around it.

Hunter would be on his way, and I'd have to deal with whatever happened.

Chapter Twenty-Six

Hunter arrived faster than I was prepared for. I had no idea where Richard went, but he was nowhere to be found in Hunter's car. By the time Hunter had arrived, we had all filed out of the pickup. Jasper and Mia were standing close together, until Hunter flashed his lights and hopped out.

He kept the door ajar and leaned with his arms rested on the top of the door. "Flat tire, but no spare?" His expression made it seem like he was calling Jasper an idiot for not having a backup.

Jasper didn't seem to notice as he leaned against the truck. "Nah, man. Used it in Texas last year and never replaced it."

Hunter slammed the door shut. "Got it. Well, what's your plan with the truck?"

"Tow company will come pick it up and take it back to the shop. So can ya give us a ride?"

Hunter jerked his head toward the car.

Mia and I exchanged glances and walked toward his car.

I froze halfway there. Hunter had a small car; it wasn't like he drove a minivan that could hold a basketball team. It was tight on a normal day, but five teenagers? Someone would be squished in the backrow of seats in the middle, and I had a bad feeling it would end up being me.

Hunter realized the same thing. "Bennett, why don't you sit up front with me?"

He paused and then nodded.

Mia raised an eyebrow, clearly surprised by this choice.

I would have been too if I didn't understand that Bennett posed a bigger threat than Jasper. Any tough feelings toward the guys weren't about him being a big protective brother, but Mia didn't need to know that.

Jasper sat next to Mia, and I managed to sit on the right side of the car. Mia didn't mind being up against Jasper, if anything, it was going perfectly.

Hunter's gaze settled on me as he drove away from the pickup.

Besides Mia's and Jasper's whispers, the only sound was Hunter's radio, which was tuned to some local station that played any local artists, but nothing that popular.

My phone vibrated against my hand. It was a text, but since everyone I really texted was in the car, I had no idea who to expect it to be from.

I unlocked my phone and checked the message. It was Bennett, *Well, this isn't how I hoped tonight would go.*

Despite everything, this made me chuckle. He had a point.

No? You didn't want to be stuck on the side of the road? These things happen though.

They do, but the timing sucks.

That's usually true, too.

I could hear the slight chuckle from the front seat and Hunter's gaze intensified as we pulled into their driveway. If I was confused before, I was worse now.

We all piled out and the boys stayed silent as they waited.

Hunter turned to us. "I'll take them home and then be back."

Mia ignored Hunter, but I had the feeling the message wasn't for him anyway. She went up to Jasper and whispered something in his ear.

He smirked, then got back in the car.

Bennett closed the distance between us. "I had a great night. Text you?"

I nodded and waved bye, but the feeling of Hunter's stare made it hard not to squirm.

Mia and I waited until Hunter's car pulled away before we went in. She closed the door behind us and sighed. "That was amazing."

I giggled. "I've never seen you so swoony over a guy before."

"Allie, he is not like any guy I've ever met around here. He's handsome, funny, and that southern accent is to die for. Did you see his butt in those jeans?"

I shook my head. "Just be careful."

Her face scrunched like she tasted a lemon. "Of course."

"Okay, I just want to make sure."

"I'm not delusional, but he really likes me. He kept playing footsy under the table."

I arched a brow. "Has he kissed you yet?"

"Well, no. But then again this was our first date, and his stupid tire blew. I'm sure he would have otherwise. Let's head upstairs, maybe watch a movie?"

"Sure."

My phone dinged and I knew before I even looked that it would be Bennett.

I had a good time tonight. Hopefully, we can do something again soon.

I smiled and followed Mia up the stairs.

* * *

Mia and I had stayed in her room after the movie, but once she fell asleep, it felt too stifling to stay there. Mia would be passed out for the night—only a bomb could wake her up now.

I took my phone off the dresser and crept down the stairs and to the back porch.

Mr. and Mrs. Baylor had gotten home an hour before from a company dinner party and had gone straight to their rooms after saying goodnight.

I breathed in the cool, crisp air as I wrapped myself in the heavy blanket Mrs. Baylor kept for the cool evenings and stretched out on the chaise part of the patio couches. It wasn't too cold yet in Chesapeake Hills, but in another few weeks, the evening could dip below the forties. Although in Chesapeake Hills, the weather tended to do whatever it wanted from year to year.

According to my phone, tonight was fifty-eight with a cloudless sky and new moon—perfect for star gazing.

I searched for the north star and the big dipper but wasn't quite sure where it was without the star gazing app our school had showed us in middle school. It wasn't long before I could sense I wasn't alone on the porch anymore.

Hunter walked around in his fleece lined zip up. "Fancy meeting you out here."

I gave Hunter a skeptical glance. "As if you didn't know I was here."

He held up two hands, palms out and sat a cushion over from where I was. "Guilty. I couldn't help myself."

I sighed and glued my eyes on the stars above me.

"Do you not want me here?"

I shrugged. I honestly didn't know how to answer his question. Even now, I wished for him to move closer. To kiss me under the stars and make me lose my bearings like before, but I also knew it got us nowhere.

"Did you know I once went to space camp?"

My jaw slackened as I faced him. "What? No, you didn't."

He chuckled. "Yes, I did, right after sixth grade."

My eyebrows knitted. "I thought that was basketball camp."

"That's what I told everyone, but it was space camp. I had so much fun, too."

I wiggled farther into the cushions. "So, why hide it?"

"Wasn't the cool thing, I guess."

"Ruin your cred?"

"I supposed I thought it would."

"And you don't think so now?"

"I don't care about my cred with you."

"And why's that?"

"I don't know if I fully understand why, but it doesn't feel like I need to pretend with you."

What was I supposed to do with that? Why did it have to be impossible for us and at the same time be everything I always wanted to hear?

He scooted closer to me on the cushion. "Allie, I know what you've said about Mia and why this"—he gestured between us both—"can't happen, but I don't want to have to resist you." His jaw ticked. "I see you all the time with Mia and I don't want to watch you date the football player. It drives me insane."

"What are you saying?"

"*I* want to date you."

"And how exactly will we do that when your sister is my best friend? I don't see her just letting us date."

He shrugged. "So, we don't tell her."

"She's my best friend. How am I supposed to hide that from her?"

"You're only hiding the dating part. Shouldn't we be able to see what that kiss meant? See if there's a reason it was so good?"

I cocked my head to the side. "So good, huh?"

A glimmer of something I couldn't name, passed through his expression. He moved closer to my face, hovering between the space, but close enough that I felt the need to squirm. "You're saying it wasn't?"

The air seemed as if it had been vacuum sealed from my lungs. "Uh ... maybe."

He moved even closer as my pulse raced.

Then right before his lips met mine, he gazed into my eyes and moved his hand to my cheek.

I tried to resist, but my eyelids fluttered close, and he kissed me.

Somehow it was even better than before. His hand didn't stay on my cheek for long. As he intensified the kiss with a nibble on my bottom lip, his hand entwined in my hair. And when he guided me onto his lap and covered us both with the blanket, I barely noticed as all the contact overloaded my brain from logical thought. The only thing that would process was how good it all felt.

Hunter broke the kiss, but his gaze told me he didn't really want to.

"Okay, maybe I distorted the truth," I said.

He chuckled and wrapped his arms around me, pulling me closer until my head fell on his shoulder. "At the risk of hearing the truth and possibly ruining this moment, do you feel this way about Bennett?"

I shook my head against his shoulder.

He turned his neck to see my face. "Mia aside, would you want to date me too?"

"Yes."

He smiled. "So, can we try?"

I covered my face with my hands. I shouldn't say yes. How could I keep such a big secret from my best friend? But I had intense feelings for Hunter, and he was right, something just worked between us. I could feel it every time we kissed.

"I don't know. It just feels wrong. I'll have to lie to Mia every time we go somewhere. I don't want to lie to her about something like this."

"It isn't lying. It's simply excluding the information until things are determined. Mia doesn't tell you every little detail about boys she likes does she?"

"I mean, maybe not every detail, but I know when she does like someone."

"Okay, so this is you figuring it out."

"I already know my initial feelings for you. I would have told her about someone once I felt this way."

His grin deepened. "That's good news."

I smacked his chest. "Stop focusing on how that's good for you. I'm serious. Mia is important to me. Your family is important to me. If this goes south, I could lose it all."

"It won't go south."

"You can't possibly know that."

He stared at my lips. "I can know that."

I groaned. "Okay, so what if things have worked so far. Mia is more than just a best friend. We spend so much time together. How will I get away to meet you and then not feel guilty that I lied?"

"I don't know, but I want us to have a chance to try."

I nibbled the bottom of my lip. This was torture. Hunter wanted to date *me*. He had said all the right things and I desperately wanted to stay in his lap and relish in what could happen. But the sinking feeling of how Mia would take the news made me hesitate every single time.

"What if we do a probationary period? It doesn't even have to be called dating, just hanging out. We can spend time together without the normal constraints and just see what happens."

God that was so tempting. It would keep things as status quo until we knew for sure. What if Brittany had been right? What if once he didn't have to chase me his feelings dwindled and then I had suffered Mia's wrath for no reason? This could test the waters and, if it mattered, then I could tell her. "It would be just until we see where this is headed. Until we figure things out. Why tell Mia unless we know ourselves, right?"

"Exactly."

"Okay."

His eyes widened and he pulled me closer. "Yeah? Really?"

I nodded. "But this must stay a secret. I can't have Mia finding out unless we decide to tell her."

"Right, of course."

I smiled. I was going to hang out with Hunter Baylor *alone*? I could hardly believe it.

"So, think you could get away for a night with me this week?"

I tapped a finger to my chin. "Hmm, I'll have to check my schedule. I'm pretty busy."

He tickled my side, which was completely unfair since I couldn't move far enough away while sitting on his lap.

"You can't play hard to get when I already know how you feel."

I giggled. "Who says I'm playing hard to get?" But one look at his face and I couldn't hold my serious expression together. "Fine, what day?"

"You have practice all week?"

"Yep, which you know means Mia and I will come back here."

"Right." He paused. "Think you could come up with a reason to go home right after like on Wednesday? Then I could come pick you up from there."

"I should be able to think of something. Maybe, I'll convince her to go somewhere with Jasper."

He rolled his eyes. "That dude is bad news."

I sat up. "Why do you say that?"

"I just get this feeling."

"Hmph. Well, I don't like to hear that."

He shrugged. "It would be a good plan though."

"Then Wednesday it is."

"Good."

"Where are we going?"

"You'll see."

I frowned. "How will I know what to wear?"

"Wear whatever. Won't make a difference."

Maybe not to him, but it did to me. This was a date with Hunter Baylor, I would only get one first date. Only one chance to make a first impression as a girl he could *date*, date, and I couldn't ask Mia her opinion. Something to obsess over later.

For now, I enjoyed the feeling of his arms around me as we sat under the blanket watching the stars. I never wanted it to stop, even though I knew it would have to.

Chapter Twenty-Seven

I had never been more excited for something in my life than after practice on Wednesday night. The plan was to head home after practice and Hunter would pick me up by five, which meant I had only an hour to get ready after volleyball. Somehow, I managed to take a shower, blow dry my hair, at least in the front so it wasn't dripping wet, then braided the rest.

I had no idea where we were going, so I wore jeans, my comfy sneakers, and a long-sleeve, mint-green sweater. I should have prepared to wear a coat too, but I didn't want to deal with the bulkiness when we got to wherever we were going.

The doorbell rang and I bolted down the stairs. Thankfully, my parents were working late, although, lately, they were always working late. If it weren't for the Baylors feeding me most nights, I probably wouldn't eat much besides cereal—at least when there was milk that hadn't expired.

At the bottom of the stairs, I inhaled deeply, released it, repeated once more, then opened the door.

Hunter had been facing the street, when he turned and

saw me, he smiled. "Did you order one large pepperoni pizza and cheesy bread?"

I rolled my eyes and nudged his arm before yanking his shirt and pulling him inside.

He surveyed the room. "I don't think I've ever been inside your house."

I chuckled. "Probably not. You're never here."

He settled both hands on my hips and pulled me closer. "Maybe that'll have to change."

I wiggled from his grasp and moved toward the stairs. "I have to grab my phone from upstairs. I'll be right back."

He arched an eyebrow. "Now Allie, don't be getting the wrong idea here. Leaving a guy alone in your house, where you'll be going upstairs?" He gasped. "I don't know what you've heard, but I'm not that kind of guy."

"Ha ha. Stay put."

He saluted me. "Aye aye, captain."

I jogged up the stairs as fast as my feet could take me. I didn't want to risk him seeing any of the old photos of me. Regardless of if he had seen me at that age, it had been a while and I certainly didn't want to remind him of my many awkward photos. Besides tonight was different. Tonight, was about seeing each other as more than just Mia's brother and Mia's best friend. It was about seeing if things worked between us, just Allie and Hunter.

Once I grasped the phone, I headed back down the stairs, thankfully he hadn't moved.

"All set?"

I nodded. "Do I-do I look okay?"

"Always. But if you mean will it be okay for where we're going? Yes."

I smiled and twisted the end of my braid. "Okay. Then I'm all set."

He opened my front door and waited for me to exit before

he closed it. I turned and locked up, then walked next to him as we approached his car.

His shoulder was close enough that I could feel a brush or two as we walked. He had changed from school, wearing light wash jeans and a black thermal, which hugged his chest and shoulders, no doubt from all the muscles of being as athletic as he was.

He opened the passenger door and waited until I got in before walking around to his side of the car. He put it in drive and sped away from my house.

We headed in the opposite direction of town, which usually went to the highway. I had no idea where we would go from there, but I honestly didn't care. He could take me nowhere and I'd be happy. Never in my entire life did I ever expect to go on a date with Hunter and now that it was happening, I hoped it lasted forever.

"Where do your parents think you are?" Hunter asked.

"At your house."

He chuckled. "They won't ask Mia?"

"Yeah, right. They'd have to be home to notice, and they don't question it. I'm always at your house."

"I know."

I eyed him warily. "Is that a bad thing?"

"Not entirely."

"*Not entirely?* What's that mean?"

"Relax. I just meant before we decided to see where things lead, it was ... difficult."

"Difficult how?"

"You know how."

I faced him, even though he kept his gaze on the road. "Nope. I don't."

"Is that so? Well, not barging into Mia's room and kissing you right then and there has been slightly harder than I had expected."

I giggled. "Mr. Senior can't resist little ol' sophomore me?"

"Guilty."

"Well, good. Now you can see how I've felt."

He arched an eyebrow. "Is that so? You imagined kissing me?"

I shrugged. "Maybe."

"For how long?"

I exhaled loudly, letting all the air drain from my cheeks. "I don't remember."

"This summer?"

"Longer."

"Interesting."

I shifted in the seat. "Yeah, I know. It's sad, pining after someone who doesn't even realize."

"Or that's what you thought anyway."

"More than what I thought. You didn't see me that way before." I gazed at his expression. "Right?"

"You're not like other girls, Allie. I'm never sure what most people's intentions are. Most girls see me as a way to increase their popularity. It becomes less about me and more about what they think my social status will do for them." He glanced at me. "I don't get that feeling with you."

I grimaced. "Does that really happen a lot?"

"More than I'd care to admit. Brittany was merely the latest."

I winced.

"Sorry, I shouldn't have brought her up."

"It's not your fault."

He removed his right hand from the wheel and placed it on my leg. "I knew better, and I did it anyway. I know her type."

What blonde and beautiful?

"Stop that."

"Stop what?"

"Comparing yourself to her."

My eyes widened. "How ...?"

"How did I know that you were *thinking* she was better looking than you? Because you wear it all over your expression. She doesn't have anything special. You're beautiful and smart, that's way better than how much she can flaunt whatever she has."

"Well, you're the only one who sees it that way."

He shrugged. "Blame my senior vision, but things won't always be like that once you're out of high school."

"Maybe."

"So, what does Mia think you're doing?"

"That was a tad more difficult. I had to convince her I had a serious project to do and that it was due tomorrow."

He chuckled. "Well, I doubt she would pick at that. She doesn't have any reason not to believe you. Plus, I'm quite sure Jasper was picking her up."

She hadn't told me that, but I didn't want to say that. I wasn't telling her about Hunter, she was allowed to have secrets too. Originally, I had thought maybe setting them up together would work, but I didn't want it to backfire and end up as another double date.

Our conversation lulled, but not in a weird way. It didn't seem awkward in the air, just a comfortable silence, like between two people who really knew each other and didn't have to have small talk if they didn't need to. In reality, we did know each other, so I guessed that made sense.

Hunter pulled off the highway and into a large shopping complex. I surveyed the stores trying to tell where we were, but I had no idea. I didn't leave town much and it wasn't like I could drive yet.

However, when Hunter finally stopped the car, we were parked next to a Dave and Buster's which didn't need any explanation. I at least knew what that was.

Hunter shifted his weight uncomfortably with his hands in his jeans' pockets. "I thought maybe somewhere out of town was a better move than hoping to not run into someone?"

"That was a smart bet. It's hard to have privacy at home."

He nodded.

Normally, I would have questioned if he was embarrassed being seen with me, but I knew that was silly. We didn't want Mia to know about anything and staying invisible in town was nearly impossible. Not to mention, Hunter was a well-recognized part of our town as a starting basketball player.

We walked toward the front doors and Hunter held the door open for me, then followed me inside. Inside the noise from the game room was immediate. There were fewer people than I had expected, but still enough to make it loud.

"I think we have to get a card to load points on and then we can play games." He pointed to a desk in the center of the chaos and led us toward the person who waited behind the counter.

I fiddled with my braid as he paid for a card and loaded it with points to play the games. My stomach flopped from all the nervous energy that coursed through my body. I had forgotten he might want to pay. We hadn't discussed who would pay for stuff on our dates and I had to admit, I hated not knowing if I should try to pay or just let him, or if I let him after I argued it a bit.

This was something I would have asked Mia, but I couldn't without telling her who the date was with and that I lied to her.

If he had expected me to pay, his expression didn't show it. He smiled as he turned around. "What do you want to play first?"

I shrugged. "I've never actually been inside a Dave and Buster's before. I've only seen the ads on TV."

"Me neither."

"Oh."

He chuckled. "But they're all supposed to be like carnival games, so the question is are you feeling lucky?"

Of course, I felt lucky to be on a date with him, but I had no idea which game to pick. I twirled slowly to survey the games I could see, and which ones didn't seem too bad. At the back to the right, was a row of Skee ball. That was at least a game I had played before.

Hunter's eyes followed mine and he smirked when he saw what my gaze had landed on. "Skee ball?"

"Yeah, why not?"

"You do remember that one summer ...?"

I did remember. It had poured in Outer Banks for so many days we had all gotten restless. The Baylors decided to take us to an arcade to play games for as long as we had tokens. Most of the games had been rigged, eating our tokens but rarely giving us any tickets or prizes. So, we settled on the Skee ball at the side of the arcade.

The three of us had played for hours, until Mr. and Mrs. Baylor peeled us away from the arcade. Hunter had won most games, but he still took the time to teach us how to play too.

"When that's all we played in the arcade, and you won? Yes, but Skee ball is still fun."

"That it is," he said, then gestured toward the game.

I lead us over to that side before someone else stole the machine. Luckily, no one did.

Hunter swiped our card in two machines. We played side by side. He threw the first ball, and of course he landed right in the middle, racking up points.

My first shot was not so lucky. I decided I would have to distract him if I wanted to beat his score. "So, won't your friends think you're ditching them?"

Hunter's gaze stayed steady on his game. "Nah. Some have

girlfriends and others have jobs. Most are pretty busy during the week."

"Gotcha, I forget it must be different once you can drive. Endless possibilities."

He chuckled. "Endless? Only as far as the gas in the tank will take you, but it does give more opportunities, I suppose." He nudged my arm. "Unless you have to chauffeur your baby sister and her friends all the time."

I gasped and feigned hurt. "How rude! We are wonderful passengers."

He laughed. "You are, I suppose."

I elbowed him back.

"So, I hope this isn't too intrusive."

My stomach lurched. That couldn't be good.

"I couldn't help noticing you're left at home a good bit by yourself. Your parents used to be around more. How come they aren't now?"

I launched my last ball and sighed when it only hit the ten-point hole. "They have their research. I guess they assume since I'm older, I don't need as much attention from them. That I can manage on my own. Which, for the record, is true. I don't *need* their attention."

"But you want it."

He didn't say it like he was unsure. He stated it like a fact.

"Yeah, I do. That probably makes me crazy."

"Everyone wants their parent's attention, Allie. Even if they pretend they don't."

I arched a brow. "Even you?"

"Of course." He tossed his remaining ball from hand to hand. "My dad was a college athlete and Mom had a four-point grade point average. They don't say it or make me feel pressure, but I have pressure on myself to do well like they did." He tossed the ball and once again landed perfectly in the middle.

I didn't even want to see his final score. The points kept going up and up on the screen. "Is that why you and Mia are so competitive?"

"Maybe. I can't really explain it for her, but I like to do well. It makes me happy and proud of my accomplishments."

"Doesn't that get tiring always having to do the best, though?"

"I suppose, but I guess because it comes from inside, I look at it more as always doing my best and if my best is *the* best then that's a bonus."

"I hadn't thought of it that way."

He shrugged. "I realize I have opportunities many people don't, so I don't want to squander it. But sometimes it can be hard to forget that winning isn't always the sure sign of success. Even if you beat everyone else, doesn't mean you always did your best."

I scrunched my nose. "I don't think that's how Mia sees it at all."

He chuckled. "Probably not, but it probably changes things not being the oldest."

He had a point. Mia complained about Hunter being a *golden child* all the time. I mean even with stupid things he won. If she had been older, maybe the pressure wouldn't have been as apparent for her.

He swiped the card on both our machines again and we waited for the balls to roll down before we could start.

"How was the book you bought by that OBX author?"

I tilted my head to the side. "You remembered that?"

"Of course. You tried for like five minutes to get that book."

I giggled. "Great. I'm sure I looked ridiculous then."

His expression shifted like it did before he kissed me the first time, sending my stomach on a roller coaster. "No, you looked cute." He leaned in close and kissed my lips briefly, before throwing his first ball.

My tummy fluttered with anticipation. Why was he such a good kisser? I couldn't think straight when he did that.

"The book was good. I finished reading it in the car on the way home."

He chuckled. "Of course, you did."

"Well, what about you? You were in that bookstore too. What'd you end up buying?"

"Just some things for school."

I stared at him in disbelief. I knew him and he was not in there for school.

He glanced at my expression and smirked. "Don't believe me?"

"Of course not. It's not the truth."

"Well, if you must know, I was looking for more John Steinbeck books. We read him in English, and I wanted to see what else he wrote."

"*Of Mice and Men*, right?"

He nodded.

"That's cool. Wasn't my favorite genre, but I thought he wrote the novel well."

I focused on the next three throws of our Skee ball game. Unfortunately, I was not so lucky today. When the points were added to our card, we moved around to survey the other games available. As soon as I saw the basketball hoops and no one around, I knew he would suggest it before he even opened his mouth.

I walked ahead of him and toward the baskets. When I faced him, he appeared amused.

"Am I that predictable?" he asked.

I giggled. "Well, it is your favorite sport. Obviously, I figured you'd want to play."

"You'd be right. It's been a while since we've all played together. You any good still?"

"I guess you'll have to wait and see."

His eyes widened, then he swiped the card into the machine. This was already a two-player machine, so we had to swipe it twice for us to play.

The machine counted down and we waited for it to say play before we started shooting any ball that we could reach.

My first shot went in, but the next two bounded off the basket. I wasn't exactly horrible at it, but I wasn't as good as I was with volleyball either. In the final ten seconds, I landed three more baskets for only four total.

I covered my face with my hands, then peeked between my fingers to see how we compared. As to be expected, Hunter had at least doubled my score.

He smiled and then rested his arm around my shoulder as we waited for the points to be added. "Want to eat?"

My stomach gurgled, like it could understand what he said. "Yes."

We walked toward the booths and waited to be seated. I had to admit the date was going well and the butterflies weren't as overwhelming as before we got here. I could get used to this.

Chapter Twenty-Eight

Hunter popped a fry into his mouth. "What are you and Mia doing for Halloween?"

I frowned. "I don't think we've planned anything. Why?"

"I was wondering if you wanted to go to a party with me?"

"A party? How will we be secretive at a party?"

"It's Halloween. We wear costumes."

That was true. If I picked the correct costume, most people would have a hard time knowing who it was, but how would I miss it with Mia? We always did Halloween together. "Maybe." I picked at another tater tot on my plate. "That might work. I'll have to think of something to tell Mia."

I glanced at his expression. Was he worried about someone finding out? If he was he didn't seem that concerned. He still appeared carefree like usual. "What will you tell your friends? Won't they ask who you brought?"

He shrugged. "If they do, I'll tell them to mind their own business."

I giggled. "Because that always works."

"I'm not too worried about them. They don't question me."

"Must be nice to be the leader."

He dipped a fry in ketchup, then chewed. "Not always. It's a lot of pressure to be the leader and have them thrust their expectations on me. I suppose this is an upside that they won't question what I say."

"Well, I'll try to make sure I can come. I've never been to a Halloween party before."

He arched an eyebrow. "Oh really? Then we must go."

"You're not going to try to get me drunk are you?"

He feigned shock. "Of course not." He reached for my hand across the table. "Honestly, Allie. I'm not like that. If you end up uncomfortable at the party, we can go."

The warmth from his hand melted any apprehension I might have had. It would take some doing, but I would go to that party with him. It might be the only chance I had to be around him when he was with his friends.

"Okay."

He smiled and caressed my cheek. "You're so beautiful you know that?"

Heat crawled across my neck and cheeks. I was never any good at taking compliments and clearly, hearing compliments did nothing to resolve my issues. "You're not so bad yourself."

He pretended to toss hair over his shoulder. "Why thank you. Want to play some more games?"

I tidied up my food, stacking the plates on top of each other, then piled any remaining trash on top. When the table was organized, I took his hand as he led us toward the games.

We stopped in front of one of the shooting games and he swiped the card twice for a two-player chance.

I ignored the story behind the game. Most always had some far-fetched explanation of terror and bombing and then

BAM! A post-apocalyptic world. The rules were always the same, only the characters changed.

Hunter glanced at me like he didn't expect me to do much, but little did he know how much I had played games like this growing up.

My dad was all about academics, but every now and then he would take me to an arcade and this kind of game always had three or four machines and were never the most occupied. I hadn't played in a while, but I knew I'd be decent at least.

"Watch the zombies ... they always come back."

I stayed quiet and hid my smirk.

The first wave ran through the building and toward us. Hunter had been almost eaten, but I managed to shoot each of them with a headshot and move us on to the next scene.

Hunter slowly faced me. "You ... damn, that's hot."

I giggled. "What? This?" I asked as I killed three more zombies.

His eyes were wide. "You've clearly played these kinds of games before."

"Yep. My dad used to take me. Just us."

"Aha, that explains it."

I arched an eyebrow. "What girls can't be naturally good at these games?"

He chuckled but didn't take the bait.

We focused on the arena and made it through a few more scenes before both of our characters succumbed to injuries. We didn't receive many points for the card, but I didn't care.

For our final few points, we used it on several random games of chance, some paid off, some didn't.

Hunter pulled out his phone and checked the screen. "Says we have like a thousand points to use in the gift shop."

"That many? Wow."

He blew on his nails, then rubbed it on his shirt. "I am a pro gamer."

I giggled and nudged his arm. "You are *so* competitive."

"Yeah, you like it."

"Maybe," I said as I hid my expression. I did enjoy his competitiveness. It always kept things interesting, even if he went a little too far. "Although, I *did* beat you at Monopoly."

"Oh, you didn't just say that."

I stood straighter. "Oh, but I did and it's true."

He squinted his eyes and pretended to glare. "I'll remember that little comment."

We squished past a few young kids and surveyed the options for prizes. There were shelves of massive size candies, some board games, shot glasses, mugs, and other items with Dave and Buster's logo and then around the top were the large stuffed animals.

Hunter reached up and grabbed the Panda bear that costed exactly 1,000 points. "This is for you."

"Really?"

He nodded and shoved his hand in his pocket.

"You don't want to spend it on several things? Like the games or candy?"

"Nah. I know how much you like pandas."

"How's that?"

He glared at me like I was an alien. "I *have* spent a decent amount of time around you over the years, Allie. I'm not totally oblivious."

"Fair point." I squished the panda in my arms. "Thank you."

He smiled as we walked to the counter to have the points subtracted from the card.

I carried the panda out to his car and shoved it on my lap once I buckled up. The panda was soft and fluffy. "Today was fun."

He smiled and started the car. "I thought so, too." He squeezed my knee, then drove toward the highway.

* * *

After our date, Hunter had dropped me off at home and I had to admit, my head had spun. Later in the week, I tried to pull it together around Mia and thankfully she didn't seem to notice. The timing was perfect with things heating up between her and Jasper. She ended up spending more time with him than with me anyway, which meant I could fill it with moments with Hunter.

Mia sat at the little vanity in her room. "So ... what are we doing for Halloween?"

My stomach sank. I still hadn't figured out something to tell her and Halloween was officially in a week. "I don't know. Why?"

Mia wriggled like she was nervous. "Jasper wants to take me to some haunted house, fright fest type of thing. I know those aren't your style."

How was it possible that the perfect excuse would land itself in my lap?

I crinkled my nose. "Yeah, you know I hate those things."

She twisted her shirt around her finger, crinkling the material. "I know ... which is why I asked."

I inhaled. "You're asking to go with him and hoping I don't care, aren't you?" I mentally crossed my fingers. If she answered yes, then I was off the hook and I didn't even have to try that hard.

She clamped her eyes shut, then peeked one open. "Would you hate me if we didn't spend this Halloween together?"

My insides rejoiced, but I couldn't let her know that. If I hadn't had plans with Hunter, would I have been upset by this? "Well, that's a big ask. Eating candy all alone, handing it out for my parents? I don't know. Seems pretty lame to me."

"I'll make it up to you. We could do a horror movie marathon before then."

"Uh, that is what you'd want too."

Mia giggled. "Right. Well, whatever you want. You name it. We do it."

"Deal."

Mia squealed. "Yay! I can't wait to tell Jasper we can go."

"Then tell him. I'll wait for you downstairs?"

She nodded then placed her cell to her ear.

I was learning that Jasper hated to text, so they chatted on the phone most nights. It was weird. Mia hated to talk on the phone. She hated to text too, but apparently it took the right person to do both and she'd comply.

I headed downstairs to wait for her. She wanted to stream the new season of a crime show that we usually watched, but I hoped to run into Hunter and tell him the news.

The kitchen was devoid of her parents, but Hunter must have heard someone come down the stairs, because a minute later, he stood in the kitchen with me.

He winked. "Fancy seeing you here."

I giggled. "You knew I would be." I peered around the corner eyeing the stairs. "We're set for next weekend."

He moved around the counter, closer to where I stood. "Yeah? How'd you swing it? Yanno, so I don't screw up the plan."

"Didn't have to swing much. She did the hard work. She just asked me if she could cancel because Jasper asked her to one of those haunted house type places for Halloween."

Hunter grimaced. "I mean yay for us, but ugh about her." He shook his head, running his hands through his hair.

"Why don't you like him?"

"Just get a weird vibe from him. That's all."

"Have you told Mia?"

He snorted. "Are you serious? You remember how she is right? She won't listen to me."

He had a point. "Well, good news is we can hang out."

He smiled at that. "Always looking on the bright side." He checked the stairs again. "Do you have your phone on you?"

I nodded and pulled it from my pocket.

He snatched it from my hand.

"Hey."

"Relax." He slid the unlock screen then frowned. "You have to unlock it."

"Tell me why first."

"I was going to put my number in ... but maybe I shouldn't."

I unlocked my phone and opened contacts. "Probably a good idea."

"Of course, it is. I always have good ideas."

"Whatever. Hurry up, would you?" I peered at the stairs. "It won't take her long to tell Jasper she can go. She'll be back any minute."

Hunter entered his number while I grabbed a pack of popcorn for the microwave. Our show marathon needed snacks and it was my duty to prepare them while she was on the phone. If I didn't have it at least started before she came down, she'd wonder what I had been doing.

Hunter slid the phone back toward me on the counter. "All done."

I glanced at the screen and noticed he had texted himself and named himself *hot shot*.

I stifled a giggle. "Hot shot? Are you serious?"

Hunter smirked just as Mia bounded down the stairs. He looked busy on his phone as Mia rounded the corner.

I focused on pouring snacks into bowls for us.

Mia eyed Hunter, but looked at me, practically floating around the kitchen.

I raised an eyebrow at her.

Mia nibbled her bottom lip and mouthed, *I'll tell you later* as she jerked her head toward Hunter.

I nodded and continued to pour. "I have popcorn in the microwave, pretzels, and M&Ms. What else do you want?"

"Nothing. I'll set up the TV," she said as she headed for the sectional.

Hunter winked, then headed upstairs.

A new text scrolled over my screen, *I can't wait for the party. Let's match costumes and get you a mask.*

My insides quivered. How was this real life?

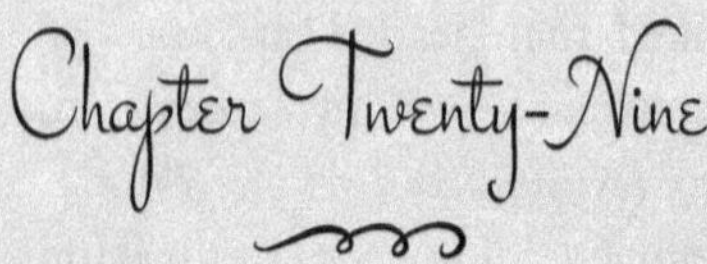

My parents thought I was with Mia and of course, Mia was with Jasper, so I had to get ready in the car. Luckily, we decided that our matching costumes would be sporty skeletons. We had masks that covered the top half of our faces and bodysuits that showed the bones. I pretended to be a volleyball playing skeleton, while Hunter was a basketball playing one. It was cute if I was being honest.

"Are you sure you don't want me to stop?"

The top of the bodysuit should have worked easily over the tank top I was already wearing. "I'll get it, just keep driving."

He chuckled. "You're a cute sporty skeleton."

I rolled my eyes as I tugged the shirt over my head one more time. "I'm not even fully dressed in costume yet. How would you know?"

He winked. "I've got X-Ray vision."

"Ha ha. How long did you work on that joke?"

"A fair amount of time."

"Despite the *time* it took, I'd retire the joke."

Hunter pretended to pout. "I thought it was funny."

A smile tugged at my mouth, but I resisted. If I could get this costume on without so much struggle, I might have agreed with him. I usually liked puns. Finally getting the shirt to cooperate, I shimmied on the pants, which worked much easier. "So, whose party is this?"

"A guy from the basketball team, Marty. We aren't *great* friends, but he's on the team, so I go."

"Anyone else I've met that I should expect to be there?"

"Richard."

My stomach churned. "Anyone else?"

"Not that I know."

"Okay, Richard will be hard enough."

"Maybe, maybe not. He's not exactly the most observant person in the world. The mask and costume should do enough to throw him off."

"What about my voice?"

He chuckled. "Richard, he's a cool dude, but like I said. He's not observant like that. I guarantee he couldn't pick out his mom's voice if you asked him to."

That certainly put a check next to meathead like Mia always said. She would love that tidbit, but I couldn't exactly tell her without making her wonder how I heard Hunter say it.

"Got it." I rubbed my hands over my legs. This was an entirely different situation than going to Dave and Buster's. We had been alone there, with no pressure from our real worlds and lifestyles. This was a huge test. Could I handle his social world? Would I fit in? Would he like me in his world?

He laced his fingers with mine, pulling our hands closer to his body. "Stop worrying."

"Am I always that transparent?"

"Maybe, but I have known you your whole life, Allie. I can tell when something is bothering you."

I scrunched my nose. "That's not fair."

"Why?"

"Because then I can't lie and say I'm fine. You shouldn't know all those quirks about my personality yet. I should be able to be nervous and you not know any different."

"Would you like me to pretend?"

I sighed. "No."

"How about I let you announce your feelings first?"

"Maybe."

He chuckled. "It'll be fine. You'll fit right in and it's a fun way to spend the night."

"Okay, I'll trust you if you really think so."

"I really do." He released my hand as we pulled into a neighborhood. I could practically feel the music's bass from the car as we got out.

"Won't that cause a scene?"

"Tonight? Unlikely. At most, the cops would come for the music being loud. If they don't see anything, they can't do much but say turn it down."

I gulped. I was fine with spending time with him and his friends, but I didn't want to get caught in a situation that broke the law.

"It will be fine. He has parties all the time. Trust me."

"Okay."

Hunter twisted his mask over his head and grabbed the basketball from the backseat before we headed for the front door.

The house was a bi-level, with light yellow siding and white trim. It looked quaint enough but seemed tiny for a party.

Hunter said hello to a few people right at the front door. So far, we hadn't walked by anyone that hadn't noticed who he was. The costume didn't even slow anyone down in recognizing him. Was this really a good idea? What if someone recognized me?

From the outside, I couldn't tell this many people could fit inside Marty's house. The rooms were jam packed with bodies in all sorts of costumes. Some were clearly going for couple costumes and other costumes seemed like they were trying to win the award for the least amount of clothing—sexy nurses, maids, and then one guy in a Tarzan costume.

Hunter leaned close to my ear. "Stay close. I'll lead us to the patio out back and it'll be easier to breathe."

I tried to answer, but my voice was drowned out by the music. So, I leaned into him as he guided us through the house instead.

He had been right. The back patio wasn't as crowded, but still had a decent setup. There was a large folding table with cups stacked on both sides. People were already playing a game of beer pong as we walked by. There were a few other tables that had flip cup games going, but Hunter didn't stop. Instead, he walked up to a blond guy with chestnut brown eyes. They fist bumped, before the guy stood.

"Hunter, my man. You came!" The guy eyed me, clearly trying to figure out who I was.

"Of course, Marty. You know I always show up to your parties." Hunter tucked me into his side, with his arm encircling me around the waist. "You ready for the season? Coach said we might start conditioning next week."

"Coach is a fool. Why would he start so early?"

"Cause he knows guys like you have let yourself *go*. He knows the team needs a kick in the ass to get back in shape."

"I'd like to see *him* run suicides."

"Wouldn't we all." He peered toward me and then back to Marty.

An eerie silence settled over the three of us, especially as another guy sat by Marty. I had no idea if I was supposed to say anything or just stand there. It wasn't like Hunter could introduce me. If he told them my name, word could get out. If he made up a name it made the whole thing feel dirty. What was I supposed to do?

Marty kept glancing at me and then Hunter.

"I'll catch up with you later. Need to get us some drinks. Flip cup later?"

"You're on, man."

Hunter fist bumped Marty again, then we headed to a quieter area. There was an old looking swing set with a kid bench under the fort section.

"That was awkward," I said.

"Marty is a decent teammate, but he has no social skills. If he wasn't a talented player, he'd be a nobody."

"Unlike you?"

"Everyone can't be as charming as I am," he said then winked.

"Is that so, *hot shot*?"

"The hottest." He puffed up his chest, then laughed. "I didn't think about how to introduce you here."

I fiddled with my top. "I was thinking that too. You can't really say my name."

He sighed. "So, what do you want me to do?"

"I guess exactly what you just did. Don't say anything. I'm sure you've brought girls to parties before without introducing them. This would be no different than that."

Hunter's gaze scanned my expression. "I can't figure out what part of that to argue first."

I rose an eyebrow. "What do you mean?"

"If we weren't trying to keep a low profile because of Mia, I would always introduce you. I don't just hide girls away, even at random parties. I don't do that. And I'm not sure how I feel that you think I would."

I shrugged.

Hunter's finger settled under my chin and raised my gaze to meet his. "I'm not sure what you've heard, but you aren't just some *party girl*. I hope you know you mean something to me."

My stomach shimmied. "Okay. You're right. I shouldn't assume."

A hand clapped Hunter on the back, the costume looked like a poor excuse for a pirate. The hat dipped low enough I couldn't see their face, but the voice was clear.

"Hunter, hey bro."

It was Richard. *Crap.*

"Richard. How's it going?"

"Good, good. You know." He peered around Hunter and stared at me. "I didn't know you'd be bringing a date."

"Yeah, you did. I told you."

Richard's face scrunched up. "You did? I don't remember, but you're probably right." He focused on me when he said, "If this guy doesn't treat you right, you come find me. I'm more fun anyway." He winked, but not well. His eyelid looked like it was spasming more than it looked like a wink. He looked around us, then leaned in. "I'm surprised you don't have tagalongs tonight."

Hunter creased his forehead. "Tagalongs?"

"Mia and Allie. They're always with you."

Hunter's eyes widened, but before he could talk, Richard spoke again.

"A shame really."

It was my turn to be surprised.

"Why's that?" Hunter asked.

"Well, your sister is rude, but her friend ... I bet she'd make a hot nurse or something." Then he walked away.

"What in the world?"

Hunter shook his head. "He's drunk, but I'll go hit him if you want."

"Already?"

"He's probably been here awhile."

I moved over to the swings and sat. "Leave him be. I don't care." I kicked the play sand under the swing set. "You know, I heard you two that day."

"What day?"

"In Outer Banks. He pissed off Mia at the pool and she went inside. Then you two were swimming. Richard had started asking about me."

Recognition flitted across Hunter's expression. "Ah, that's why you practically bolted from the chair."

I pushed off the ground, launching my swing into a rhythm. I pumped back and forth until I moved quickly. "It freaked me out. I didn't know what it meant that he considered me and then your answer."

Hunter crossed his arms as he stood in front of me. "Richard can be an idiot when it comes to girls. He doesn't always respect them as well as he should. He sees them as conquests, and I knew you weren't like that."

"Right."

He grabbed the chains on the swing and slowed me down, until I barely moved, and his face was inches from mine. "But that four-wheeler ride with you had my brain on overload for days."

His lips skimmed mine as he steadied his face near me. "I could feel your hands on my body and the warmth soaked in through my shirt. It was intoxicating."

I gulped as his lips moved to my neck.

"You have no idea how much I think about you, Allie Duncan." He said my name almost as a whisper against my skin.

My body tensed and sent tingles to every spot he touched.

"I-I ..." I squeezed my eyes shut and forced myself to say it. "I couldn't think either. Being that close to you practically drowned all my brain cells and short circuited the wiring. If you had asked me my name, I doubt I would have been able to tell you."

"Good," he said as he straightened and outstretched his hand.

"What do you mean good?"

"It's no fun if I'm the only one on the edge."

I giggled. "You're terrible."

"Maybe, but at least I'm honest." He pulled us toward the house and found us sodas. I had figured he would drink something. I had heard things about him, but tonight had me doubting all of that. No one even offered him alcohol. I couldn't tell if that was because he had to drive me back or that was just how he was.

We moved to a back room, close to the music, but not as earsplitting as the front rooms. He found us a seat on a couch, and we sat extremely close to each other. I couldn't tell if he was protecting me or wanted to be close still.

"So, I have to ask you something," I said and then sipped my soda.

"Hmm?" Hunter's gaze settled on my face, not wandering around the room. It was like we were all alone.

"Why do you really come to these?"

"Appearance, I guess."

"But why? You don't have to maintain appearances. You'd manage that all on your own. You're Hunter Baylor."

"That might work now, but we all start somewhere. I wasn't always a senior and star high school basketball star."

"You've always been popular."

He cocked his head to the side. "Says who?"

"Me. I've known you my whole life, too. You've always had so many friends."

He shrugged. "Maybe, but it didn't always feel like that.

Popularity is fickle and the more you try to appease everyone, the lonelier it feels."

"Then why keep appearances?"

"I guess old habits are hard to break. And besides, if it means I get to take you out and spend time with you, then that's a sacrifice worth making."

"I must be good company."

He pulled me closer onto his lap and leaned toward my ear. "The best." Then he shifted and stood. "I'll be right back, okay?"

I nodded and watched as he filtered through the crowd and then disappeared. I pulled out my phone and checked my texts. Nothing from Mia so far so I sent her one, *How's it going?*

The dots appeared and then her message, *Amazing! I'm having so much fun. I so owe you, but he is seriously so sweet, Allie. I* really *like him.*

I smiled. I was glad she was so happy. Hunter might have his feeling, but he probably didn't think anyone should be with his sister, so what did he know really?

I'm glad. You'll have to tell me everything later. I'll let you get back to it.

She sent a thumbs up and nothing more. A moment later, Hunter had returned with a plate of snacks—pretzels, chips, and other random party food.

I smiled when he sat. I only wished I could tell Mia about my night too.

* * *

Hunter and I were in his convertible parked down the street from my house. My parents thought I was with Mia, and I didn't want them to see me get out of his car. That would have made no sense to drive me two seconds down the road when I usually walked.

And if I walked from the Baylors after he parked, I didn't want to risk Mia getting home from being with Jasper and seeing me either. Although if I really thought about it, this spot wasn't a much better idea either, but oh well.

Hunter's thumb circled around the inside of my wrist. "I had a really nice time tonight with you."

"Me too. Plus, now I can say I've gone to a Halloween party."

"That you can. Although I'm sure it was only a matter of time before someone would ask you."

"What do you mean?"

"Mia's right. Many of the upperclassmen guys have noticed you this year."

My eyes widened. "Mm-hmm sure."

Hunter turned my face toward his. "Don't do that."

"Do what?"

"Doubt yourself like that. I hate to see you assume you aren't enough."

I shrugged.

"Seriously, Allie. I feel lucky you are even interested in me."

My stomach twisted. I always thought Hunter wouldn't pay attention to me because of who he was. I didn't know how to accept those words from him. They went against everything I thought I had known about myself.

"That's just hard to process."

"Well, get used to it, because it's true."

The time on the dash read—ten. I sighed. "I should head in. My parents will expect me soon."

Hunter leaned against the back of his seat. "Time to turn into a pumpkin already, huh?"

I giggled. "Read many fairy tales there, hot shot?"

He smirked. "Of course, they're classics. You must read the classics."

"If you say so."

"I do."

I nudged my bag on the floor filled with my costume. "I guess I'll see you Monday."

Hunter leaned over the console toward me, as I did the same.

I stared into those beautiful emerald eyes, before I closed my own and waited until the brush of his lips met mine.

At first, he gave me a light kiss, our lips barely touching. Then his hands roamed through my hair as he pulled us closer together. He intensified the kiss as he nibbled on my bottom lip, his one hand roaming over my arm, sending shivers through my body.

When we pulled away, we had to slow our breathing, with goofy grins plastered over our faces.

"And on that note, I'm getting out of the car."

He nodded, although his eyes gave me another message entirely. "See you, Allie."

I closed the car door before I convinced myself to stay any longer. Getting caught by anyone while making out with Hunter would not help our case.

Once I was on the other sidewalk, he flipped the car around and headed toward his house, waving as he drove by.

I walked the short distance to my front door, the front porch lights were off, but I knew my parents were home.

The door was unlocked, so I pushed it open, then locked it. I kicked off my shoes and went to the main room. Both the main room and kitchen were dark, but I could hear voices down the hallway toward the back of the house.

I shouldn't have even been surprised that they would be holed up in their office.

The door was ajar, so I pushed it open farther, letting the hallway bask in the light from their desk lamps.

"I'm home."

Mom looked up first and smiled, before tilting her head back over the papers in front of her. "How was it? Did you and Mia get lots of candy?"

"Nah. We only went in search of the big candy bars, but they were out before we got there."

"Maybe next year kiddo," Dad said as he rubbed his eyes.

"Did either of you hand out candy?"

"Nope."

I groaned. "You put it in a bowl on the front porch, didn't you?"

"Yes, why?"

"Did the Jones's boy take it all? You remember last year, don't you? He dumped the whole thing in his bag after five minutes."

Mom's eyes widened. "I don't remember that. Maybe that's why there was a lot of honking. We saw it was empty at seven and brought it in and turned off the lights."

"You're lucky no one egged the house."

Dad shrugged. "Oh, well, there's always next year."

I shook my head. "I'll let you two get back to work. I'll be upstairs."

"Okay, honey," Mom said.

But they had already refocused themselves on their work. If I hadn't dismissed myself, their silence would have done it for me soon enough.

I trekked up to my room, dropped my bag after pulling out my phone and flopped onto my bed.

I asked my smart speaker to play music, while I scrolled through social media.

Many of my classmates had posted pictures of their costumes while posed in big groups. Some looked like they had a party of their own, until I came across pictures from Marty's house. I searched every image for traces of Hunter or me, but luckily I found none.

My phone vibrated and then scrolled a text message across my screen, *What are you up to, beautiful?*

My cheeks flamed, regardless of the fact I had just seen Hunter, he texted me.

Sitting in my room. Talking to you.

I wish you were here instead.

Me too.

Do you think you could ever picture spending time with me here without Mia?

Maybe. It's hard to go down that road because Mia doesn't know.

That makes sense, I suppose.

Was he disappointed? I didn't want him to think I didn't want to. I was fully enjoying spending time with him. *So, what would you have normally done tonight?*

Nothing fun. I would have still been at the party maybe, but not having any fun.

I doubt that. You would have figured something out.

Maybe, but it can't compare to tonight.

☺ I shifted off my bed and walked to my clothes drawers. I pulled out a clean pair of pajamas, then went to the bathroom to do my nightly routine. When I finally went back to my bed, I had two messages waiting.

Want to watch a movie together?

You could pick it.

A movie? *How would that work?*

Pick a streaming service and a movie and we can watch it at the same time.

I giggled. I would have never pictured Hunter offering to do something like that, but then again, I didn't picture this either. So, what did I know?

Okay, but what should we watch?

Anything you want.

I sighed. What did I want to watch? I didn't want something sappy and romantic, that would just be awkward. I searched for funny movies, until I landed on *The Proposal.*

What about The Proposal *with Sandra Bullock and Ryan Reynolds?*

I waited for the three dots to tell me he was responding, then he finally answered, *Done.*

Okay, get it ready and then hit play in five minutes.

Deal. And Allie?

Yeah?

Next movie we watch together.

Deal.

I snuggled into my covers and hit play just like we said. We texted back and forth through the movie, mostly our reactions to certain scenes. When the movie finished, we texted goodnight. I didn't think I had ever been that happy in my life.

Chapter Thirty

It was moments like this that I thought the universe had a dry sense of humor. On Monday, my history teacher announced a partner project. And of course, for all the possible projects with all the possible partners, Bennett had to be mine.

Ugh.

We had arranged to meet after school to do the project. Jasper had willingly decided to drive us to Hal's and Mia was only too thrilled to drop us off at the diner and leave us stranded.

Ugh ugh ugh.

"Any ideas on what you want to do for the project?" Bennett asked.

I stared at my notes from class. The project was to create a presentation on a U.S. president and discuss their reforms and legacy.

"Not a clue. You?"

He shrugged. "I'm sure the big ones would be easy."

I scrunched my nose. "Easy, but everyone will do Lincoln, FDR, and Washington. That'll feel so redundant."

"Okay, so who then?"

I tapped the pencil against my chin as I practically burned the images of each president into my retinas. I just wanted to finish this project and get home. "Truman?"

"Sure."

"Okay. Want to split up the sections? Then we can put our information in the google slides and it'll be done sooner."

Bennett smiled. "Trying to get rid of me?"

I nearly knocked my soda over. "What? Of course not."

He chuckled. "I'm kidding. You just seem in a rush."

I exhaled loudly. "I just want the project done. Doing projects on dead presidents isn't my idea of fun."

"Fair enough." He eyed me warily. "I haven't seen you much lately. Everything okay? I know the last time we hung out things didn't exactly go as planned, but are you okay?"

I stifled the urge to cringe at his statement. I knew this would be a lousy night. I had avoided Bennett like the plague after that night, but not because of him, because of Hunter. Things just *worked* for us after that night, and I didn't do much of anything else.

"Yeah, I'm good. Sorry. Just trying to keep up with classes and volleyball. That's all."

"Right. You guys have the championship game this weekend. Are you nervous?"

"Not yet. Ask me that day."

He laughed. "I'd be nervous. So much pressure."

I shrugged. "Yes, but it's a team thing. Either we'll play like we should and gel or we'll blow it. Can't change the energy that will or won't happen."

Bennett's eyes widened. "Wow. I think you might be an alien."

I cocked my head to the side. "Is that a compliment? Aliens are ... uh bad?"

"Sorry. What I meant is I think you're the only person I

know who would see things like that. I guess I just meant it in the sense that it's a foreign idea, not that you're weird."

"Thanks." I dipped my head to focus on the textbook in front of me. At least we had raided as many books as we could find on presidents at school before heading to Hal's. If I had any say in the timing of this project, then we would be done in an hour, maybe two if we had trouble finding something.

My phone buzzed against the book. "Sorry," I said as I tried to silence the phone, but I still managed to catch the screen. I had a new text from Hunter, *What are you up to? Mia just got home and you're not with her. I hate that Jasper offered to drive you all.*

I smiled, then checked to see if Bennett was paying attention before I texted back.

Partner project for school.

I hate those. Good partner?

I guess. It's ... Bennett.

Bennett, hmm. Is he behaving?

I bit my lip to keep my laugh from escaping. If I laughed there was no way Bennett would miss that.

We're just doing a project. We're reading a textbook right now.

Partner projects can get flirty. There could be sideways glances and footsy under the table.

I sent him an emoji of me rolling my eyes followed by, *Hunter, relax. You're the one I want.*

He sent me a *Grease* gif. I smirked and shoved the phone in my pocket. The phone continued to buzz but I ignored it as I stared at the words on the page. I was supposed to be finding the major reforms Truman had in his presidency, but instead of seeing words like bills and management, I could only hear the song from *Grease* and see that smirk Hunter liked to make when he thought he was so clever.

Buzz. Buzz. Buzz.

My self-control was crumbling. After the tenth buzz, I broke. I scrolled through the messages.

What's he wearing?

What are you *wearing?*

Is he still doing the sad puppy dog look to hook you in?

How's it going?

I aced sophomore year history. I could help. I could be your expert source.

I shook my head. He was relentless. I peeked at Bennett. His gaze stayed focused on his textbook.

Would you stop? I'm turning my phone on silent. The longer this project takes, the longer I'll be with him. Maaybe we could meet on the trails later, but I must finish this first.

Fine. Text me when you leave.

I turned the switch to silent, then shoved the phone back in my pocket. No more distractions.

Although, it was pretty cute that he was jealous about Bennett. Even if he was just pretending, it sounded like he was a little worried.

"Okay, I typed the early life slide and just finished the interesting facts slide. Want to check them real fast?"

I scrolled to his slides and read. "Looks good. Thanks."

"Of course. We're partners."

I smiled. I guess I should have been thankful he was interested in even doing his half of the project. Most partners I usually had did nothing and I had to pull it all off and then carry them through the presentation. Help was a welcome change.

"I'm just used to having no show partners. I always get stuck with a free loader."

He laughed. "Me too." He glanced at me then looked away. "You know, I could be a good partner for more than just projects."

My eyes widened and my jaw slackened. Did he just say what I thought he said?

He ran a hand through his hair. "Wow, Allie. I'm sorry. I didn't mean for that to come out the way it did. I figured I would do this differently. I uh ... well, I like you. I think you might like me a little too. And I just thought maybe we could date and be a couple."

My mouth gaped open. "Bennett ..."

"I know it was sudden and that the double date didn't really go well. But you're a special girl. I can't stop thinking about you."

"Bennett, I think you're cool, but I'm not sure we should date." My heart sunk as I watched his hopeful expression crumble.

"Right, yeah, of course. I'm sorry."

"Bennett, I'm—"

"No. It's fine. Seriously. I'll be right back. Need to head to the restroom." He stood and walked away.

I let my head relax on the table after he walked away.

Stupid. Stupid. Stupid.

I should have been more sensitive, but I had no idea he would ask me that. I meant what I said. He was cool, but Hunter was the only one I wanted to focus on. He was like having the whole ice cream cake, and Bennett was only a few pieces. There was no comparison.

He had disappeared for at least ten minutes.

I used the time to finish most of my slides and text my mom. She agreed to pick me up in ten minutes and that was my escape. I could finish the remaining sections at home and then all we had to do was practice our information separately. It would be fine.

When he sat, his body language seemed to shift. He didn't seem as open and carefree as before.

I hated that I could have hurt him, but I couldn't string

him along when I knew he had no chance if Hunter was in the picture.

"Bennett, my mom will be here soon to pick me up. I thought maybe we could practice separately, and I'll have the remaining slides done tonight. Does that work?"

"Yeah, sure."

I tried to reach out, but he withdrew his hand from the table. "I'm sorry."

"No worries. Honestly."

I glanced at his expression one more time, then closed my books and put them in my bag. I stood, left some cash on the table, then headed for the front door to wait outside. I felt horrible. Rejecting someone who was a decent person felt like the worst thing in the world.

The path was somewhat of a blur. I couldn't get the image of Bennett's expression out of my head. He was crushed and I caused that. I sighed sending my breath floating away in front of me as it met the colder air.

Suddenly arms wrapped around me and lips kissed my cheek. "There you are."

I smiled weakly. "I didn't want to wait by the road. Anyone could see."

Hunter's gaze scanned my expression. "What's wrong? Did something happen with Bennett?"

"Kind of."

"What'd he do? I'll knock him out if he hurt you. I don't care who finds out."

"Hang on. No need for violence. He didn't hurt me. I hurt him."

Hunter's eyebrows rose.

"He asked if we could be a couple. I turned him down,

obviously, but he looked so hurt."

"Oh. He'll get over it, Allie."

"You didn't see his expression."

"Do you regret turning him down? It wouldn't be a relationship you'd have to hide."

I held Hunter's arms closer to my body. "No. I told you before. I like you. I just feel so bad. He didn't take it well."

"That's understandable. You're a special girl, but you did the right thing if he's not what you want."

I sighed. "I wish I could get his expression scrubbed from my memory."

Hunter spun me around to face him. "Well, maybe I can help with that." He lowered his head so our lips could almost touch. Then he pulled me toward his body as the space between our mouths closed.

His kiss was full of want and need. It was like no matter how long our bodies stayed entwined, and our lips touched, we weren't close enough. His arms held me close as we made out on the trail, smack dab in the middle.

We broke apart when a biker rang their bell. *Oops.*

I leaned my head on his shoulder as we walked forward. "That helped a little."

"Only a little? Hmm."

I giggled and raced toward our bench. He, of course, beat me, but I didn't care. We sat; my legs rested over his.

"I was so stupid the last time we sat here," he said.

"Why?"

"Because I should have asked you out instead of asking about Brittany."

I shrugged. "Everything happens for a reason. Maybe that night needed to happen to force us to be honest about our feelings. Without it, who knows what'd we still would be doing."

"Maybe, but I was still stupid."

I giggled. "It's in the past ... but yes you were."

Hunter tickled my side. "I'll remember that."

I burst into a fit of giggles. I was too ticklish for my own good and Hunter knew it, which was completely an illegal move. "That's cheating, you know."

"Nope. Fair game."

I glared and crossed my arms.

"So, I want to come to the championship game to watch you play."

My eyes widened. "Won't that look a little suspicious?"

"Nope. I always drive you two to practice and I've been to your games, too."

"Yeah, but you don't pay attention when you're there."

"I do pay attention, just not as much as other people."

"AKA, not paying attention."

"Okay, so I pay attention. I look like a good big brother. No one will ask any questions when my little sister is on the team."

"Fine. But, Hunter, you must be careful. Mia knows the difference. You can't be cheering and all."

"And miss a chance to show school spirit?"

I rolled my eyes and leaned on him. "You know what I'm saying. We can't tell her yet and I don't want her to find out some random way. That would be the absolute *worst*-case scenario."

"I promise. Okay? I don't want to jeopardize this either."

"Then I'll see you there."

"I'll be the one driving," he said and then winked.

We sat on the bench, my legs over his lap for a long time, until the cold became too much to bear. We walked together as far as we could, then separated before hitting the neighborhood road. He gave me a quick kiss and headed toward his house. I couldn't wait for us to be together in broad daylight with no masks and no lying.

Chapter Thirty-One

Despite what I said to Bennett, I was so nervous for the game. This was Sammie's last chance to play for school and in some ways, she was passing the torch to me. It was weird to know that at the end of the game today, I would be finished volleyball for the season.

I hated waiting until the next year, but volleyball was only for a season. It had to end sometime.

Mia nudged my arm. "You ready?"

I nodded as I slipped my sweatpants over my spandex. It was November and far too cold to just go outside in my uniform. "Are you?"

She smirked. "Always."

I grabbed my bag and hoodie and followed her out of her room and down the stairs. My stomach shimmied as I knew I would see Hunter. Just like he said, he agreed to drive us to the championship game and Mia hadn't even batted an eye.

I was glad he had been right because I wanted to see him today, but he would be insufferable knowing he had been right. Another trait he shared with his sister.

At the bottom of the stairs, Hunter stood, holding two

bottles of water. "You two ready? We must leave now if you want to make it in time."

"We'll be fine," Mia said.

Hunter rolled his eyes. "I'll be in the car."

I waited for Mia as she grabbed a granola bar and then we headed outside. She took a big bite. "So, you never told me how it went with Bennett and your project you had to do together."

I grimaced. I hadn't expected her to ask me about that already. "It was a project," I said as I opened the car door and hopped in.

She snorted. "Just a project? Now you really have to tell me. There's no way that nothing happened as you worked on that project."

Hunter's gaze met mine in the rearview mirror, then shifted to the road. He already knew what had happened, but he had to pretend he had no idea and that he didn't care.

"Mia, just drop it. We had to complete a presentation and find research. Most of the time I typed on my laptop, and he typed on his. Or we looked for information in our separate books."

"I can't drop it. I know something happened because Jasper said Bennett hasn't been the same since."

I clenched my hand. "Well, if you know so much then you already know what happened."

Mia's face scrunched. "I just wanted to know what to expect today when we saw them."

"I highly doubt he's coming."

"Says who? He practically slobbers over your attention. Of course, he's coming."

After his face crumpled when I rejected him, I wouldn't be surprised if he stayed far away from me for forever.

My eyes pleaded with Hunter.

He coughed. "I must focus on the road. Can you please stop arguing about some boy and help me navigate?"

I knew he did that for me because I was uncomfortable, but it worked. Mia shifted her gaze to the phone giving us directions and helped call out the turns and exits on the highway.

We arrived at the gym, and I released the tension my muscles held. I didn't like being trapped in the car with all the secrets floating around that my best friend didn't know. It was exhausting and quite frankly made me *almost* want to stop it.

The strap of my bag creased into my skin, leaving bumpy ridges. I tossed it over my shoulder and made a beeline for the gymnasium. Mia stood waiting at Hunter's car for Jasper, but I didn't want to wait another second. The sooner I entered the gymnasium, put my knee pads on and my sneakers, the sooner my head could focus on the game and not on the boy drama.

When I opened the doors, the noise assaulted my senses. I could hear whistles, cheers, shouting, and volleyballs smacking the floors as they were spiked or served to the other side. Two games were already in progress on the far ends of the gymnasium. I knew it was bigger than our high school gym, but I had no idea it would be so busy. Everyone in our county and a few of the surrounding counties came to this gymnasium for their championship games.

Someone gasped from behind. I turned to come face to face with Brittany—someone high on my list of people I didn't want to see yet.

"This place is huge," she said.

My jaw slackened. She hadn't talked to me about anything since homecoming. "Yeah it is."

Her expression registered who she had said that to and I could tell the second she realized I was the enemy. Her face scrunched up like she had just sucked on a lemon, then she pushed past me toward our bench.

"She doesn't know how to let things go does she?" Hunter asked.

I startled. "When did you get in here?"

"Soon enough to see that exchange."

I shrugged. "It happens."

"Well, I'm tired of her being so dramatic just because she didn't get her way with me. I'm not some prize to be won and then lauded over people. Things would have gone south with or without you."

I giggled. "Is that so? You'd have realized she was horrible eventually?"

"Maybe later than I'd like to admit."

Mia burst through the doors, Jasper dangling on her arm.

Hunter caught sight of them and rolled his eyes. He moved toward the bleachers, leaving me alone just as Bennett strolled through the doors too.

My stomach tried to leap from my body.

His gaze settled on my face, then immediately dropped to his feet.

Mia nudged my arm. "Look who I found in the parking lot." She looked past me; her eyes widened. "Woah. Did you know there'd be this many games happening at once?"

"Nope. Crazy right?"

She nodded.

"At least the noise will drown out the nerves."

"For you maybe."

"Hello, Allie," Jasper said as he dipped his hat. Then he leaned close to Mia's ear to whisper something.

She giggled and kissed his cheek. Her arm slipped from his, then went around mine. "Let's go get ready." She waved to Bennett and Jasper as she practically drug me toward our team.

Bennett stayed silent. He didn't smile, didn't wave, didn't

do anything but pretend that a gymnasium floor was more interesting than an actual human being.

Our team was huddled on the right side of the closest court. Large curtains partitioned the different sections, but I could still see through at certain intersections. This was by far the largest game I had played in this big of a place. I had already counted three courts, but my view was blocked from the remaining ones. There could easily have been two more.

Our coach called us into a huddle to give us a pep talk before we started warmups. We just had to be better than the other team more times. It sounded simple, but this was the championship game. This wasn't playoffs. The other team was the best team in their matchups. We needed to expect anything to happen today.

* * *

Mia leaned close in the huddle. The other team had just called a timeout during the second game. We were up by two points, twenty to eighteen. If we won this game, we won the championship.

I peered over the huddle toward the bleachers. Jasper leaned forward, eyes on Mia. Bennett's posture was the opposite, he looked as disengaged from the game as he could be.

Hunter's posture mirrored Jasper. He wouldn't admit it, but he looked nervous.

Mia's hand settled onto my shoulder and squeezed.

I smiled back.

We did our cheer and headed back to the court. I was in with Brittany and Mia. Brittany was surprisingly making things easy. If I hadn't known any better she almost seemed friendly, but there was no way that could last long—not toward me anyway.

I scooted close to Brittany. "The left back position is wide open every time. If I get a chance to set you. Target that spot."

Brittany eyed the position and then readied her stance for the serve.

I was a setter; it was my job to help the rest of my team. If I didn't point out a chance for us to score a point, then I wasn't doing my job. And no matter how much I couldn't stand Brittany, I wanted to be the best player I could be.

Mia's eyes widened as I walked to my place before the referee blew the whistle.

I shrugged in response.

The whistle blew and the other's team server readied her serving stance. This particular player liked to slap the ball once, bounce twice, then serve it over the net. I was in the back middle, and it was my job to receive the ball, pass to the front, then move to be setter once the ball was in the clear. It was the busiest position for me because I had to constantly stay vigilant for the ball. If I moved before I should, I left a hole.

The serve crested over the net, landing perfectly in front of me. I moved forward, bumped the ball to the front line, and Kayla, another senior, spiked it over the net. Then I moved to the front row as the secondary setter moved to the outside position.

The other team set up their bump, set, and spike returning it to our backline. Mia was quicker. She lofted the ball to give me plenty of time to get under it and set it over to Brittany's position.

I inhaled and held, hoping she would be in place to spike the ball in their hole.

Brittany jumped and spiked the ball in a perfect diagonal to their back corner. The sound of the ball smashing into the floor, ricocheted off the curtain and back to our court.

Our team did a little cheer and rotated. It was our serve

again and our best server was up. Four more points and the championship was ours.

The first serve floated in the air toward their backline and hit the floor before anyone put hands on it. Twenty-two to eighteen.

I crouched for the second serve, readying myself to move to the front line if the ball made it back from the other team. This time the serve flew over the net and then seemingly dropped right on the other side. The other team was caught too far back after the first serve. Twenty-three to eighteen.

I touched the floor preparing my body to launch as our team served the ball, rocketing it over to their side. This time their libero snagged the dig, but no one had followed her for the second hit, letting it hit the floor. Twenty-four to eighteen.

My heart kicked up in my chest. This was game point. If we earned this point, we were the champions. I snuck a glance toward the bleachers, finding those emerald eyes. Hunter's face was a carefree grin. Our gazes met and he winked.

I forced my gaze back toward the other side as my teammate served the ball. The force of her hand on the ball made a loud thwack. The other team tried to shift to follow it. One person off their back line bumped it up toward the setter. She pushed the set too far out and her spiker missed as she wound up.

We won!

The referee blew the whistle as Mia's body collided with mine. We jumped up and down, then moved toward the middle to shake hands with the other team. My cheeks felt sore from the persistent smile that didn't dare to leave my face. This win felt better than anything we won on the freshmen team.

Our coach shouted our praise and told us to be ready to celebrate on Monday instead of practice, then he dismissed us. I pulled my sweats and other shoes on as I tried to slow my heart rate. We kept wishing each other warm smiles and huge hugs and high fives.

Mia jogged over toward me with only her knee pads down by her ankles and her good sneakers slid off and replaced by big comfy slippers. "I'm going up to see Jasper a minute. Want to come with me to say something to Bennett?"

I shook my head. "Go ahead. I'll wait for you by the car. I'll let Hunter know you'll be out soon."

She tapped my arm and sprinted up the bleachers to where he stood waiting for her.

I watched as he enveloped her in a huge hug and spun her around. They looked so cute together. I was happy for her.

I slunk out the gymnasium doors and headed for Hunter's car.

Hands snuck around my waist and pulled me close. I spun around. "What are you thinking?"

Hunter chuckled. "Relax. Everyone is in there basking in the glory of your team. No one but *you* has really left the gym."

I resisted the tug of a smile and made my gaze grave. "If someone saw you, we would be screwed."

"Well, they didn't, and I want to congratulate my girl on her team's win."

"*Your* girl, huh?"

"I like the sound of it. Don't you?"

My lips pulled to a smile. I couldn't resist that. "Yes. So, what does that mean?"

"It means I think you should be my official girlfriend."

"And what about Mia?"

"We'll figure that out. Together."

I backed into his car and leaned against it as he stood in front of me. He surveyed the parking lot and then lowered his head as his lips were feathery light on mine.

I relished our first kiss as an official couple, then reality set in. I placed my hand on his chest and scanned the lot. Just because I couldn't see anyone didn't mean they couldn't see us. "Okay, but no more of that until we're alone."

"But—"

"And don't say we are alone. We're in the middle of a parking lot. Anyone could walk out of those doors at any minute and catch us. Including your sister. Promise me you won't tell her until we decide how to."

He raised his hands, palm out. "Okay. I promise."

"Good."

"Can I at least tell you how hot you looked out there?"

I giggled. "Maybe, but not too loud."

"Oh." He pretended to pout, then a mischievous grin spread across his face. "So, I can't shout it?" He cupped his hands around his mouth and inhaled deeply.

I mushed his hands together with mine. "Don't you dare, Hunter Baylor."

"Or what?"

"Or ... I don't know, but I'll make you regret it."

He chuckled. "I'd like to see that."

I shook my head. "Let's just get in the car."

"Okay."

"Mia will be out soon by the way. She had to say something to Jasper before she left."

Hunter rolled his eyes as he pulled his seat up for me to crawl in the back and then pulled it back down to sit. He wiggled his eyebrows at me from the rearview mirror. "So, when can I shout it?"

I huffed dramatically, even though I was happy he was excited to share it with everyone. "I don't know yet. We need a plan."

"A plan, got it."

"I'll think of something. Maybe after she has a date with

Jasper or something. She needs to be in a good mood. And maybe I should tell her first."

"Are you sure?"

"No, but I'll think on it."

He started the engine.

I looked out the back window toward the doors and watched as Mia walked out arm and arm with Jasper. Bennett was nowhere near them. He must have left before they did or was in the gym still. The guilt still laid heavy in my stomach, like rocks that slowly sunk to the bottom of the river.

Oh, well. It was over. I needed to remember I couldn't change the past. Instead, I needed to figure out the plan to tell Mia. I didn't want to waste time if Hunter wanted to be a couple. I just didn't know how to tell her. It had to be me, but would she understand even if I was the one to tell her?

I wasn't sure, but I had no choice but to try if I wanted to be with him.

Chapter Thirty-Two

At school on Monday, everyone came out of the woodwork to give our team high fives and congratulations. People I didn't even know knew my name said hello and great job. It felt nice, but also strange to have such recognition. Our team's party instead of the practice had also been fun. We had pizza and drank sodas, then played a scrimmage amongst each other. We had laughed so hard, it made our stomachs cramp from all the activity.

The next day, people still congratulated us, but not as much. Hunter and I had walked past each other several times that day. It was like he had decided to take every chance to go to his locker and walk in the direction he knew I would be. If he was alone and so was I, he would brush my hand or arm as he passed. If we weren't alone, he would make eye contact and give me one of those smiles that melted my insides all the way to my toes.

The final bell rang, releasing me from my last class. I pushed my way through the hallway toward my locker one final time. What I hadn't expected was for Mia *and* Brittany to be waiting for me.

I glanced toward Hunter's locker, but it was clear. He had either already stopped or hadn't made it there yet. I would see him soon enough on the way back to their house anyway, so it wasn't a big deal.

I glanced at Mia and tried to make eye contact with her enough to ask her with my eyes why Brittany was there, but she wasn't facing me head on to see.

"Hey," I said as I turned the dial on my locker.

"Oh good, I ran into both of you at the same time," Brittany said.

I resisted the urge to roll my eyes. As if she hadn't intended to run into us both. It was my locker, who did she expect to see?

"What for?" Mia asked.

I smiled and hid my face as I looked inside to grab my books.

"I wanted to let you both know I'm having a party Friday for our championship win. I thought it would be fun to celebrate with the team. You can bring whomever you want."

How weird that she was inviting us to a party. Although I supposed she had to since it was for the team. How would it look if she didn't?

"Oh, that's so cool. Thanks, Brittany," Mia said. "I'll bring my boyfriend, Jasper."

"Cool. Allie, you can bring your boyfriend too."

My stomach lurched. *My what?*

Mia slapped my arm. "You're boyfriend? Bennett asked you out and you didn't tell me?" She squealed. "This will be so much fun."

Words wouldn't escape my mouth. Why did Brittany think I had a boyfriend? And how was I supposed to tell Mia no he hadn't when he had, and I had told him no?

Brittany settled Mia's jumps with her arms. "Bennett? No. Allie's boyfriend is …"

Time froze. It literally froze in that second. My stomach stopped digesting. My lungs stopped breathing. And my heart stopped pumping blood through my veins, because there was no way she would say ...

"Hunter."

Mia's face contorted in confusion. "Hunter?" She burst out laughing. "Brittany, did you get hit with a volleyball? Allie isn't dating Hunter."

Brittany's carefree and kind expression turned icy. So, this was her plan all along.

"Oh no? The kiss at the end of the championship game looked pretty convincing to me."

My body unfroze and everything shifted. It was like someone had bought an industrial washing machine, threw me in, and turned it on high spin. My head was fuzzy, and the floor seemed to tilt.

Mia's jaw slackened as she looked to me to deny what Brittany said, but words wouldn't come. "I-I ..."

"They looked so cozy. It makes sense, what with him running after her at homecoming. That's like a whole month of dating right? How sweet."

Mia's expression hardened. "Brittany, I don't know what you *think* you know, but Allie isn't dating my brother. Now we have to go, see you at the party."

Mia turned her body to nudge Brittany away. She closed my locker door and shoved me down the hallway. I didn't know that I wanted any part of the next conversation.

Mia glanced over her shoulder.

I couldn't. I didn't want to know if Brittany was there or not. How could I have thought sneaking around behind my best friend was a good idea? I was supposed to be the one to tell her. Not *Brittany*. Of all people this was the worst scenario.

"She's gone." She stopped walking and gazed at my face.

I averted my eyes to my feet. If I looked at her, she would know. And if she knew, she would get angry. I knew how Mia was. She was my best friend. If I didn't look at her, I could contain my feelings, push them down, and convince her later when I had time to process everything.

But that wasn't possible.

She pulled my chin up to face her. "What was Brittany talking about, Allie?"

Tears threatened to spill from my eyes. Her face became blurry as they tipped to the edge, but not quite spilling over.

"It's true. She's telling the truth. You're dating my brother!" Her last sentence was a shout. Other students turned in the hallway. We were drawing attention.

She zipped up her jacket, turned toward the exit and sped walked as she shoved her hands in her pockets.

My feet stalled and then carried me toward her. I had to get to her. To explain. I had to tell her it wasn't as bad as Brittany made it sound. I had to fix this.

Mia's short legs carried her quickly, but my stride was slightly larger, and my pace was panicked.

I could see Hunter leaned against his car waiting for us as he scrolled his phone.

Mia wasn't slowing down.

Hunter looked from Mia to me and back again. I could tell he was trying to understand the mood even from where I stood.

"Mia!" I shouted, but she didn't bother to turn around.

Hunter met my gaze, and I shook my head. His expression cleared and recognition slid over his features as he guessed what had happened.

I made it to Mia before she got in the front seat. I grabbed her arm grasping at the red wool coat.

She threw me off. "Don't touch me!"

"Mia, please. Can we talk about this?"

Hunter moved closer, but I shook my head. I didn't want her to go off more.

"Now you want to talk? *Now?*" She wiped a gloved hand down her face. "You had a whole month to talk, Allie. At least according to Brittany."

Hunter winced and clamped his mouth shut.

"It's not what Brittany thinks."

"No? So, tell me, Allie. Have you kissed Hunter? Have you gone on dates? Snuck around without telling me?"

I twisted the zipper on my coat, the tears teetered dangerously close to spilling out. "I-We ..."

"We!" she shouted. "There's a we? Damnit, Allie. How long have *we* been friends?"

I cringed as she got louder and more people passed us, gazing at the scene. This was like a bad dream.

"A long time."

"Our whole lives! Our whole lives and you couldn't bother to tell me you had feelings for him. So how much is right? How much does freakin' Brittany know that I don't about my own damn best friend?"

My heart felt like it might break. I couldn't even look at Hunter. "We kissed."

"When?"

I glanced at my feet.

"When?"

"Homecoming."

Mia threw her hands in the air. "Were you even sick? Were you two laughing at me as you snuck around behind my back? Did you come over to spend time with me or see *him*?"

Hunter moved closer. "Mia, it wasn't like that."

Mia glared at her brother. "I don't want to hear anything you have to say right now."

"Mia—"

"Not a damn word, Hunter! Or so help me."

Hunter shut his mouth, but he pleaded with me in his expression. I couldn't look long. I didn't want to see how he felt about this. If I had to take on his feelings too, I might drown under all the weight.

"I wasn't sick, but I left because Brittany said some nasty things to me that night. She told me I was a charity case for you and Hunter, and that Bennett would find out soon enough."

Mia's hardened glare didn't falter.

"I walked home. Hunter had heard her and left to check on me. When we kissed, we both agreed it would be the first and last time."

Mia's icy stare melted a little. "So then how did Brittany see you two kissing this past Saturday if that was it?"

"Because we broke our agreement."

Mia turned and opened the car door.

Hunter stared between us.

I moved closer, but Mia rounded on me. "What do you think you're doing?"

"I ... Today we're supposed to go to your house."

She shook her head. "Not anymore you aren't."

"Mia, you can't be serious," Hunter said.

She stared at him. "You're my brother and *my* ride. Get in the car and let's go home."

"And what about Allie?"

"Not our problem." Mia got in and closed the door.

He looked at me over the top of his car as I stood alone in the middle of the parking lot. He pleaded with me.

I shook my head. "Just go. I can walk."

"But—"

"Just go, Hunter. Before she takes it out on you too. I couldn't handle that."

He looked defeated, then nodded as he climbed in.

I stood there dumbstruck as my whole life just imploded

around me. A mere forty-eight hours ago, my life had been so amazing. I had been so certain we would come up with a plan to tell Mia and then she would adjust. This. This was nowhere on the radar.

His car pulled away and I headed back toward the sidewalk. I didn't know the last time I had walked home, if ever. Thankfully, it wasn't as cold out today.

And honestly, I needed the walk to figure out how the heck things had gone so badly so fast.

Mia had reacted worse than I could have imagined. How would I even date Hunter now? I couldn't date him without her being nuclear level pissed at me. I didn't know if she would ever forgive me. And the worst part was I had no idea how to make it better. I had betrayed her. Lied to her and hid something so important in my life because I couldn't be honest. She was my best friend. I should have done better. I should have stayed away from Hunter—no matter how green and inviting his emerald eyes were.

Chapter Thirty-Three

That night I stared at my phone every single time it vibrated and even when it didn't. If I didn't see Mia's name, I didn't bother to read or respond. I had sent Mia five texts when I had finally gotten home. I sent three messages on different social media accounts, tried to call her and FaceTime her and nothing was answered. Even the messages still only said delivered, instead of read or seen.

It was excruciating.

Hunter had texted a few times checking to see if I was okay, but I couldn't bother answering those either.

I was half tempted to go walk to Mia's house and knock on the front door. It was ridiculous that we lived this close to each other and didn't resolve this now. She had to talk to me. We had been best friends for life, surely this wouldn't end our friendship, right?

A blanket laid over my head until a quick knock rapped from the front door downstairs. I leapt from my bed and ran for the door. Maybe Mia had changed her mind? Maybe she was here to talk.

I opened the door. "Mia, I'm so glad ..." But the person staring back at me wasn't Mia. It was Hunter.

Hunter's face relaxed as he saw me. "Let me in, please?"

I hesitated, but I supposed I knew he deserved some answers. He could have pieced things together, but I owed it to him to let him know we could never be more.

I moved aside as he passed into the house. Once he was far enough out of the way, I shut the door and went to the kitchen for a soda.

"What happened?" he asked.

"Brittany ruined everything."

He moved close to me, but I scooted away from his touch. "She was waiting at my locker with Mia. She wanted to invite us to a championship party on Friday. She said we could invite whomever we wanted to. Mia had said she would take Jasper, then before I could say anything Brittany told me I could take my boyfriend."

Hunter cringed. "Oh man."

"Oh, it gets better. Mia squealed thinking she meant Bennett. Before I could figure out how to say no, Brittany cut her celebration off and told her she was mistaken. That my boyfriend was you. When Mia thought it was a joke, Brittany told her she saw us kissing on Saturday at the game and that it made sense considering you came after me at homecoming."

Hunter eased himself against the kitchen counter. "Shit."

"Yep. Then you pretty much heard the rest."

"I didn't realize it was that bad."

I sipped my soda and stared at the can, even though none of the ingredients registered. "Didn't she ask you anything?"

"No. Mia refused to talk in the car. I tried and she drowned me out with the radio. The louder I got, the louder the music. She practically jumped from the car before we came to a full stop at the house. Then she ran upstairs and locked her room. Her radio went on and she hasn't come down since."

"What's she listening to?"

His brows furrowed. "Why?"

"What was the song?"

"I don't know, Simple Plan?"

"Welcome to my Life?"

He nodded.

Crap, crap, crap. Mia only listened to that when she was murderously angry and upset. That was a bad omen.

Hunter pushed off the counter and reached for my hand, but I pulled away again. "Please, stop doing that."

I turned and headed for the couch. "My parents will be home soon. I don't want to answer any questions about what happened. I think you should go."

"Allie, just wait. We can figure this out."

"I can't wait. Mia is pissed and in case you don't know your own sister, that won't change quickly. She holds grudges like it's an Olympic sport. I refuse to give her more of a reason to maintain that distrust. We can't be together. Maybe if things had changed or gone differently, but this can't happen."

"Because of Mia? Really?"

"I should have known this would be our fate when I had my crush on you. You are her brother. I'm her best friend and we lied. I betrayed our friendship by dating you, lying about it, and sneaking around. How will she trust me or even listen to me if we keep going on like nothing happened?"

"And what, none of my feelings matter? It doesn't matter that I want to be with you?"

I flinched. I never expected him to fight for this, but I had to make things better with Mia. I just had to. "I wouldn't say they don't matter, but Mia needs to know that we aren't dating. I can't ignore how upset she was."

"I'm glad to know where I stand." He backed up toward the door.

"Hunter—"

It was too late. He had already left. Now I had upset them both. Just what I needed, both upset with me, but if Hunter didn't understand how important my friendship with Mia was, then he needed to move on.

I couldn't screw up all the years we had each other's back for him, even if he was all I had ever dreamed of. It was one thing when I could pretend Mia might have been okay with us together, but after seeing her reaction, there was no chance I could ignore her expression as it crumbled.

He would come to his senses and realize dating a sophomore was moronic anyway. Then he would go to college and forget me with all the new and more mature women there. It was better off this way. And let's be real, we had been delusional to think anything else would have happened anyway. This was our fate and if I was the only one to recognize it, then so be it. I would carry that burden until he realized it too.

I had to get Mia to forgive me. That was all that mattered now.

* * *

For the first week after our fight, I showed up at Mia's locker before and after each class. I trailed her at every day after school dismissal and I called and texted her at least once a day. But just like before she refused to respond or acknowledge my existence.

Hunter ignored me too, which was good. I was glad he had listened to me finally, but it still felt too soon for him to let go completely. I guess Brittany was right. As soon as the chase was over, he lost interest. I certainly didn't see him fighting for me as hard as I was fighting to keep my friendship with Mia.

I hadn't bothered to go to Brittany's stupid party. What was I supposed to do? Show up and beg Mia to listen to me the whole time? I didn't want an audience to watch that. Besides, Mia went with Jasper. I didn't want to crash that for her.

I glanced outside the window of my mom's car. Now that both Baylors hated me, I had to find another way to get home. I couldn't walk anymore unless I wanted to be an icicle by the time I arrived home. The wintry weather had officially moved into Chesapeake Hills, and I didn't want to tempt it any more than I had to.

"Want to have an early dinner at Hal's?"

I stared at my mom. She barely had time to pick me up, let alone go to an early dinner. "Why?"

She laughed. "Are you saying no? I thought it might be nice to go and eat something. I was always starving after school."

"Okay. Sure."

Something was up, I just hoped it had nothing to do with the Baylors.

We parked on the side, and I zipped my coat before getting out. The chilly wind whipped around me as I shuffled toward the door.

Mom held the door open for me and I ducked under her arm. The inside was toasty from the heat. A hostess placed us in the fifties section, and we took our sides in the booth.

Mom unwrapped her scarf and placed it on the booth. "I could almost go for coffee or hot chocolate."

I rubbed my hands together. "It's definitely chilly."

Mom buried her face in her menu as she decided between her two usuals. Once the waitress took our order, she eyed me suspiciously.

I wiggled from the uncomfortable attention. "What?"

"I'm just wondering if you will tell me what's up with you

and the Baylors. Never in your entire fifteen years of existence have you not been picked up by them this many days in a row and now suddenly, I'm picking you up every day."

"They're just busy."

Mom crossed her arms. "Busy? That's all, huh?" She tapped a finger to her chin. "That's funny because when I called Gwen, she told me that Mia has been trapped in her room after school and she doesn't have the slightest idea why. Whenever she asks Mia about you, she practically shoots lasers from her eye sockets."

I cringed. That was seriously not good. She wouldn't even tell her mom what was going on?

"So, let's start over. What's the deal?" Mom gave me her you-better-tell-me-the-truth-right-now-or-else-stare.

I didn't want to tell her. She had been nonexistent this whole school year so far. I could have used her advice when it first happened. Now that everything exploded she wanted to help? "Nothing."

She stared at me like she wasn't believing a word I said. "Now, Allie. You have never been one to lie to me."

I shrugged.

She eyed me suspiciously.

"Why does it matter?"

She cocked an eyebrow and reached for my hand. "Because you're my daughter and I love you and clearly something is wrong."

"If you didn't have to pick me up every day you wouldn't have even noticed," I mumbled.

"What was that?"

"Nothing."

"I see you, Allie. I know that your father and I work a lot. Even more so lately, but we still care about you and want you to be okay."

"Then why are you always gone? I've eaten by myself for

the last several weeks. I ate most of my meals at the Baylors. You two are never home."

The skin by her lip twitched. "I guess we've been busier than we realized."

I shrugged. "I know your research is important."

She gripped my fingers. "It's never more important than you."

I stared into her gaze, trying to see the truth in that statement. I'd be lying if I said I hadn't thought it once or twice before.

Our food was placed on the table, and we ate a few bites, but her expression seemed pained. Should I trust her?

I gulped. "We got in a fight."

She paused mid-bite, a smirk on her face. "Really? My PhD didn't see that one coming." She nudged my arm. "I'm always here for you, Allie. I just want to understand what happened."

I exhaled and stared at the peeling paint next to our booth. "Hunter and I kissed."

"Oh, so you finally went for it with Hunter. I bet he's a good kisser."

My gaze snapped back to see her expression. "Mom!"

"Don't be so shocked. I have a pulse. I'm not dumb. In case you haven't noticed I'm quite clever and observant." She waved at me to continue.

"So, we kissed and may have started hanging out without Mia knowing."

Mom grimaced. "Not the best choice. So, how'd she find out?"

"By a girl at school who hates me. She outed me in front of Mia and then I didn't know how to tell her. She screamed at me in the parking lot at school then made Hunter drive her home and leave me there."

Mom shook her head. "That wasn't nice, even if she was upset."

"I'm not mad she left. I would have too. I was the wrong one."

She sipped her tea. "And what about Hunter?"

"What do you mean?"

"What did Hunter think you should do?"

"He thought we could figure it out together."

"And you said?"

"No."

Her brows furrowed. "Why?"

"Mia was mad, Mom. You didn't see her face. How can I work it out with Hunter when she's so mad?"

Mom's expression shifted, but I didn't recognize it. "Allie, do you really expect Mia to sacrifice your happiness just to stay friends?"

"I betrayed her. I owe it to her to leave Hunter alone. It's her family."

"And what about you, Allie? You've been crushing on that boy for years. If she didn't notice that's her fault. You don't have to tell her when you like someone, and you can't change who you fall for. Best friend or not, she should be happy for you."

"Well, maybe she would have been if she found out from us."

"You two definitely screwed up the delivery, but it doesn't mean you should cut him out." She leaned closer and grabbed my hand. "Does he make you happy?"

I nodded.

"Then figure out a way to make up with her and still be with Hunter because I'll tell you one thing. You'll regret every day not dating that boy. Especially if you and Mia make up."

I didn't want her to tell me that. Moms were supposed to help us do what's right. What's right was helping Mia after I betrayed her. How was getting my cake and eating it too the right way?

She tapped my hand and then released it. "Think about what I said. I would hate for you to wake up after all this settles and realize you missed an opportunity you can't get back."

She might be older and possibly wiser, but she didn't know Mia the way I did. I had to fix things with her or I would regret *that* for the rest of my life.

Chapter Thirty-Four

It had been three weeks since our fight and I couldn't take it anymore. I bundled up in my scarf, hat, gloves, and coat and walked to Mia's house. If she wasn't home, I'd wait outside until she was. I had to talk to her. Absolutely had to.

The air was brisk, winter settling in a month early from the Winter's Solstice. Several houses in the neighborhood had already started decorating for Christmas. A few only had their lights, some had the blow-up reindeer, Santa, and trucks with a Christmas tree in the back already up.

Personally, it went Thanksgiving and *then* Christmas, but this year I didn't mind an early dose of the joy the lights gave me. Memories of previous Christmases circulated around my brain. The year Mia and I were ten, her parents had rented a carriage to take us up and down the neighborhood to see the lights. The next memory was from when we were twelve and we stayed up on the twenty-third until midnight to exchange presents. Christmas eve morning was ours, since Christmas was with our families.

There were too many years of watching the lights and the parade to count.

I shook the thoughts from my head as I approached their door. Hunter's car was in the driveway, but he wasn't who I was here to see.

I knocked on the door and held a breath as I waited to see who would answer.

Hunter.

Seriously? It had to be him of all people?

He crossed his arms as he recognized who was at the door. "Mia's not home."

My face fell flat. "Any idea when she will be?"

"I don't give out my sister's information to people she isn't friends with."

Ouch. I hadn't expected the negativity from him.

"Do you not know or are you just going to withhold the information?"

"Either way, it won't help you."

I gripped the bridge of my nose. "Seriously, Hunter? Can't you understand I'm trying to make things right." I sat on the front stoop and faced away from him.

The door shut and that sound echoed in my ears. I seriously messed up. How did one event change my life so inextricably that I couldn't fix it?

I had sat on the stoop for an hour before the door opened again. I turned, surprised to see it was Hunter holding a woolen blanket. The blanket launched from his hand onto my head.

"What the heck?"

"Mom was worried you'd get sick. She wanted you to have the blanket."

I eyed him warily. "And what? You offered to give it to me? Yeah right, Hunter. If she had been worried, she wouldn't give me a blanket through you. I'm not an idiot."

"Either take it or don't. I'm just delivering the message."

I moved it around my legs, the only part not properly bundled in my coat. I stared at the street, willing a car to arrive that carried Mia.

I was suddenly aware of another warm body next to me on the stair. I turned to face Hunter. "What are you doing?"

"Why are you sitting here? She won't talk to you."

I crossed my arms and huddled my body in close. "Because it's the right thing to do. I screwed up and now I need to fix it. If she can so easily ignore my texts, calls, and social media messages, then I'd like to see her ignore me face to face."

He snorted. "It's Mia. You yourself said she can hold a grudge longer than anyone."

"Not the point. I would regret not trying. We've been friends since birth."

"So *that's* worth trying for, but not us?"

I winced. "Hunter, don't do this."

"Do what, Allie? Are you really going to pretend that our sneaking around meant nothing?"

"Of course, it meant something, Hunter."

He reached for my hand. I didn't have the strength to pull it away. "Then why aren't you fighting for this too?"

"You're better off without me, Hunter. I'm a sophomore. What will you do at the end of the year? So, we date and then you go to college? How will we make it through that? It's better to part now. Nothing happened, no damage done."

He released my hand and stood. "No damage done?" He tousled his hair with his hands. "There's plenty of damage already done. But I hear you. This is what you want. End it before you can feel what we could be. Cut things off before you could *potentially* get hurt. Makes perfect sense." He turned toward the door, then glanced back before entering. "She's not coming home tonight. You might as well go home."

All the air whooshed from my lungs. He let me sit here for an hour and didn't bother telling me she wouldn't be home. Was it a game to him? And how dare he get upset with me for making that decision. It wasn't easy giving him up. Didn't he realize what kind of choice that was for me? Didn't he realize that I would have given anything to be with him? It just wasn't working out for us.

I stood and folded the blanket. I left it on one of the chairs on the front porch and walked back to my house. My head stayed tucked inside the lip of my jacket. I didn't want to see anything else that would remind me of times with either of them. Thanksgiving was in a week and everything I usually had to be thankful for was gone, and it was all my fault.

Chapter Thirty-Five

I pushed the lumpy mashed potatoes around my plate as my dad told the same Thanksgiving story he had been telling for as long as I could remember. Mom still beamed and laughed at the little jokes here and there. How did she do that even after hearing the story for so many years?

Dad looked at me expectantly.

"I don't know, what?" I asked. It was my line in the story.

He kept going without missing a beat, but Mom eyed me from across the table. I might be fooling Dad, but I certainly wasn't fooling her.

I was miserable and I was sure she could smell it like a bloodhound smelling rabbit in the forest.

Unable to convince myself to bother eating anymore, I stood from the table. I scraped the remaining food on my plate off into the trashcan and ran the water over it to get the last pieces of stuffing and gravy desperately clinging to the plate.

It was funny. That's exactly how my insides felt. Desperately clinging to any possibility that Mia might answer me ... finally.

If Hunter had told her that I came by that night, she

didn't act like she knew. She still ducked into the other direction whenever I came down the hallway at school. Hunter was barely ever at his locker. Had he only ever visited it that much for me? Or was he purposely avoiding it now?

I wasn't sure, but it didn't matter anyway. I told him to go away. I pushed him to the edge. Any avoidance on his part was mine to carry.

"You know a running tap can waste upwards of four gallons every few minutes. That's a lot of wasted water," Mom said then nudged my side with her hip.

I shut off the water and placed my plate in the sink, then crossed my arms and faced her. "I'm sorry I'm ruining the holiday."

She placed her hands on each shoulder. "You aren't ruining it for me. I am spending time with the two people I love, even if you may be slightly vacant in thought." She tilted my chin so that my gaze met hers. "Mia still not listening to your attempts to apologize?"

I shook my head as tears threatened to spill over.

"Then you need pie."

I stared at her dazed. "Pie? I don't even like pie."

Mom laughed. "The pie isn't for you."

My brow furrowed. "Then who is it for?"

"Put your coat on." She rustled around the kitchen. The distinct sound of aluminum foil stopped my movements as I searched for my coat. "Arnie, Allie and I are heading over to deliver some pie. I'll be right back."

Dad looked up from his plate. "Okay, dear. Tell the Baylors I said Happy Thanksgiving."

"Will do, hun. A game of Scrabble when I get back?"

He smiled.

Mom shuffled me out the door even while my coat was half on.

"The Baylors? The pie is for them? Mom, they won't even let me inside the house."

Mom tucked her scarf into her coat, then walked forward at a fast pace. "Oh, that may be true. But Gwen is a sucker for apple pie, and she loves me. She will let me in, then what you do with that open opportunity is up to you." A mischievous grin spread across her face.

I had to admit, it was a solid plan. Better than any I could muster. The adults weren't fighting, and I never knew Mr. and Mrs. Baylor to be rude. They wouldn't turn down a guest, especially on Thanksgiving.

Mom's pace was faster than I had imagined she would maintain. Maybe she was right, and I didn't notice as much about her as I thought I did. We arrived at the Baylors and without hesitation she walked right up to the front door and knocked.

Hunter opened the door.

I sucked in a breath at his appearance. He was dressed in khakis and a dark green long-sleeve button up. He looked hot, even after everything, my heart raced just at the sight of him.

"Mrs. Duncan?"

"Well, hello dear. Grab your mom for me?"

He nodded and left the door ajar.

I could hear laughter from the other room. It sounded happy. The ache that swallowed my heart felt the exact opposite. I didn't just miss Mia; I missed her whole family. They were my family too and I forgot that when I made the choices I made. If things didn't change, I would lose them all.

"Janet!" Mrs. Baylor shouted. "Come in, come in." She hugged Mom then moved aside to let her in. "Allie! I've missed you. Where have you been?" She hugged me too and pushed me inside and then closed the door.

I winced at her question. It meant neither of her children had told her what had happened. I didn't know what that meant. Was it not final if their mom didn't know? Or did it mean they didn't want her to know *yet*?

"Mia's in the family room. We were about to start a movie. Would you two care to watch with us?"

My mom eyed me and then jerked her head in the other direction. "Why thank you, Gwen. How sweet. I'm afraid I can't. Arnie wants to beat me at Scrabble."

Mrs. Baylor giggled. "He still believes he can win?"

Mom shrugged. "I let him now and then."

I gasped.

Mom turned to me and put her finger to her lips. "Don't you dare tell him."

"You're bad, Janet. That poor man." She faced me. "Allie? How about you?"

I twisted the zipper of my coat around. "Sure, but only if Mia says it's okay."

Just then Mia rounded the corner. The grin she had slid off her face as she saw me.

My stomach dropped to my feet.

Mia stopped and crossed her arms. "What is *she* doing here?"

Mrs. Baylor looked from Mia to me and back again. Then she averted her gaze to my mom.

Mom shrugged.

"Mia, that's no way to speak to Allie. She's your best friend," Mrs. Baylor said.

"Not anymore."

Mrs. Baylor's eyes widened.

Mom nudged my elbow.

"Mrs. Baylor, Mia's right. We had a fight, but I was hoping we could talk." I pleaded with Mia.

Her expression didn't change. She seemed just as mad as she had that first day.

"Mia?" Mrs. Baylor asked.

Mia screeched and stomped up the stairs.

Mrs. Baylor plastered a grin on her face. "One moment. I'll be right back."

She hustled up the stairs in an impressive speed for the height of the heels she wore.

I heard a door slam and I flinched.

"Try to do what you can. If it doesn't work, I have another pie at home for us." She gave me a hug and then slipped out the front door. I had to do this alone.

I felt ridiculous standing in the middle of their foyer, so I went off to the other side of the stairs to sit and wait for someone to return.

Muffled voices emanated down the stairs, but nothing I could understand. I sighed and sunk farther into the couch cushion. Eventually Mrs. Baylor came downstairs with Mia in tow.

Mrs. Baylor looked around then found me on the couch.

I stood.

"There you are. Mia is here to listen."

"Thank you."

"I'll be just in the other room. Shout if you need anything." Mrs. Baylor gave a stern look to Mia, who responded by sulking toward the couch and plopping down.

When Mrs. Baylor was out of sight she said, "You have five minutes and then I'm going back to the other room and you're leaving."

At least it was something.

I took a deep breath and then prayed this worked. "I'm sorry. Truly, Mia. I was wrong. I was wrong to date Hunter. I was wrong to hide it. I was wrong to kiss him back. I was wrong to lie about it. I should have never gone down that road. I knew better and I gave into the temptation."

Mia snorted. "You still think this is about Hunter? About *dating* him? Allie, seriously?"

"I ... what do you mean?"

"You *lied*! And then that twit told me about it. She knew information about my best friend and brother, and I didn't. I'm mad because you kept it a secret as if I would control who you can date. Do you not know me, Allie? Do you think so little of me that I would have demanded you drop feelings for him? I'm pissed you didn't tell me when you had those feelings!" Her voice broke. "How could you not trust me to tell me something so important to you?"

"I thought falling for Hunter would be against the rules."

"What rules?"

"Our friendship. You two are so competitive. I saw what happened when Maureen liked Hunter. She never came back to the house again. You shunned her."

Mia's face scrunched. "Maureen ... Oh my god! You thought that was because she liked him? I never talked to her again because she *stole* from me."

"But when you saw her in Hunter's room you were furious."

"Yeah, because I could see the bracelet she had taken in her pocket as she sat on his bed. I didn't care if she liked Hunter. Lots of girls fawn over him, I'm used to it."

"So, you wouldn't have cared? You wouldn't have felt betrayed?"

"I don't know if that's the best description. I might have been surprised. I might have needed to adjust a little and I certainly wouldn't have wanted to see any PDA of any kind, but I wouldn't have been mad."

"Oh."

"You really thought I'd be mad if you told me how you felt?"

"Yes."

"Then why did you do it? Honestly, the lying is the biggest

betrayal. We were always honest with each other. That all feels too hard to trust now."

"I'm sorry. I was so used to pushing down my feelings because I thought you'd hate me, that when it happened, I convinced myself that you'd be mad. I didn't even know if things would work out, so I didn't want to chance your wrath if things were lousy."

She arched an eyebrow. "So, why let it go on for a month?"

"It just happened. We only saw each other a few times and by the time we had the championship game we discussed how best to tell you."

She knocked me with the pillow. "I still can't believe you thought I would be mad about the two of you dating. You're a bigger dummy than I thought."

I giggled. I knew it made no sense, but her using dummy instead of something worse was funny.

Then before I knew it, Mia was laughing too.

Then we were laughing so hard we were almost crying. When we finally caught our breath and wiped our eyes, I felt better. The tension had been released that I didn't even realize had been building for the last few weeks.

"I guess I could have listened a little sooner," Mia said, then exhaled loudly. "I was just so mad that Brittany had been the one to tell me. She looked so smug when she told me Hunter was your boyfriend. Then when she had been right. I saw red." She nudged me. "It should have been you to tell me."

I looked at the floor. "I know. If it helps, we planned to tell you ... soon, but Brittany said it all before we figured out how."

"Figures that her timing would be perfect to execute her little plan."

I shrugged. "Honestly, yes, it sucked, but I'm glad you know. I hated having the weight of that secret between us. You know, Bennett did ask me out and I had to turn him down and not tell you because you would have killed me not knowing the whole story."

Mia arched an eyebrow. "He asked you out?"

I nodded. "At the project meet up while we were at Hal's. God, Mia, he looked like a crushed puppy dog. I felt awful. He couldn't even look at me afterwards."

"Explains his apathetic behavior at the game."

"I told you I didn't expect him to come."

"Are there any other secrets? Anything I don't know?"

"I don't think so, not unless you want *detail*, details."

She gagged. "Not if they involve my brother and making out."

I giggled. "Then no. But I swear Mia, it's over."

She scrunched her nose like she smelled something gross. "What do you mean over?"

"I told him to forget it. He's a senior, Mia. What would we do when he goes to college? Have a long-distance relationship while he would be around other women? No. I told him your friendship was more important."

She smacked my arm. Hard.

"Ow! What was that for?"

"You! Are you serious? You essentially told him to get lost. Are you crazy?"

"What? I didn't want you to think I was betraying you more. Then I started thinking and it made sense to end things. He wanted to be my boyfriend, but what happens in a few months? I think he would have regretted that choice."

Mia's expression became almost feral. "You are more than a dummy. You are completely certifiably insane." She stood and paced the room.

"I don't understand."

"You! I don't know whether to support you or bang your

head against the wall for being that idiotic toward my brother."

"I'm not following."

"Clearly. Allie, if he asked you to be his girlfriend, those feelings won't evaporate. He doesn't just date anyone."

"But the girls?"

"Those girls are never his girlfriend. Sure, he dates, but if he was willing to label whatever you two had, you should have taken notice to that."

"But I thought you'd be mad."

"Well, I'm not. So, what will you do now?"

"You're saying you're fine if we date?"

"I've had some time to adjust to the idea. I think I could manage. I will kill you if I see you two being all lovey dovey, but you're my best friend and he's my brother. I think you two would be cute together." She gasped. "And we would be sisters if you two got married."

"Woah, woah, woah. Hold the phone, Mia. We aren't even together right now. I'm fifteen. Marriage is not on the table."

She giggled. "Fine, but still."

"And besides, I really upset him. There's no way he will forgive me for how I handled things."

"He could."

"Would you?"

"I mean, I did with the lying." She nudged my arm. "We're cool and if we're cool then maybe you two could be cool too."

"You didn't see his face. He told me he saw where he stood."

She winced. "Okay, so not the best starting point, but if I know my brother, then I know he hasn't just ditched those feelings."

"I don't see how that helps me. When he answered the door, he didn't even glance at me with any kind of warmth."

"Let me work on him for a few days. Maybe I can convince him to come meet with you."

"Are you sure you want to do that for me?"

"I told you. I was never mad because I wouldn't be okay with you two together. I didn't like that you lied and didn't tell me yourselves. And if you make each other happy, I don't want to stand in the way of that."

"My mom was right."

Mia laughed. "They usually are. You should have *seen* my mom's face when she came up to get me. I have never seen her that upset with me before."

"Remind me to thank her."

"You were always her favorite."

I pushed her shoulder and she laughed.

"Want to come watch the movie with us?"

I shook my head. "I don't want to intrude. And before you say I wouldn't, I don't want to risk anything until *all* the Baylors don't hate my guts anymore."

"I didn't hate your guts."

"Could have fooled me."

"Whatever. I'll let you know about my progress."

I walked toward her front door. "Okay. And Mia?"

"Yeah?"

"I'm really happy you're still my best friend."

She leaned in and hugged me. "Me too."

I waved as she closed the door, then hurried home to that other pie Mom promised me. Now all I could do was wait.

Chapter Thirty-Six

The text I had been waiting for didn't arrive until the Sunday after Thanksgiving. We all had to return to school the next day, but I had been twisted inside with worry about how successful Mia really would be.

I had said some awful stuff to Hunter. I even tried to convince him and myself that we would be better off not together. What if she hadn't been successful?

Thankfully, I got her text, *Hunter is hesitant, but I got him to agree to talk to you today.*

When? Where? I can be ready in five.

Slow down. He said one o' clock at your spot on the trail. Which ew by the way. That sounds terrible.

I laughed at her reaction. I could picture her expression as she typed that. *One o' clock it is.*

And when you two makeup, do it before you get back here so I don't have to see all the mushy stuff.

I sent her a rolling my eyes emoji. *Who knows if we will get back together, but I don't want him to hate me anymore.*

I have no idea, but he agreed, so now do the best you can with the opportunity. Text me if you need me.

I will. You're the best.

Duh :P

I showered, got dressed in warm baggy sweatpants and a long-sleeved sweater. When it was only twenty minutes from one o' clock, I grabbed my coat, said bye to my parents, then sprinted toward the bench by the lake. I wanted to be sitting there waiting for him on that bench.

As I approached, I realized that would be impossible. He sat facing away from me.

I took a deep breath hoping to settle my nerves, but nothing short of his forgiveness would fully settle them.

He slouched over his knees, his forearms resting on his legs. His foot jiggled.

It was a good sign we were both nervous. If he didn't care, then he wouldn't need to be nervous.

My feet crunched over the frozen ground as I took the final steps and sat.

He leaned back and glanced at me.

"Hey."

"Hi," he replied.

Great start, Allie. "Thank you for meeting me."

"Well, Mia was pretty relentless about it."

"Oh." My insides were a jumbled mess. I knew I had hurt him, but for him to sit next to me and it feel like we were lightyears apart hurt more than I could say. "Mia and I are better now."

"I'm happy for you two. I know it was important for you to have her friendship."

"It was. Or is, but Hunter when I came to your house on Thanksgiving, it reminded me that all of you are important to me too. You, Mia, and your parents."

"I would have thought you'd realize that sooner."

Ouch. "I deserve that. But Hunter, haven't you ever been in a fight with your best friend and nothing else seems clear?"

"I don't have a Mia, so I can't say I've had that experience, no."

"Well, can you imagine it?"

Hunter sighed. "I don't fault you for fighting for your friendship with my sister, Allie. It's part of who you are."

"But you fault me for not fighting for you."

He nodded.

I nibbled my bottom lip. "I'm so desperately sorry, Hunter. I ignored your feelings in all of this, and I should have done better."

"Yes, you should have." He combed his fingers through his hair. "I mean I should have seen it coming though. I saw how much you doubted yourself, I should have expected it to transfer over to us. After I came to your house, I could have pushed harder with you."

"No. I'm the one who told you nothing could happen. You just listened."

"I shouldn't have listened. I could see you didn't mean it. If I would have pushed ..."

"Then you wouldn't be you. I had to stumble through this on my own, Hunter. I just wish I didn't push you in the same process. I should have let you help solve the problem. We could have gone together to talk to her." I leaned back against the bench. Even with my coat and sweater, I could feel the cold metal seep through to my skin. "On a scale of one to totally ruined forever, how bad did I mess up?"

Hunter chuckled, then covered his face. "You're infuriating you know that?" He sighed. "I don't know, Allie. You basically told me I was better off without you and that I would forget about you when I went to college. That doesn't exactly encourage trust in a relationship."

I winced. "I did say that didn't I?"

"Yeah, you did, and I get it. You two have been best friends for years and I don't want to ruin that. I don't, but jeez, Allie. I really like you and you stomped all over my attempt to help and support you." He tousled his hair with his hand. "I was so worried about you when I had to leave school. I hated knowing that you had to walk home and when I came by you didn't even seem fazed. You seemed like you deserved it somehow. I don't know what to do with that."

"Like? As in present tense and still true?"

"Is that all you heard?"

"No. I heard the rest, but present tense would mean there was a chance."

He gazed into my eyes, almost searching for the truth in them.

The intense attention inflamed my cheeks.

"What do you want, Allie? Like a gun to your head, what do you want?"

Was it really that simple? Could it really come down to what I wanted? Because I wanted Hunter with every fiber of my being. If I was being honest, I always wanted Hunter. "You."

"Why?"

"Because I could stare at your emerald-green eyes forever and still never get tired of the darker flecks of green and blue near your pupil. I could never get tired of that radiant heat that your smile inflicts on me. And most importantly, I would be lost without who you are in my life."

His head leaned toward me until his forehead rested on mine. "I want you too, Allie. I want you as my girlfriend, but what if you and Mia fight again or something goes wrong. How do I know you won't just shut me out and run away?"

The closeness clouded my thoughts, but my answer was easy. "Mia and I will get in fights, and I will try to run, but I promise to make sure to come back too. I can only try my best."

He twisted a strand of my hair around his finger. "Your best, huh?"

I nodded the best I could while our foreheads still touched.

"I suppose ..." He kissed my nose. "That will ..." He kissed my cheeks. "Have to do ..." He kissed my lips. The kiss was soft and gentle. It wasn't fiery and claiming or quick and insincere, but he lingered as our fight flowed out. As if our kiss restarted it all.

"Are you sure?" I asked.

"I'm sure that these past few weeks have sucked. I'm sure that you've entwined yourself into my life and my family's life and we missed you and want you back in it."

I smiled. "How sucky? On a scale of one to—"

Hunter's fingers attacked my side in a tickle strike.

I gasped for air as I tried to recover before he attacked again.

"It sucked, okay?"

"Okay," I said and giggled.

He pulled me closer to him on the bench. "There's like this war raging inside me. Being next to you is all I've wanted these past few weeks, but I can't shake how quickly you let me go."

I entwined my fingers with his, ever so slowly, so he wouldn't pull away. "I know. I hate that I did that to you when I was so worried it would happen to me. I guess you were right. I was trying to cut ties before I had the chance to get hurt."

He squeezed my fingers before placing a kiss on my palm. "I would have never dropped you like Brittany said. You are too important of a person to ever treat that way. Even if things didn't work out, our families are still friends, and you will always have that place in our lives."

"So how do I get you to trust me again?"

"Time." He lifted our hands. "This helps. Maybe we take it slow and let things fall into place?"

"I can do that."

"Want to head over to my house?"

I nodded.

He smiled and stood. I would spend as much time as he needed rebuilding his trust in me, because I had been foolish. I would never underestimate Hunter Baylor again, no matter what happened.

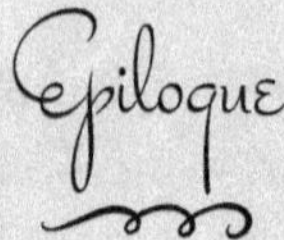# Epilogue

Big, fat, fluffy flakes drifted down, speckling the sidewalks with blobs of white. It was my favorite time of the year, and this year was better than usual.

I pointed to the house across the street, glittering with LED Christmas lights. "Look at that one!"

Hunter chuckled. "You've said that about the last five houses, Allie."

"And your point? It's beautiful."

"Yeah, you are."

I rolled my eyes. "I'm serious. Look at that. They decorated every inch of their roof and front porch. That's talent."

"That's expensive."

"Ugh, you are such an adult sometimes."

He shrugged then wrapped his arms around me from behind. "Its aesthetic is pleasing. Happy?"

"I guess." I sighed and leaned against his body. Even with our extra layers, I could feel his muscular chest supporting me. The last almost month had been perfect. Hunter and I hadn't needed to sneak around anymore. Mia went on a double date with us and didn't barf, which she used for the next week to remind me how much of a good friend she was to make such sacrifices.

And Hunter and I had gotten over our hiccup ... or I guess my hiccup of not feeling worthy enough to be dating him and expecting that things would go wrong.

"Whatcha thinking about?" he whispered.

"Us."

"My favorite subject."

I giggled. "You're so corny."

"You love it. I know you're a hopeless romantic. I pay attention to what books are on your shelf in your room and which ones you sneak out during my basketball games."

I gasped. "I would never."

"Blue cover, white title," he said with a smug expression.

"Fine, maybe I snuck it out once during your last game, but your team was crushing the other team. I didn't think it would matter if I missed one or two points."

He laughed. "I guess you're right, besides, I can't complain since you've showed up to every game so far."

"It's only four games, it's not like the whole season."

"Yet." Still wrapped in his arms, Hunter lowered his head so our lips could touch as I looked up into his face.

The kiss was G-rated compared to others, but it still held so much emotion in it. Things were comfortable between us. I trusted him and he trusted me ... finally ... and that felt amazing to say the least.

The snow picked up and we stopped when a flake landed in my eye.

"You want to head back?"

"Are you crazy? This is my favorite night of the year."

He pulled me closer. "Okay, if you say so."

It was a few days before Christmas and we were continuing the annual Baylor adventure to see the lights in the neighborhood, only Hunter and I had been the only ones to agree to actually do it this year.

Mia was out with Jasper and Mr. and Mrs. Baylor didn't want to risk falling from the pending snowstorm.

I couldn't let the tradition end, so Hunter had agreed. Although, he wouldn't admit it to many, I think he secretly loved the tradition too. The snow only made it that much more magical. I couldn't remember the last time we had a white Christmas. Chesapeake Hills didn't get many of those. Our snowstorms were usually in February or March, not December.

The wind picked up creating a curtain of snow.

"Allie, I know you love the lights, but this is more than flurries."

I sighed. "I guess, but we only saw half the neighborhood. The best house is still that way."

He turned me to face him and held my gloved hands. "Come back to the house and get warmed up, we can sit by the tree and exchange gifts."

I eyed him warily. "Who says I have a gift for you?"

He chuckled. "Well, there was a wrapped box sticking out of your closet the last time I was there."

I crossed my arms. "Who says it's yours?"

He tapped my nose. "Because I know you. And you and Mia decided to buy tickets to a concert for each other instead of a box type present, so that leaves your parents, but then it wouldn't have been haphazardly shoved in your closet because that's expected."

I narrowed my gaze. "You're too clever. Maybe you should stop watching detective shows and reading psychology books."

"You're cute when you're defensive." He tapped his finger to my nose. "And don't think I didn't see that Gladwell book on your shelf too. When'd you buy that?"

"Outer Banks."

His eyes widened. "You waited this long to tell me?"

"So, what if I did?"

He reached his hand toward my side.

"Don't you dare."

The skin around his eyes crinkled with his mischievous expression, until a large gust of wind nearly knocked us over. "Are you ready to give in?"

"Fine. But I expect some chocolate syrup and whip cream to top my hot chocolate."

"Of course, you do. You don't have it any other way."

A smile snuck across my lips as we walked back to his house arm and arm. He had a point though. It was snowing a lot harder than was called for. If it didn't warm up too much, we'd have the perfect white Christmas.

Mrs. Baylor opened the door for us before we even made it to the porch.

"Oh good. I'm glad you two turned around. It's looking much wilder. I wouldn't want you two to be in it, when it's like this."

"That's what I said," Hunter responded.

Mrs. Baylor smiled then looked to me. "I'm sure he had to pry you away from the lights."

He stifled a laugh.

"Guilty."

"Well, get those wet clothes off and sit by the fire. I'll grab you two some hot chocolate." She winked then walked toward the kitchen.

I unbuttoned my coat and unwrapped my scarf, while Hunter shimmied out of his snow boots.

I toed off my sneakers and tiptoed around the wet puddles toward the couch. The window in the living room had the curtains drawn back—a perfect view of the falling snow. Little specks of green and brown burst through the white, but rarely.

The snow had certainly picked up speed. I had no idea how I would get home in that.

Hunter plopped onto the sofa with a wrapped box in snowman paper.

"I'll be right back."

He arched an eyebrow and waited as I headed to Mia's room. Even if he did know I had gotten him something, he hadn't seen me sneak it into her room the other day. I had planned to give it to him tonight when we had finished walking around the block.

I grabbed the green wrapped box with a red ribbon and strolled back down the stairs.

He still sat in the same spot, staring out the window until he heard my footsteps. He grinned as he saw the box in my hand. "Seems someone else is clever, too."

I smirked. "You can't know all the secrets."

He arched a brow. "Is that so? Well, challenge accepted."

I giggled and sat next to him on the sofa. "Is it silly to get something this early for each other in our relationship?"

"We've known each other our whole lives, Allie. I don't think normal rules apply here."

"True. At the same time?"

He nodded, waited a heartbeat, then passed my box over as I passed him his.

My fingers itched to tear the paper apart like a bear smelling its dinner, but I didn't want to look too crazy. The truth was I hated not knowing something, so I was dying to know what he would have bought me.

After much self-restraint, I slid the gift from the paper and out fell three books—all by my favorite Outer Banks author, none of which I owned yet. I shrieked. "How did you know I didn't have these?"

"I pulled up Mrs. Wagner's number in Outer Banks. She knew what you had purchased from her before and let me know that you had been waiting for this one before you bought the other two."

"I don't know what to say."

Hunter's grin was the biggest one I had ever seen, aside from maybe after the night he had kissed me for the first time. "I know. I'm the best boyfriend ever."

I leaned forward and kissed him. "You really are."

He grinned and finished opening his present, while I read the blurbs on the back of the books. I couldn't wait to tear open the cover and read the first page.

The paper stilled and I waited as he ripped the tape from the box. Then he pulled out my present—a dark purple zip up hoodie with his basketball number on the front and Raiders embroidered underneath it in white thread.

I had gotten lucky that the lady agreed to complete the project in two weeks. Usually she was booked solid, but I gave her a little extra for it to be done quicker. It had turned out perfectly.

His gaze hovered over the stitching and then he met my gaze. "Allie this is ... too much."

I waved him off. "Please. You're a basketball legend and it's your last year, I wanted you to have a way to remember it, even if you keep the number in college. Plus, the inside is fleece and super cozy."

He eyed me warily. "No stealing this, deal?"

I laughed. "Deal. Although it'll be hard. It's seriously comfy."

He stood and tugged it over his head, then pulled it down.

Just like I thought, it fit perfectly.

He pulled me up by my hand and hugged me, before settling his chin on top of my head. "Merry Christmas, Allie."

I peeked up at his face. "Merry Christmas, Hunter."

He leaned down and teased my lip with a light kiss that barely lasted.

Mrs. Baylor clinked the mugs together and we separated.

Her eyes twinkled. I could only imagine what she wanted to say to us, but she kept it to herself.

We thanked her before she excused herself. I blew lightly on my mug before sipping to test the temperature. Satisfied it wouldn't burn my entire lip, tongue, and esophagus, I drank a little more.

My gaze drifted toward the books and a chuckle made me break it. "What?"

"You can read it now."

"How?" I shook my head. "You know what, never mind. Are you sure?"

He nodded and sat on the couch, then patted his body for me to sit with him. "You're cute when you read and you're here. I like just being with you, we don't always have to be doing the same thing together."

I smiled and thanked the universe. Several months ago, I had convinced myself I could never be with Hunter Baylor no matter how much I liked him. And now I couldn't believe how lucky I was to have a boyfriend who was satisfied with me cuddling up to him on the couch while I read the books he had bought me. It didn't get much better than that.

Nuzzled against his body, I cracked open the book and began to read while he sat with me and sipped his hot chocolate—one month down with so many left in our future.

The End

Please consider leaving a review if you enjoyed the story. Keep reading to see a sneak peek of the next story in Rosewood County: If Only He Was Mine.

If Only He Was Mine
Rosewood County Standalone Book 2
Releases June 2023.

Chapter One

The adventure date book stared me down—those books that were for *couples*. Yep, those. The ones that made a couple closer with their cutesy activities.

According to my cousin, Andrea, this was the *best* birthday gift ever.

Except, I was single. *Hopelessly* alone.

So naturally I said, "Thanks, Andrea! I can't wait to complete the dates with my *boyfriend*." The words tumbled from my mouth. No sarcasm, no hint of a joke.

What had I done?

The insults swirled in my brain: *You're such a nerd. You're such a prude. What a bore!*

I wasn't popular, fun, or cool. I didn't have some underground appeal to people that made me cool in a non-school way. I had over a four point oh GPA with my APs and I was proud of that fact. I studied and competed in competitions for *nerds*.

My cousin's blemish free skin and penetrating gaze stared back at me. I hadn't known Andrea to ever be silent. It wasn't a trait she tried to improve, either. "Marley Wix! Are you hiding a boyfriend from me? Your own cousin? How could you do such a thing." She peered around my family's living room. "Where is he? Shouldn't you invite your boyfriend to your eighteenth birthday party? That only seems right."

I groaned. My insides were on fire. Why did I say I had a boyfriend? Why did I put myself in this position? I was smart. Couldn't I find a better way to get back at her for this gift she bought purposely to upset me?

Nerds didn't have boyfriends. I hadn't been kissed. I hadn't been on a date. These were the facts of my life choices and I had accepted them.

But Andrea used these facts to taunt me. She didn't have the family freckles or the unruly curly-not-to-be-managed hair. She had pin straight blond hair, although my mom told me it was dyed.

It didn't matter. She was a knockout and she knew it. She had guys for different months of her schedule. Who would complement her at prom? Who would be the best as school president? It was obnoxious.

What was worse? The guys knew about each other and they didn't care. A chance at a Wix was legendary, except for me.

"He couldn't make it. He had to go on a trip with his family."

"For the weekend? Conveniently on your birthday?"

"Of course, Andrea." I posed for a selfie, then texted it to Sage. "See? He'll love it. He's made me a lot more adventurous."

Andrea crossed her arms. "If that's so, you won't have any problems finishing it by graduation then."

My jaw slackened, but I resisted it. Andrea couldn't know I was sweating from this proposition. Graduation was in almost a month. How could I finish all those dates when I didn't even have a boyfriend? This was the dumbest thing I had ever done. "Of course, easy."

She clapped her hands. "Yay! I can't wait to see all the pictures and meet this *boyfriend*." She stood and sauntered toward the kitchen, probably to lick icing off my cake, even though she'd deny it later.

I surveyed the other boxes on the table. My aunts and uncles had come to spend time with me. Mom had insisted on a party since it was my eighteenth, but my best friend, Sage, couldn't come. Just more proof I was a nerd.

"Mar, come in the kitchen. It's time to sing and have cake!" Mom shouted.

I pushed up from the couch and walked to the kitchen. Both of my aunts and my one uncle, Andrea's dad, were crowded around my parents and the cake. Andrea and I were the only children so far, which was weird for four siblings, but my aunts hadn't settled down yet. They were also much younger than their brothers, and had high ambitions for their careers.

I didn't mind being one of two, but I sometimes wished I had more family my age that I could get along with. Andrea wasn't my cup of tea and I wasn't hers.

"On three," Mom said. She counted, then everyone sang me happy birthday. "Make a wish, Mar."

I smiled, closed my eyes and blew as hard as I could to get all eighteen. I didn't usually wish for much, but this year, I needed help.

I wish for a way to prove Andrea wrong. Find me a way to complete that book!

I opened my eyes as they clapped, then Mom shifted the cake to another plate and cut pieces for anyone interested. At least it was my favorite, yellow cake with raspberry sauce and buttercream frosting in the middle and then more buttercream frosting on top. Everyone else left the kitchen, except my parents and me.

"How's your day going?" Dad asked.

I smiled. "Great, thanks."

I couldn't tell him about the gift Andrea gave me. He didn't like when people were passive aggressive. In fact, he didn't like admitting we had money. It wasn't like they had grown up wealthy. The way my dad told the story, he barely had enough clothes to last the week, but he worked hard and became a trauma surgeon.

My mom was a lawyer and between them, they had earned a fair salary over the years, but they didn't flaunt it. Our house wasn't a mansion. It was a regular ranch home with three bedrooms and two baths. They had a two car garage and a basement that wasn't even finished.

We didn't have a pool or live in a gated community. My parents believed in experiences, not things, which was fine by me. We always went on vacations once a year, but to be so successful, their schedules were strange. Half the time, my dad would get in at midnight and my mom would be leaning over the kitchen table staring at a deposition.

I couldn't have asked for better role models, though.

He ruffled my hair as he walked past. "Did you open all your presents?"

"Not yet. Had to stop for cake."

"Well, let's get those presents opened!"

"Okay, Dad."

"Hank, leave the girl alone. You just want to see what your brother bought her."

Dad grinned sheepishly. "Don't use your lawyer interrogation tactics on me, Erin. I just want Marley to enjoy her day."

Mom crossed her arms. "Sure ya do, big guy. Sure ya do." She pushed him toward the doorway. "Go wait out there."

I shook my head. No matter how much older I became,

they always acted like that—playful, almost like teenagers. If I didn't know any better, I'd have never guessed they'd been married long enough to have a grown daughter.

Their marriage was solid, envious. If I ever fell in love, that's what I wanted.

Mom wrapped her arm around my shoulder. "Now that he's out. What was the deal with Andrea's gift?"

My eyes widened. "You don't miss anything."

"If I did, I'd be bad at my job."

"It's nothing I can't handle."

She gazed into my eyes, searching for any moment of weakness. "If you're sure."

"I am."

Her expression shifted, a lighter smile and not as intense of a stare. "Well, let's go see what else you received. You know your dad. He'll be opening them if we leave him alone too long."

I giggled and followed behind her. I didn't know how, but I meant it. I'd find a way to get out of this mess with that ridiculous book.

* * *

"Mar, have you lost all you sensibility?" Sage asked over the phone.

I twisted my fingers around the tassels from my favorite teal pillow.

"Why do you let Andrea get you down? So what if she's boy crazy, you don't have to be."

"I know, I know." I huffed. "It was my eighteenth birthday, you know? I felt like I needed to defend myself and I was tired of the pitying looks."

"Who cares if she pities you?"

Sage didn't understand. We were so similar in so many

ways, but Sage didn't give a damn about what other people thought. She'd be hippie and carefree one day, punk rock the next and not bat an eye. I was envious of that. Sure, I was comfortable being a nerd, but did *everyone* have to define it badly? Why was doing well in school a bad thing? Did we not become successful later on?

"I do."

"Oh, Mar. I'm sorry." She exhaled loudly, letting the silence hang between us. Soft music played in the background. "Well, I'll think of some options. I don't want that twit to win."

"You're the best, Sage!"

"Obviously. I'm sorry again I missed your party."

My bed creaked as I shifted my weight to my stomach. "It's not a big deal. Your dad needed help at the store. That's more important."

"I guess. They always need help though."

Sage had worked at her father's bookstore. When she was little she would sweep or organize some of the shelves by the cash register, but now it felt like every weekend she had to slave away there. I missed my best friend. This was supposed to be the time of our lives, instead I only saw her in one class and after school for a few clubs. It just wasn't the same.

"And you're a dutiful daughter helping out."

"Ryan doesn't have to help, *ever*."

Ryan was Sage's brother. "Well, Ryan is practically a delinquent anyway, right?"

"Not the point." Sage's voice was filled with tension.

Ryan had always been a sore subject. He was three years older than us, but never finished high school. Instead he had decided to party and smoke pot instead of go to class.

"You're right, but soon we'll be at college and that won't be your problem anymore."

Shouting emanated from Sage's side of the phone call.

"Hey, I got to go. Mom wants me to finish my homework and eat dinner before school tomorrow. We should brainstorm, then come together tomorrow morning before class and figure out what to do. We'll come up with a solution. Okay?"

"Okay."

Sage hung up and I tossed my phone on my bed. Hugging my teal pillow to my chest, I stared out my bedroom window. Smaller kids in the neighborhood were using the remaining daylight hours to play a hockey game in the middle of the street.

Even *they* had more of a social life than I did. I sagged farther into my bed. What could I do to fix this? If I told Andrea the truth, it would be worse than just finding a way around it.

I leaned over my bed and pulled the book from underneath, my hand brushing the white and black rug that my bed rested on.

The book felt substantial. It's cover, glossy and black, was smooth in my hands. I flipped through a few of the pages, glancing at the dates. Nothing seemed too crazy. Maybe Sage had a guy friend I could steal to do the dates?

What was I saying? Sage and I were each other's only friends. Her I-don't-give-a-damn-attitude didn't exactly encourage large amounts of friends.

There had to be a solution I couldn't see. So like with everything else, I decided to let it go and wait for the moment to strike. Anytime I would get stuck studying, I let it go. I did something else, then came back and things were clearer. I hoped that it would work with this too.

Thank you SO MUCH for getting this far on book six. Allie and Hunter have a special place in my heart and I couldn't have written it without the help of so many people.

I have had the honor of working with many wonderful people for this novel. First, I want to thank my publisher Creative James Media. Their continued support makes me forever grateful.

I also want to thank Staci Petroski for her edits of this novel. Alt 19 for the amazing cover work.

To my beta readers: derangedeasterbunny, PK, and DKM. All your notes and feedback are invaluable to me. Thank you for putting your effort into helping me.

Finally to my family for supporting me, even when I split my time between them and my characters.

Marie McGrath lives in a small rural town in Maryland. She hopes to inspire others with her stories. When she isn't listening to her own characters, you can find her deep in any novel she can get her hands on, especially YA and contemporary fiction. She loves the color turquoise, lions, and listening to music.

Please consider leaving a review after reading.
Goodreads Review
Amazon Review

For the latest news and updates, please sign up for her
newsletter from her webiste.

Twitter: @Marie_McGrath_
Instagram: marie_mcgrath_
TikTok: marie_mcgrath_author
Website:
https://mariemcgrathauthor.wixsite.com/books